First published by Blasted Heath, 2013
copyright © 2013 Douglas Lindsay
This edition by Long Midnight Publishing 2017

All rights reserved. No part of this publication may be reproduced or transmitted in any form or by any means without permission of the author.

Douglas Lindsay has asserted his right under the Copyright, Designs and Patents Act 1988 to be identified as the author of this work.

All the characters in this book are fictitious and any resemblance to actual persons, living or dead, is purely coincidental.

www.douglaslindsay.com

ISBN: 978-1-54961-211-4

A PLAGUE OF CROWS

DOUGLAS LINDSAY

Prologue

They'd probably have viewed things differently if Detective Inspector Leander had kicked the fuck out of me, rather than the other way round. All right, regardless of the outcome of the manly posturing and handbags that it ultimately came down to, I have to hold my hand up, take responsibility for my own actions, and admit that I was banging his wife.

But surely they would have taken into consideration that he's a workaholic deadbeat loser who had forgotten his wife existed, and that I was only giving her what she deserved... had I not put him in hospital with a fractured jaw, a couple of broken ribs and a punctured lung. And, you know, people make a lot of the punctured lung, but Jesus, lungs get punctured all the time. Guys puncture lungs when they're playing football, and they play on. Break a rib, damned good chance that you'll puncture a lung along with it. God, you've still got another one. How many do you need?

He decided not to sue me, which is something for which I am apparently to be grateful. Well, I wouldn't have had to puncture his lung if he hadn't cracked a bottle of wine over my head. Good thing he hits like a girl.

He had seven weeks off sick. That must have been fun around the house, just the two of them. Maggie running after his every need. They must have had some interesting conversations over the breakfast table.

Under other circumstances I might have felt bad when he confronted me about it. I'm not a completely heartless wanker. I felt some level of guilt about the fact that I was fucking the wife of another guy at the station. But Maggie... if you saw her, you'd know. How could I not?

Leander oversnagged. And I mean, seriously oversnagged. I saw a wedding photo of them around the house, and fair enough, on their wedding day they looked kind of natural. Almost like a couple. But over the years he's worked too many hours, suffered too much stress, drunk too much, smoked a few too many God-knows-what, and he's just running to sad middle age; Maggie, on the other hand, is a few years younger, never had kids, works out, doesn't drink, and just keeps getting hotter.

I doubt I'm the only one. Don't care now, didn't care back then. Whatever, I was the one Leander found out about. We were both in the Whale one night, which was stupid, don't know what I was doing in there drinking with all our lot, and getting worse and worse for it. He asks me if I've shagged his wife. I say no, in the drunk kind of way that pretty much says 'Oh yes!' – but I'm thinking, *you know anyway, you sad sack, so it doesn't matter* – and then he minces off to a corner to sulk for a while, before coming back and beaning me over the napper with the bottle. Chaos and mayhem ensue.

Chaos, the whining Nancy boy, ended up in hospital with a punctured lung, while Mayhem got nicked. They weren't really ever going to charge me with anything, but they suspended me until I got help with my issues.

Fucking issues.

August

1

She hasn't said anything for upwards of ten minutes. I'm the one who's supposed to be talking, although I haven't opened my mouth since I sat down. I've barely looked at her as that just increases the awkwardness. This isn't comfortable for me. I've no idea how she finds it. She's probably used to people clamming up and going all silent movie on her.

Silent movie? What the fuck? Actors in silent movies didn't sit all sullen and miserable. They overacted like all kinds of shit to compensate for the silence. So I'm not sitting here like I'm in a silent movie, I'm just like everyone else who's been told to go somewhere and who doesn't want to play.

I'm looking at a picture on the wall. A painting. The top half is red, the bottom half orange. I keep waiting for her to ask me what I think it represents.

Does she care that I'm not interested in her psycho-drivel, or does she just see it as easy money? She can sit here doing bugger all for an hour and at the end send a bill for four hundred quid to the police.

I start to wonder if I could be a psychiatrist, and how long the training lasts, and if there are any modules from which they'll make you exempt if you're already a certifiable nutjob.

Sadly I haven't even been certified as a nutjob. I think someone just wrote *pain in the arse* on my file and thought that if they suspended me and made me talk to someone I might become less of a pain in the arse. How was that ever going to happen?

'What do you think it represents?' she says.

Ha!

Every week I mean to bring a Psychiatrist Bingo card with me, rather than just the one in my head. *My mother. My father. Childhood trauma. Why do you think that is? What do you think it represents?*

Of course, if I was playing actual Psychiatrist Bingo, she'd have to ask me what I was doing, and if I told her then she'd have to ask me what I felt about the fact that I was choosing to do this, and how did I think it impacted on our time together.

Time to go. I stand up. I contemplate walking out without even looking at her, but I can't stop myself glancing her way. It's a warm day and she's just wearing a light blouse on top. Open at the neck. I look at her breasts. Small, enticing.

Oh, God... Stop it. Stop doing that thing. It's not about her breasts.

Enticing, for crying out loud. Get a grip.

We look at each other for a moment. It feels like she can read my every thought. She knows I've been playing Psychiatrist Bingo, she knows I just glanced at her breasts, and she knows I liked them and immediately chastised myself for looking and for thinking about it.

Nevertheless, she's wrong about the most fundamental thing. She thinks my time in Bosnia left me with Post-Traumatic Stress Disorder. I like to tell myself that that's the case. I have Post-Traumatic Stress Disorder. I don't speak to anyone about it, but if I did, that's what I'd tell them.

Me and my PTSD. That could be the title of my autobiography. *My PTSD And Its Part In My Downfall.*

But I'm lying to myself. The whole time I'm lying, because I don't have PTSD.

I have guilt. And I have shame.

I leave, closing the door behind me.

*

When I'm in town for the weekly psych sessions, I always go to the gym. I punch a bag for an hour, and take a shower. I'm washing the rest of the week, but this is warm water, rather than a testicle-freezing stream at the bottom of a mountain.

I punch a bag, I have a shower, I have a hot meal, and then I get the train back down to Tarbet and walk off into the mountains.

The guys at the station probably think I'm sitting at home, watching sport all day, getting pished and finding myself as many women as possible. But in fact I'm living in a tent, have barely touched alcohol in four months, and spend most of my time wandering the hills and catching dinner. Yep, catching dinner. I can trap, skin and cook a rabbit. That's some ancient fucking skill-set going on right there. When society breaks down, and the infrastructure of the western world collapses, I'm going to be stoked. Everyone else is going to be queuing up for the last box of frozen chicken pieces in Tesco, and stabbing folk in the back to get it, and I'm going to be dining on fresh meat.

In this modern world, there's probably a name for what I'm doing. Everything's got a name. In my head, however, it doesn't have a name. It's just what I'm doing this week. This month. I doubt it'll last into the winter, although I'm not giving Dr Sutcliffe anything on which she could recommend that I be allowed to return to work.

I just don't think they should have suspended me in the first place.

So, I don't know that I'd give what I'm doing a name, as such, but I've lost nearly twenty-five pounds, and I'm marginally less likely to die of a heart attack than I was a few months ago. Off the fags as well. What a fucking loser.

My mobile rings for the first time in over two months as the train pulls into Helensburgh station.

2

Sitting in the station café waiting for DCI Taylor to get the coffees in. Feeling, as I do most of the time these days, remarkably fresh and healthy. Bright. Sharp as a fucking tack. Haven't had coffee in three weeks, but the boss has come down here for a chat and if I drink water or some sort of fruit smoothie like the twenty-year-old wankers drink, he'll think I've lost it.

He comes back with two Americanos and parks himself across the table. First time I've seen him in three-and-a-half months. Hasn't changed.

Of course he hasn't.

'What's with you?' he says. 'Been to the Med or something?'

Ah, yes. Got a bit of a tan.

'Out on the hills every day. Windswept.'

'You've got a Scottish tan?'

'Aye.'

'Fuck me…'

He shakes his head and looks away. Glances around the café. Checking out the rest of the clientele. I know the look. Making sure there are no journalists. We take a sip of coffee at the same time.

'You're coming back to work,' he says, before he looks at me.

Strangely I hadn't expected that. I hadn't given any thought to why he would get on a train to the other side of Glasgow just to come and see me, so this possibility never entered my head. Not sure what else it was likely to have been, though.

'What if I don't want to?' I say.

I'm not sure what it is I've been doing the last few

months, but I'm not finished.

'You're still getting paid, aren't you?' he says sharply.

Very true. I don't *need* to be living in a tent.

'You start tomorrow morning at eight. I expect you'll spend the night in bed with God knows who, but wherever you lay your hat, you'll need to get out of there in time to get back to work.'

Don't immediately say anything. Another drink of coffee, look at the road outside. Traffic and people. I've grown used to the solitude of the hills.

'Surprised Doctor Sutcliffe thought I was ready,' I say.

Must have fooled her into thinking I was normal by doing what most blokes would have done. You know, by not saying anything. And staring at her breasts.

'Sutcliffe thinks you're so fucked up you're practically retarded. You've buried your past deeper than most war criminals bury the bodies, is what she says.'

Jesus. That didn't take much. Suddenly it's all back there in my head, the thing that I manage not to think about while I'm sitting on a quiet Scottish mountainside, looking out over the hills and lochs, the sea in the distance.

'So why are you bringing me back?' I ask. Just to keep the conversation going. Don't want to wallow. Wallowing can lead to many things, none of them good.

'I need you.'

I stare across the table. Don't know what to say to that. Don't even feel like sarcasm or bursting into some bloody awful romantic song.

He's got a bag beside him. I'd noticed the bag, what with me being a detective 'n' all. He reaches into it and pulls out an iPad.

'You been following the news?' he asks, as he keys in the code.

'In my world, America's still fighting in Vietnam.'

Seriously, I haven't the faintest idea what's happening in the news. And I like it that way. I've been sitting on the side of hills, staring into space, listening to Bob. Bob's timeless. News doesn't come into it. Occasionally on my trips up to Glasgow I've seen the odd Evening Times billboard, but invariably it'll be some pointless story about the city council or about some Hollywood movie filming in the centre because it so beautifully approximates an apocalyptic war zone without any extra work being done to it, or there'll be a story about some Old Firm player I've never heard of before.

That's my news.

He's found what he's looking for, looks up at me.

'There were three bodies found in a small wood up above Cathkin four days ago.'

Why is he bringing me this? I don't want to know about bodies in a wood. I've seen enough dead bodies in woods. It might have been a long time ago, but those bodies are still burned in my brain. It wasn't like it happened yesterday. It's like it's still happening, like there's something I could be doing about it.

'One police officer, one social worker, and a journalist.'

'One of ours?' I ask. 'The polis?'

'No. A constable from out Royston way.'

'The papers get it all?'

He hesitates. He's looking at a photograph. I'm looking at his face, not trying to see the photograph upside down. I don't want to see the photograph.

'They got a bit about there being three deaths in mysterious circumstances. One of them was a journalist after all, we could hardly keep it a secret. But the exact details of the murders… no. We've had to do some serious business to keep the lid on. Just making sure they don't go for some human interest angle. The public only ever care when the press want them to.'

He turns the iPad round. I'm still looking at his face. Finally I lower my eyes.

The photograph is of a clearing in a wood on a bright morning.

There are three cadavers in the picture, all sitting upright in a small triangle, facing each other. They have been strapped to wooden chairs, presumably while they were still alive, so that they would remain sitting upright throughout the process of their murder.

Despite the clarity of the picture, it still takes some deciphering at first glance, especially when I don't know what it is I'm looking at. From the angle that the picture has been taken, two of the faces are visible, the other showing the back of his head to the camera. Blood has run down and dried on the two faces. It's hard to make out what's going on with the other head.

The most obvious thing about the three victims, yet the thing that takes the longest to decipher, is that each of them has had the top of their skull removed. Cut clean away to reveal the top of the brain. What is visible, however, is not clear. On all three of them, what can be seen is a bloody mess.

'There are more,' said Taylor.

I hand the iPad back.

'Nice job,' I say. 'Bleed to death?'

'No,' says Taylor. 'The killer did a good job. Very precise. Managed to expose the brain without causing too much bleeding. Any that he did cause, he immediately cauterised with superglue. Knew what he was doing.'

'Quality,' is all I find myself saying, like I'm a football pundit talking about... fuck I don't know, just not anything that ever happens in Scottish football, that's for sure.

I look back at the picture, which is now upside down. Having my attention, Taylor turns the iPad round and flicks it onto another frame. It's a close-up of one of the victims. The photograph has been taken from a slightly elevated angle, looking into his face from the front and just a little above.

The face is dirty with congealed blood. The eyes are missing. The top of the brain is a bloody mess, but there appears to be a lot of it missing too. Weirdly, and this really is fucking weird, the photograph isn't grotesque. Not to me, at this moment. It looks like a damned good special effects job.

I take a slurp of coffee, start wondering if they have

anything decent to eat here. He goes to flick over to the next picture, and this time I push the technology away from me.

'Don't show me anymore.'

It's the woods. I don't want to see the woods.

What's the matter, Numbnuts? Traumatised by Winnie the Pooh when you were a kid?

He looks at me, then turns back to the iPad. Another glance at a picture or two, then he turns it off and slips it back into his bag.

I have to ask.

'What happened to the brains?' The words sound empty. I take some more coffee.

'Birds ate them. Crows.'

He glances out the window as he says it, as though he can't look me in the eye while saying something that bizarre. Grotesque. Or maybe he's looking to see if there are any crows outside. I don't follow his gaze. There are usually crows. There are always crows.

'The guy controlled the crows?' I say. This has got a bit of life back into me. This is too weird to be real. 'That's like some sort of Steed and, what's her name, Emma Peel, kind of shit.'

'No, don't think so,' says Taylor. 'It's not the Avengers. He tied the victims up, stuck them out there in the wood, removed the scalp *in situ*, and then left them to it. Exposed brain. Almost an experiment to see how they'd go. The most obvious way would have been that they'd've bled to death. But as I said, he'd done a good job, made sure that wouldn't happen.'

'Why didn't they do something? Topple the chairs over, crawl through the wood. Something…'

'He cemented them into place.'

'Fuck.'

'Cemented them into place and left them there. I suppose he took the chance that they could be found and rescued, but as it was, they were found by birds. Glistening live brains proved to be too much of an attraction.'

'But they wouldn't feel the brain getting eaten, right?'

'Probably not. They were facing each other. They would have been able to watch as it happened to the other two, and they'd know it was happening to them. Who knows what part of the body went first.'

'Well, they could watch if their eyes didn't go first. I presume that was the crows too.'

Taylor nods. I hold his gaze for a moment and then look down at my coffee. Suddenly don't feel so much like drinking. I'd already given up on going back to the fresh air and the solitude of the side of a Scottish mountain, but now that reality strikes firmly home. Back on the job, and at a hundred miles an hour.

'So I'm cleared by Sutcliffe,' I say.

He shakes his head.

'No. You need to go back and see her first thing tomorrow morning.'

'What?'

'And you need to talk to her. I don't care what you say, just be... normal.'

I continue to stare across the table. This is bullying, right? This is new millennium Britain, and he's bullying me into coming back to work when I'm not ready. I could sue him. Right now. I could make a phone call and have a lawyer wedged a foot-and-a-half up Taylor's arsehole before he leaves the café.

'Whatever,' is all I can manage.

*

We don't talk for a while sitting on the train on the way back up to Glasgow. My tent is still up and waiting for me at the bottom of Ben Vorlich, in the lee of some trees. Some part of me still thinks I'll be going back there, but the further the train gets from Helensburgh, the closer we get to Glasgow and on our way to Cambuslang, the more I know that I won't be going back.

Not sure what happens to tents that are just left lying.

Maybe someone will report me missing and there'll be hundreds of people searching for me for months. It'll be on the news, and I'll be watching it, thinking, *miserable fucker, you deserve to be lost*.

I should probably call someone about the tent.

The warm afternoon passes by. At all the stations there are women in summer clothes.

'So you've been hill walking?' says Taylor after a while.

'Aye.'

I answer without looking round. Watching the world go by, like a kid on his way home with his dad. *Black Crow Blues* has started playing in my head.

'Where were you staying?'

'In a tent.'

'You've been living in a tent for four months?'

'Aye.'

'Jesus. Thought you'd smell worse.'

'Had a shower today at the gym.'

'What've you been eating?'

'Rabbits and shit.'

'You've been catching rabbits?'

Look round at last. Shrug.

'You've been catching rabbits?' he says again.

'Aye.'

'Eating them raw, cooking them?'

'Cooking them.'

'Jesus, Hutton.'

He shakes his head and looks out the window.

'What does rabbit taste like?' he asks eventually.

'Don't know. Rabbit.'

'Thought it was supposed to taste like chicken.'

'Doesn't taste like chicken.'

He glances at me again, and then we both look out of the window as the warm summer's day passes by. All we can see are the banks of the railway line.

'Are you sure they were rabbits?' he says.

3

I have three MP3s on the go. One for studio Bob, one for live Bob, one for bootleg and miscellaneous Bob. (Bootleg and miscellaneous Bob is naturally largely live too, although it does include some of Bob's songs performed by other artists. I know, I wasn't sure about that either. It felt like I was debasing the MP3, or that I should have a completely separate fourth MP3 to accommodate them. But really, it's just versions where the artist has done a solid stand up job, like Tim O'Brien's *Farewell Angelina* or George's *I Don't Want To Do It*. Don't go thinking I've got that woman singing *Feel My Love* or any shit like that.) I had no way to charge them when I was out on the hills other than when I came up to town every week for my psych, gym and dinner afternoons. I'd get them charged while I was there, then listen to them at will over the next few days, then start to ration myself as it got closer to the town trip and the charge started to run low. I bought one of those Ray Mears books, but there was nothing about how to charge your MP3 whilst living wild.

I tried building a shelter one day, thought that would be a natural extension of what I was doing. Do away with the tent. Had even begun to imagine that I might be there, trying to see myself through the winter out in the wilds, even though the winter was some way off. Anyway, my shelter was shit. I slept under it a couple of nights, but that was only because it wasn't raining and the wind wasn't blowing. As soon as some weather happened I was back in the tent.

Suppose I could have stuck at it, but I was too busy catching rabbits.

It's 7.30 in the morning, Taylor and I are heading up to

the woods to check out the site where the bodies were found. It's been closed off to the pubic for three days, will remain so for quite some time. Eventually they'll have to let it go – for no other reason than we won't have the manpower available to keep people away from it – and then the tourists will arrive, the great ghoul collective who like to visit murder sites. Weird bastards the lot of them. I mean, I get stopping to stare at something as you drive by or if you just happen to be walking down the same street on which someone got gunned down. But going out of your way, and in some cases a long way out your way, to check out where someone got stiffed...

It's a short drive. He needs me to speak to Sutcliffe again before I get authority to come back to work, but she's not free until ten. He can't wait. I'm just an observer for the moment. If we come across any other crime while we're out there, I'm not allowed to produce my I.D. and nick some bastard.

Bob's playing on the CD. Another Side Of. *I once had a girl...* Never liked that song, although it might be just because I read somewhere that Bob wished he hadn't written it. If that's what Bob thinks then, subconsciously or otherwise, that's what I think. I also wish he hadn't written it. Whatever. It'll be over in eight minutes.

I know Taylor doesn't like it either, but he doesn't believe in skipping tracks.

Had a quick look through the folder, got an outline of the case. Three victims. One police officer, Constable Goodwin from Royston. 33 years old, divorced, no family. The journalist, a staffer on the business pages of the Herald, Morris Tucker, 29, degree in business from Stirling University, no kids, one girlfriend. Due to get engaged next year, she said. I've been married three times without being engaged once. If you're going to do it you might as well just get on with it. These two, they were engaged to be engaged. That's just spinning it out for the sake of attention and presents. Well, if the lassie got any pre-engagement presents, she might as well give 'em back.

The third was a social worker from the centre of the city. Lived in a small flat not far from Bridgeton. Nothing noticeably to connect him to the other two, just as they weren't connected to each other. Angus Sparing, 42. Wife and kids. Three of the little bastards. Given how shittily social workers get paid, it might not make that much difference to the family household him not bringing any money in.

That's me not considering the effect of the father and husband being gone. No empathy. That's one of my issues, apparently.

'You know Bob's playing the SECC in a couple of days?' says Taylor, casually.

'What the fuck?'

He doesn't say anything else. He's driving. Pretending to concentrate. Haven't seen Bob in two years.

'How come nobody told me?'

That's kind of a stupid question, which Taylor's only too happy to answer.

'You've been living on the side of a mountain shagging sheep,' he says.

'You get me a ticket?'

'Yes.'

'Seriously? You got me a ticket?'

'Well, I got two tickets. To be honest, if I'd found some woman to ask in the last month I would have asked her, but we're now only two days away and the ticket's still free, so the chances are it's yours. So, it's slightly disingenuous to say that I got you a ticket, but you can have it if you like.'

I nod. Good man. He was never likely to ask a woman. I mean, really, you hit it off with some new bit of skirt at our age, the last thing you want to do is scare them away by offering to take them to see Bob. Living legend 'n' all that, but really, not designed for getting women into bed.

'We should talk about the case now,' he says.

Although we don't.

'I didn't shag any sheep,' I feel the need to point out.

*

The entire wood has been cordoned off. And you know, it's a wood in central Scotland not too far from Glasgow, so we're not talking about the Black Forest here. It's a few acres worth of trees where not many people go. I don't even know who found the bodies, but it'll have been one of the usual suspects: a dog walker, kids playing or illicit lovers. Although I'm not sure kids go out playing in woods anymore, so that probably rules that one out.

The victims were placed in a small clearing. A natural clearing, and not a bespoke space created for the task at hand. The killer dug out three small pits. He took three large wooden armchairs and sharpened the base of the legs. He then planted the three chairs in the ground adjacent to the holes. We don't know how far in advance he did this, but the whole thing seems to have been well thought out, so presumably he had it all set up before he arrived on the spot with his victims.

It's like serving a full Scottish to a group of people. There are so many things that don't take long, like bacon and frying eggs and making toast, that you can't start those and then start setting the table and making the coffee and whatever. You do as much preparation as possible before you start so there's no last minute panic.

So this is what he did. He killed three people like he was making bacon, sausage, egg, tomatoes, haggis, mushrooms and toast for fifteen people.

He prepared his area, and then he brought his victims out to it. They had all been drugged, so that he was able, one by one, to take them from the back of a van – the nearest identifiable tyre tracks suggest a Ford Transit, but you know, they suggest in a vague, well maybe, maybe not, kind of a way, so that's not exactly piling on the evidence. They had each already been strapped into chairs, then he placed the chair legs in pre-prepared holes in the ground, placed the feet in the larger pits in front of them, and filled all the area around the legs and their feet with concrete. The concrete set.

This was no movie-type bondage situation. In movies, people always find a way to wriggle their way free. Of course they do. Most of those types of movies wouldn't happen if Bruce Willis didn't have a convenient paper clip secreted away up his arse. But this was no Bruce Willis movie. Bruce Willis was not getting out of this.

Once he had them in place, he got to work with a saw. They reckon he used the proper tool, something like the electric bone saw that a brain surgeon would use. In the old days that would have helped narrow it down because it would have been much easier to trace anyone who bought a GPC Electric Bone Saw, Oscillatory & Rotary Model, but in these times when you can buy nuclear weapons over the internet from a guy shipping armaments, machine tools and cosmetics from his bedroom in Almaty, it's an entirely more convoluted ballgame.

Pretty easy to have someone bleed to death on you while you're removing the scalp, and he hadn't gone to all this trouble so that these people would die before the fun started. He had superglue to hand to stop any bleeding, but this fellow knew what he was doing, and he didn't need to use the glue very often.

We're not sure at what stage he woke them up. We're not sure if he stayed to watch. Perhaps he stood in front of them to intimately share his triumph with his victims. Perhaps he watched from the sidelines. Perhaps he just walked off, left them to it.

How did he know that crows would come and eat their brains? Can't say. He did select, with foresight one must presume, an area with crows nests in the trees. Maybe he'd trained those crows. Maybe he'd been leaving brains lying out in these woods for months, getting them used to it. Maybe he just left them there, assuming that the birds would look down, be curious and have a nibble, decide that they quite liked what they tasted.

Either way, he had these three people staring into each others' eyes, bound and gagged and helpless. And the first time a crow landed on someone's brain, put its feet on the soft surface and took a peck, the one to whom it was happening very possibly was unaware, depending on whether the crow landed on the edge of the skull or completely on the brain. But the other two would have watched it, and that person would have known something was happening. And then, as word travelled around the crow community, and the flock descended, they would have been covered in birds and through the mass of flapping wings they would have watched as the blood started to run. Probably not much space on the average scalped human head for more than two crows at a time, so there would have been a lot of avian squabbling.

Scalped? It's a bit more than scalped, isn't it? Superscalped, they'd call it in McDonald's.

Would any of them have stayed alive long enough to start losing various faculties of their bodies as their brains slowly disappeared? Baird and Balingol, the pathologists, don't have an answer to that yet.

'You all right?' says Taylor.

We're standing on the spot, looking down at the three chairs. He doesn't know my story. He doesn't know what happened to me in the Balkan forests eighteen years ago. I try not to think about it, and try to suppress it as much as possible. Maybe I don't really know any more.

What *happened to* you? That's one way of putting it.

But this, this doesn't bring it back anyway. I saw some horrible things. Horrible. But they were random and spontaneous, brutal, vicious. Barbaric and indiscriminate acts that spoke of the general depths that humanity will sink to in wartime.

This is cold and calculated.

Genius.

'Sure,' I say. 'This is some fucking guy we're dealing with. Scary. And I mean, really fucking scary. With your usual nutjob kind of bloke, woman, whatever, there's a physical aspect, some sort of thing where you imagine that it'll come down to a fight and you'll be able to take them.

It'll be brute force. If it ever gets tricky, there'll be a way out. But not this. This is one cool fucker we've got here. He gets his hands on you…'

Taylor's nodding.

'Let's just concentrate on catching him.'

'We know it's a man?'

'No,' he says. 'We're just making an assumption for the moment. My mind is open. Just don't want to be saying *him or her* every sentence. We'll call him *him* until we know otherwise.'

'A bit like God really.'

He glances up at me, looks to see if I'm being serious or anything, then shakes his head.

'Fucking Hutton,' he mumbles.

4

I'm staring at the same painting as before, but this time I've only just sat down, and I've only looked at the picture because I was following Sutcliffe's eyes.

'What do you think it represents?' she asks.

After spending some time back with Taylor I realise that part of the problem was that I just hadn't been speaking to anyone. I'd been out of practice. I'd stopped talking altogether, found that I didn't really need it, so that when I pitched up here at Sutcliffe's office, I was just thinking, what's the point? I'm getting by just fine without saying anything.

A few months ago, I may well have thought that Sutcliffe and her ilk were the real nutjobs and that it was all a waste of time, but I'd at least have made some effort in talking to her, even if it was just to try to get her into bed.

I look round at her and smile. Still haven't had any alcohol, eyes are bright, the hillside tan is still a few days away from fading. Suddenly I'm talking to an attractive, intelligent woman and I'm full of myself.

'Just a painting,' I say. 'Red on top, orange on the bottom. It could be a red sky over the desert, it could be strawberry jelly on top of orange jelly, but you know, I think the artist just thought it looked nice and he – or she – left it up to the viewer to make up their own mind about its meaning. In fact, they might not even have got as far as thinking that anyone would read meaning into it. But, of course, you stick a picture on a psychiatrist's wall and it immediately has to mean something.'

She smiles, doesn't nod or anything. She makes a quick note – although I reckon she's just doodling a bloke with a button nose and a moustache – and then looks up.

'My daughter painted it when she was six.'

Ah. She has a daughter. Doesn't mean she's still with the father, but it might not be a good idea to go hitting on any more married women. Just yet.

'How many times did you sleep with Detective Inspector Leander's wife?'

'You think I counted?'

'Possibly.'

'Seventeen.'

'Did you just make that up, is it a guess, or did you really count?'

'It's a guess. But a fairly good one.'

'Did you ever think about DI Leander? What this would do to him?'

'No.'

'Why not?'

'I was too busy sleeping with his wife. It was sex. It happens. She's gorgeous and, as far as anyone knows, doesn't keep it to herself. I wasn't the only one. Am I proud of what I did? No. But the sex was great.'

'You were aware that it was becoming a scandal around the station. You'd been told to stop.'

Now that's true. It had started to get a bit uncomfortable. Taylor was getting pissed off at me. Everyone knew. Everyone. DS Hutton was shagging the DI's wife. Open secret. That was awkward. I did almost think about ending it one of the times that Taylor told me to, but then she called up and invited herself over and she stands on the doorstep of my flat, and I'm thinking, you know, I'm solid, this is it and I'm going to tell her she has to leave and that we're finished, and then she opens her coat and she's wearing black underwear. Just, you know, the kind that's supposed to go straight to a man's cock. And it does. And I sleep with her.

That was a couple of weeks before the bottle of wine at the Whale incident.

'Have you got a problem with sex?' Sutcliffe asks,

when I don't say anything.

Hmm. Well, I haven't had any in the last four months.

'I don't think so,' I say.

She glances down at a thin file, looks at a couple of pieces of paper.

'Your history suggests otherwise,' she says. 'You seem insatiable. It's peculiar in a man your age.'

I give her the dead pan after that one. Saying nothing, although the words 'you can find out for yourself if you want, darlin'' aren't far from my lips.

'There's not much in your file about your time in Bosnia,' she says, cutting to the big one. But I'm in a good place today. Back in the zone. Back in the denial zone. 'You've never talked about it.'

'No, you're right.'

'Why is that?'

'It was horrible,' I say, but without accessing any of it in my brain. 'There's nothing about it that I want to talk about.'

'But there's some suggestion here that that's your problem. Your time there, your time spent in a war zone, it has impacted on you ever since you came back, made you reckless.' She takes another quick glance down. 'Even though it was a long time ago. If these things aren't dealt with properly, they can hang around in the head for a long time. Forever.'

Nothing to say to that.

'Reckless is a bad word for a police officer. Your affair with Mrs Leander, accompanied by a host of other incidents and affairs and marriages over the years, all point to an inherent recklessness.'

I'm staring across the room at her. She's only four yards away. And she's right. I was reckless before I ever got to Bosnia – given that I went there just to check it out and have a look at war, death and suffering first hand, it was implicit in my even going – but I've been a lot worse since.

'Do you have examples of any cases in which I've been involved where it's negatively impacted on the outcome?' I ask.

Aye, there's the rub.

She doesn't immediately answer.

It's been close a few times, and maybe there'd be some legitimate suggestion that I should be dealt with before I negatively impact, rather than after, but really, there it is, there's the fucking rub. I always get by.

'You don't think you negatively impacted the work of the station by hospitalising Inspector Leander?'

'He hit me over the head with a bottle of wine.'

'You slept with his wife.'

'An act of love and affection. It was him that brought violence to the table.'

She gives me a bit of an eyebrow for that one, and well deserved. *Love and affection? Tuck it in, Hutton, you wanker.* Still, I've got her pegged as a tree hugging liberal, the type who wants to believe in people, the type who wants to think there's good in everyone and that everyone can be rescued.

'I was wrong,' I say, finally getting around to coming out with the kind of standard arsewipe that Taylor was looking for me to say. 'I shouldn't have slept with Maggie and, at the very least, I should have stopped when the Chief Inspector told me to stop. Leander only did what any self-respecting man would have done.'

Apart from the fact that he took weeks to do it and then he came at me from behind my back because he's a pussy.

She's melting. Piece of cake really. I haven't quite put the ball in the net yet, but I've made steady progression into her half. The main thing now is to concentrate and not blow it by asking her what she's doing after work.

5

Three o'clock, my first afternoon briefing. The keys to the castle have been returned to my good keeping, and I can once more join the police fold, once more strike boldly forth and legally kick the fuck out of people. Wouldn't have happened so fast without Taylor demanding it, but he's now the senior DCI around these parts and he's risen to the challenge. Knows what he's doing, gets results.

This'll be the first time he's had to find the killer of three people who've ultimately had their brains eaten by crows, however.

Seventeen people in the room. The walls are covered in the pictures Taylor tried showing me on the train. My head's in the right place now, which it wasn't yesterday. I can look at this shit without wanting to shut down. It's a constant adjustment process.

I'm sure I'll start drinking again soon enough, and I've already bought my first packet of fags in over a month; on top of that, an hour alone with Dr Sutcliffe has got me thinking about women. It's been a while.

With serenity comes lust.

That there, what I just thought, has got to be some ancient piece of Chinese philosophy.

Mind on the job. Taylor stands before us.

'We're welcoming back DS Hutton today,' he says, pointing a desultory finger my way. They've all noticed me already of course. No one nods or says anything. One or two of them might have been glad to have me back, but I'm not the friendliest bastard in these parts. I'm just another copper in a room full of them. Well, I have slept with three of the women, but fortunately none of the WAGS.

Of the three women, I used to be married to Sergeant McGovern, so you know, you can take sex for granted. It lasted less then a month – I mean the marriage, not the sex. I know I'm a bit fucking full of myself sometimes, but not even me... Then there's Constable Grant. Bit awkward. Had sex once as a result of there being a bit too much alcohol consumed on both sides. But then, I'm rarely embarrassed about it, while Grant could barely show her face around here for the next week. Assumed I'd tell everyone, and seemed downright shocked that I didn't. And then there's Constable Carr. That one was a bit more long term. And when I say long term, I mean four weeks. Maybe five, if you count the part where we weren't talking to each other but hadn't actually acknowledged that she thought I was complete bastard.

So, on the SexPossibility-ometer McGovern is out, what with her being married to the other McGovern at the station. Grant, well she respects me a bit more now because I didn't publish a full account of our all-nighter in the Sun, but she's still pretty embarrassed about the fact that she got nailed by someone who's fifteen years older than her. And Constable Carr still thinks I'm a complete bastard.

Which leaves the four other women in the room to be considered.

I'm supposed to be listening to Taylor.

'... planned out, to the last detail. Sgt Harrison, how's it going on trying to establish a link between the victims?'

Sgt Harrison glances at her notepad. Best sergeant around these parts and several steps ahead of the likes of me in the promotion race. And it is a race.

'Nothing,' she says. 'I think we can probably go so far as to draw a strict inference that these people definitely did not know each other and were not connected in any way whatsoever.'

'You've spoken to...'

'Done the rounds, been across the board. You can never be completely sure, of course, because how can you know?

Not everyone documents every minute of their lives, albeit even that seems to be changing... Nevertheless, although Sparing worked in social services, we can't really call him a social worker. Apparently he only did that for a couple of months, couldn't handle it, and ended up as support staff. Paperwork. Had no connection with the police. Had never, his family says, had reason to speak to the police. Not, of course, that Goodwin worked in his area anyway.' She flicks the notebook, waves a rather mournful hand across it. 'I'll give you more details later, if you like. But these people didn't know each other.'

'OK, thanks. Morrow, how's it going at pathology?'

Detective Constable Morrow also has a notebook. A quick glance round the room. Everyone has a notebook. Seriously, everyone in the room is sitting there with a fucking notebook in their hands. Pen at the ready. Jesus.

I, of course, don't have a notebook. I suddenly feel like I'm standing naked in the middle of the street. The weird thing is that they've all got the same notebook. I mean, all right, there's the standard police issue, but there's more than one notebook in the police service, and there's usually someone brings something a little idiosyncratic to the table. It's like some weird satanic worship thing where I'm the only one not involved.

'They're sure now that Tucker died first,' says Morrow. 'Quite possibly as much as an hour before the others.'

'So the journalist didn't suffer too much...' says Taylor ruefully. Dark, but well said.

'Relatively speaking, no. The other two both showed signs of surviving much longer, and with much greater brain degradation, before they died.'

Man, that's one of those situations where you're going to just hope that you go quickly, isn't it? Sometimes you're going to want to hang on as long as possible – say for example, if you're dying while Scotland are playing Brazil in the World Cup Final – and sometimes you're going to just want to fucking peg it.

Maybe they clung on, their nerves twitching and bodily

functions failing, in the hope that they'd be found. That they'd get to live on, live another day, live out their days in a quiet suburb, watching daytime television and visiting their therapist.

'Anything else?' asks Taylor.

'They're keen to point out the quality of the workmanship. They got a brain guy in from the Western to take a look, and he said the work was done with surgical precision.'

'So do we think we're looking for a brain surgeon?'

'Not necessarily. It wasn't as if the bloke performed surgery on the brains. He was just a dab hand at removing an area of the skull without inducing fatal bleeding. He could have practiced on animals. And maybe on humans. I did wonder if there were missing persons that he might be responsible for, where he practiced his craft before going public.'

Taylor stares at him for a second, then looks at the floor. Thinking it over. That's a decent thought from Morrow, but it's a tough one to move on. Does he put one of his officers on something that might be a complete waste of time? Where would you start?

Well, with a list of missing persons obviously.

'Give it a go,' said Taylor. 'Yep, you know, don't spend a week on it or anything, but just stick your toe in the water.'

'Yes, Sir.'

'Constable Grant, you help him out. It'll be one of those you'll-know–it-when-you-find-it things.'

'I'm used to that,' says Morrow, immediately shaking his head at the comment.

Taylor ignores it, glances around the room. Eyes settle on DI Gostkowski. When she says her name, she still pronounces the *w* as a *v*, so it can't be too long since her family left eastern Europe, although there's no trace of an accent. She's the number two here, and he hasn't referenced her yet. Wonder what he's had her working on.

She was brought in to replace Leander because, when

he was finally able to return to work, he didn't want to come back here. Thought everyone would be talking about him. Which they were. He was packed off to the other side of the city. Just as well, or it would have been me being packed off to the other side of the city.

'Stephanie, how's it looking on possible revenge motives?'

She manages to talk without looking at her notebook. That's the talent that comes with being higher up the pay scale.

'Blank,' she says. 'Sergeant Goodwin… well, you don't know what kind of petty grudge people are going to bear, but there's really nothing there. A regular policeman's life…' She shakes her head. This time she does glance at her notebook, although she's not actually looking at it. 'A regular police officer's life, no stand-out cases. Recently he's been spending a lot of time going round schools, speaking to youth groups.'

'If this is revenge, it's old, been a long time in the planning,' says Taylor.

'I know. It's hard to imagine that any of the people he's arrested over the years would want to do anything other than put a brick through his car window.'

'All right. Tucker. He's a journalist. He must have fucked someone off. I'm fucked off at him and I'd never even heard of him…'

She answers without any trace of the black humour that Taylor has just introduced into the conversation. I start to drift away, crossing her off the list as I go.

Did I say list?

She's too … I don't know… serious is probably the word. She's a grown-up. You know the sort. Has that air of humourless responsibility about her. You can imagine she's been this way since she was eight. Then later, when all her friends were doing standard teenage things, like getting drunk and listening to indie bands and smoking weird shit and getting annoyed at things that happened a hundred years ago and being outraged at that year's genocide, she was looking disdainfully upon it all and writing in her diary the precise plan of how she was going to become Chief Constable of the Met by the time she was forty-seven. And a half. Marry George. Take two months off to have a child. Harry or Imogen. She probably had the kid signed up to the nursery school of her choice even before she met George.

No, I don't want to get involved with DI Gostkowski. And given the events that led her to be posted here in the first place, it's probably a good idea to leave well alone.

She's still talking.

With Sergeant Harrison being as interested in women as I am, that pretty much leaves Constable Corrigan and Sergeant Jones. Don't know either of them particularly well. They don't usually get dragged into this kind of shit, but it's obviously all hands to the deck. Corrigan looks like she's barely out of school. Really not a great idea for me to be hitting on girls that are damned near twenty-five years younger than me anymore.

Which leaves Sgt Jones. Bobbed blonde hair. Bit of a, I don't know, thirtysomething policewoman cut. And she's young enough amongst our lot to still be pretty fit. Slim. Not bad looking. I don't think I'd be over-snagging. Just need to overcome the fact that she'll know all about me and will more than likely not want anything to do with me.

DI Gostkowski is still talking. I like to think I've heard enough to make a judgement in the case, thereby excusing myself from listening.

Wonder what Jones is doing after work.

6

'What d'you think?'

Taylor and I are sitting in the pub. Our usual. Not the Whale, where the rest of the gang are likely to be, if they're at the pub at all. The younger police officer tends to spend less time in the pub and more time at the gym. Fuck's sake. Of course, I'm banned from the Whale, so it's not as though it's an option. Shouldn't have gone there in the first place.

'For the moment, you're fucked,' I say.

First vodka and tonic in a long time. Since the Leander thing. God it feels good. Crisp and cold and fresh, and perfect on a warm summer's day. There's something to be said for living on the side of a mountain being a Buddhist monk, but not as much as there is to be said for a crisp, cold vodka tonic.

'You're forgetting you're back on the team, Sergeant. You mean, *we're* fucked, not *you're* fucked.'

'I stand corrected, Sir,' I say, acknowledging him with a small movement of the glass.

Taylor looks pissed off, takes another sip from his pint, glances around the bar. There's football on the TV. Never seems right in early August. For me the football season doesn't really get going properly until it's pishing down, freezing cold, and the Thistle are playing against Cowdenbeath in a mudpit.

'Care to elaborate?' he says. 'I didn't bring you off the substitutes bench to state the bloody obvious.'

OK. Still getting back into the groove.

'Everything about this says planning. Planning to the absolute n^{th} detail. A perfectly executed crime. This is a scary fucking guy. None of your drunk aggressive, not even your psycho, can't-keep-his-knife-to-himself type. This is cold and devious. This is... you know, it's the equivalent of the German death camps against the Rwandan thing. Rwanda, a bunch of guys with machetes going about their business, making no attempt to cover up what they did. It was brutal, nasty, vicious. There was no artifice. The Germans. They burnt bodies, they dug deep graves, they used camps and then tore them down when the Russians closed in. They had a system. They systematically murdered. And that's what this guy is doing. He has a system. He's going to do the same thing again. We have no idea when that'll be, but *he* knows exactly when. Exactly.'

Taylor is looking at me while I talk. Face expressionless. I know it's why I'm here. To say what he already knows.

'And worse than that,' I continue, 'he'll already know who he's going to kill, and they won't have any idea. Maybe he's already taken them.'

'We should be looking for missing persons,' says Taylor. 'And not the usual kind, the seventeen–year-olds, the ones who'll have gone out on the piss and ended up on the bus to Aberdeen or in the wrong person's bed.'

'If he really didn't know the three victims and he selected them at random, then we're about to find out if he just selected any old person or whether he has a gripe against these professions. Did he choose social worker, policeman and journalist for a reason, or might it just as likely have been butcher, baker, candlestick maker?'

'We need to get ahead of the game,' says Taylor.

'We always do.'

'So we start by establishing if any police officers have gone missing in the last day or two, because the way he carried out that first murder, he must have grabbed the victims some time before they died. There had to be a gap.'

'Were any of them reported missing?'

Taylor stares at me for a second than shakes his head, drops his eyes.

'He had that covered as well. None of them were missed.'

'Why?'

'A combination of things, and it all points to the fact that this was immaculately planned. Either they lived alone, or the ones who didn't had time off work previously planned. They had arranged to go away. It was… it was like he was inside their lives, knew what they were doing, knew that he could secret them away and nobody would notice. How do we counteract that?'

'He was doing it online? Facebook, that kind of shit?'

He stares at me again. 'You weren't paying attention at the briefing, were you?'

Look a bit sheepish.

'Fuck, Sergeant, head in the game. The next time you're in the same room as a bunch of women, stop trying to work out which one you want to sleep with.'

Hide behind my drink. No one likes to get read like a damned book.

'We're checking it out, but we've found nothing so far.'

'So, realistically, we're not going to know if there are any officers missing?' I ask, to move the conversation on from Facebook.

'No.'

'What do we do about that, then?'

He takes a long drink. Drags his hand across his face.

'If it was just the one station, if we knew it was on our patch, we could introduce a system... I don't know, a checking-in system, a buddy system… But shit, we can't city-wide. And what do we know? Maybe it's country-wide. Maybe the next one'll be in the south of England. Or in France. This level of planning, how in the name of God are we supposed to know?'

V&t to my lips. Getting near the end, and it's losing a little of its crispness. Clearly I'm going to need another one.

'He knows,' I say.

Taylor drains his pint and places it on the table. He

looks into it as the last of the froth hugs the side of the glass and slides down.

*

Second night back at home. Already changed the sheets, did a bit of a tidy. Glad I did it yesterday, as I've already reverted to where I was four months ago. The weeks of clean living and communing with the Gods of the Scottish highlands have gone. I woke up yesterday morning at the foot of a mountain. This evening it feels like a hundred years ago.

Brought a prostitute home with me. I know. Filthy. Picked her up in town. Had to drive on the back of four v&ts to go and find her. No hookers on the streets of Cambuslang and Rutherglen anymore.

She wanted to do it in the car. I wanted her to come back to my place. She refused, which is quite right of course. These people are mental if they go home with anyone. Being a bit pissed, I showed her my badge. She still refused, but at least began to enter into negotiations. I paid through the nose in the end. She wouldn't come until I'd gone to a cash point and got several hundred. It's just sweetie money to me at the moment, because I've got four months wages in there that I've hardly spent.

Back to my place. I made her shower first. Didn't ask how many she'd scored earlier in the evening, didn't want to know. I was gallant enough to shower too. After all that, it was worth it. Every penny. Great tongue on her, absolutely beautiful body, she had the decency to try to earn her money and got stuck into it. Great fun.

A fair compensation for feeling like a complete and total loser for having to go to her in the first place.

Called her a cab, then fell asleep as soon as she was gone. The door was locked and I knew she wouldn't be coming back.

*

Went to see Bob the next night. He didn't disappoint. Not that he ever does. He disappoints some people, of course. The nostalgia brigade, not the fans. The kind of people that go and watch Cliff Fucking Richard and McCartney, the Rolling Stones even. They go along to hear *Hey Jude* and *Livin' Doll* and *Jumpin' Jack Flash*, expecting it to sound exactly like it does on their *Best of The '60s* CD, and by fuck, sure enough those guys are still peddling the same shit and still managing to sound exactly like they did in 1965.

Bob doesn't sound like he did in 1965. His voice is completely shot. Anyway, it wouldn't matter, because he changes the arrangements all the time, and these sad fuckers go along thinking that he'll walk on stage with his acoustic guitar and start warbling his way through *Blowin' In The Wind*; well he'll do you *Blowin' In The Wind* often enough, but it'll be with a full band and a completely different tune, if it's even got a tune, and to the uninitiated he'll be halfway through before they pick up a line they recognise, then they think, *fuck me, this is shit, what a waste of £75*, and they'll storm out and if they can find someone to tell how shit they thought it was they'll do so.

That lot, those people, they can take a fuck to themselves. Bob owes you nothing.

November

7

The games involving the Old Firm got a bit nasty at the weekend. Clyde pitched up at Ibrox on Saturday, and a few of their fans thought it might be fun to have a go at the Scottish lower division superpower. It was brief but nasty. I mean, seriously. Fucking Clyde. The Sunday Mail said that parts of Govan looked like Aleppo, which was just incredibly stupid, not to mention completely inaccurate.

Then, in the interests of even-handedness, some Aberdeen fans got the bug on Sunday, and rocked up at Parkhead looking for a fight, and a little of that spilled out our way, although by then I don't think they were Aberdeen fans, just drunk guys who thought they'd get into a fight because everyone else was. A few injuries, but they all got what they deserved.

Sure, every now and again you'll get an innocent walking down the street who stumbles into a gang of orcs and gets the complete fuck kicked out of him. I might occasionally feel some sympathy for that guy. If he exists. As long as he's not wearing a scarf or a strip, in which case, what did he think was going to happen?

Most of them go looking for it, though. They're looking for the fight, expecting to win in the first place or, failing that, expecting the emergency services to clear up after them. Generally, I think we should just let them bleed. You want to fight for whatever dumb-ass cause you think it is you're protecting, then on you go, but don't expect the rest of society to clean up the mess for you.

Some might argue that the same should apply to people who smoke and drink too much, and end up draining the

NHS of all its funds. The healthy living are supporting the rest of us hard-living chaps. Maybe those folks would be right. I'm just hoping to peg it from some other cause before I get cancer and die a horribly protracted death, dragged out over several years with just my estranged family to pop in and see me once every few months.

Walking back upstairs after a two-hour interview with a bloke who bricked another bloke in the head. The other bloke is in a coma. Our bloke is in custody. Not getting out any time soon, although personally I'd just let him go. Let him back to his feral homeland, where he might well be about to suffer much greater retribution than the courts will be able to visit upon him.

One of those lost generation types. Broken home. Abused as a child. Generally didn't go to school, left officially at sixteen with sod all to his name. Never worked. A child of the benefit system. He can afford his Ibrox season ticket though, albeit they're giving them away like sweeties these days.

That he lives out our way, and not on the other side, does not speak well for his chances. He's also got a self-defence defence as he was being chased. So, all in all, the usual thing. On the surface it looks a clear-cut case of a ned bricking another ned, and then you get into it and there's all sorts of subtext.

The summer seems a long time ago, but sometimes I look back fondly on my days sitting on the side of Ben Ime, watching old people trudge by and Tornadoes low-flying and clouds coming in from the west. Happy days.

There's talk of a redundancy round coming up. They'll be looking for volunteers. I'll need to do the maths. The other side of the coin, the side where one doesn't take redundancy, is that there ain't going to be any less crime committed, but there will be fewer officers around to do anything about it.

To be honest, the lump sum on offer is going to have to be pretty fucking low for me not to go for it. But then, there's a damned good chance that the lump sum on offer will be pretty fucking low.

Back to my desk. The paperwork seems to have grown in my absence. That was one of those things that got mentioned in my annual report. It was made part of my objectives. *Deal with paperwork in a more timely and organised manner.* I even said that I'd do it. I've now had to add that I'll try not to get into fights with anyone from the station, so I've been concentrating on that one. The paperwork thing has slipped.

Morrow is sitting across the desk, head buried as usual. I'm really pleased he's not one of these officious cunts – and I know that's a word that a lot of people hate, but it is the actual dictionary-defined term for people who are just too organised – although naturally his paperwork pile isn't quite as apocalyptic as mine.

'Any word from the hospital?' I ask, slumping into my seat. Not hungover today, but beginning to think that on days when I'm not hungover, I have a kind of anti-hangover feeling caused by withdrawal.

He shakes his head without looking up. I stare at the paperwork for another moment or two. It's breeding. It's breeding so much that I can actually see two pieces of paper humping each other trying to produce more paper. I'd probably get a bollocking from someone if I poured water over them.

Straight back up again and over to Taylor's office. He's in his usual position. Sitting at his desk, albeit this time he's staring at his computer screen rather than at the ceiling. As police officers go, Dan Taylor is slightly more cerebral than others. Not that I want to imply he reads – I don't know – fucking Kierkegaard or anything, but he thinks a lot. Likes to take his time, think things through. He doesn't rush, doesn't jump to conclusions. Spends a lot of time staring into space. Working things out.

I'm more of an Action Man type of police officer. Leap in, punch a few people, a bit of shouting, sort things out. Taylor stares at the ceiling. I believe his methods are more effective than mine. Mine is more fun.

Today, however, he's looking at the computer screen. There's an intensity in his gaze. He'll be looking at a single image, trying to see the thing that everyone else missed. Or looking at a photograph, attempting to read the lie behind the eyes.

He hasn't noticed me yet. Given that I've pretty much just come in for a chat, and the vague hope that seeing me will remind him that he has an interesting case to investigate, I contemplate turning and walking back out again.

Decide that that's just what I will do. Watch him for a moment. Hesitate before leaving. There's something in his face. He's not trying to work something out. There's dread in his eyes, rather than curiosity or inquisitiveness.

'Chief Inspector? Everything all right?'

He doesn't answer for a moment, then finally says, 'Close the door,' without looking up. Shut the door, glance out at the office as I do so. In the far corner I can see three of the guys standing around a computer screen. None of them look happy. One of them is staring over in our direction.

'What is it?' I ask.

He doesn't answer. I watch him for a moment, the strong uneasy feeling growing. I realise that the guys out there are looking at the same thing as Taylor. I look back at them through the office window and can see they've been joined by a fourth, and I know I no longer need Taylor's permission to go and look at what he's watching.

Round the side of his desk with a strange feeling of fear. I've had to watch a lot of really nasty shit online in my time in this job. How bad can this be? And yet I know it's going to be awful.

I stand behind Taylor and look over his shoulder. Recognise it straight away, entirely because it's such a clear picture. Well shot using an expensive digital camera. The scene from the woods. Three people cemented to the ground surrounded by a chaos of birds. It appears that two of the victims are already dead. Maybe they're all dead, but the third is twitching massively beneath his bonds. Body convulsions. But it's impossible to tell whether the person is panicking, or whether the crows that are squabbling over his brain have hit the appropriate nerve, causing him to spasm.

Watch it for a few more seconds and then turn away and return to the other side of the desk. Notice that there are now seven people around the computer and that there are others on their way over. The entire office is being drawn in that direction.

'How?' is all I ask.

'Fuck,' is all he says in reply. Indeed, it isn't a reply at all, more an expression of oncoming disaster.

'Not sure how quickly this'll…' he starts to say, but I point in the direction of the gaggle around the computer and a brief moment of resignation and defeat flashes across his face. Doesn't last long, and he stands quickly.

'Fuck it,' he says. 'We're already behind the curve with this, we need to start getting a grip. I'm going in to speak to the Super, you get them together. Meeting Room A, ten minutes.'

He walks past me, stops at the door.

'Make it five,' he says, and then he strides off in the direction of higher authority.

8

Back in the operations room. This is what we've feared for the last three months. Worse, indeed, given that we didn't know the killer had filmed the twitching, bloody horrible deaths.

We don't know exactly when it started, but instantly the Plague of Crows is all over the internet. The Plague of Crows. That's what he's calling himself. Wanker.

Twitter, Facebook, Blogger, YouTube, all over. Every single social media site you can think of, hundreds of them, names being thrown around that I don't even know exist. Now, all right, that doesn't really mean too much. I couldn't begin to care about all that shit, but the young 'uns around here, and the experts, a lot of this is new to them too. And the guy has accounts coming out of his arse. The Plague of Crows is a new presence in the world of social media, he's well prepared, and suddenly he has unleashed a clusterfuck of online horror.

Straight off, we're diving in there, trying to get sites closed down, things taken off. Not from this station, of course; this thing flew straight to the top. This is the kind of thing that will have had the First Minister feeling his testicles squeezed. The police, however, look worse than anyone.

A few months ago there were three people killed in the woods, and we did a deal with as many influential people as we needed to play it down. And now, there on every single computer monitor in the damned world, is proof that we lied.

People love that shit. The media love that shit. Those who didn't know anything about it will be exploding in a masturbational paroxysm of police-hating frenzy, and those who knew but had been persuaded to keep quiet will now be unleashed.

This isn't the worst thing, of course. The media deciding that the police are a bunch of lying fuckers? We get that every day. 'We'll never trust the police again,' say public who believe everything they read in the papers. Yeah, whatever.

'Why now?' says Taylor, standing at the head of the room.

We haven't met like this to discuss the summer deaths since last month. It was full on for a few weeks, then it began to tail off. There really was nothing to find. The guy who'd done it, had done it well. Eventually we had to acknowledge that there were other crimes being committed. I got taken off it about four weeks ago. Taylor's still going, however. He has worked on nothing else for three months. The superintendent has been quite happy with that, aware of just how shit this whole business has the potential to be.

There were two things we've been scared of all this time. One was that the truth behind the killings would get out and a shit storm would be unleashed. The other was that he'd do it again.

'Is he going to do it again? Has he already done it, and out there, right now, there's a small group of people strapped to chairs, shitting themselves? We need to know. We need people looking, we need to work on the basis that the three victims targeted the last time were done so because of their professions. So let's start looking to see if any such people are missing. And not just around here, or around Glasgow. This could be all over. We've got…'

The door opens, the Superintendent comes in. He nods at Taylor, who immediately steps back and cedes the floor to the boss.

His name is Connor and he came down from Aberdeen when the vacancy arose. No way they were promoting anyone from around here. Given the stories that were going around about us being a complete bunch of fuck-ups and the total shitbucket of criticism that came the way of all of us once the full story of that tube DCI Bloonsbury was known, they were dedicated to sending in a hard bastard to clean up the joint.

Didn't really help with me banjoing a fellow officer just a few months after Connor pitched up. Taylor must have really had to fight my corner, although there have been plenty of times in the last few months when I would have been grateful if they'd just left me sitting on my mountain.

So Connor comes in expected to be the hard man. A tough senior copper, sorting out the mess left by the previous incumbent who, in the opinion of most of these senior dinosaurs, suffered horribly from being a woman. We're not supposed to like him. We're supposed to think he's a wanker. If we like him he'll be doing a poor job.

Well, he's doing a brilliant job.

'We failed on this in the summer, gentlemen,' he begins, 'and now it's coming back to bite us on the arse. No one, and I mean that, no one... no one is to take any leave, any days off sick, anything, any-fucking-thing, until we have this man nailed to a fucking cross. We need twenty-four hour days, seven days a week...'

Because that's how people work best.

'... let no man stand aside at this time of need...'

Jesus suffering fuck. Quick glance round the room. Everyone is looking at him with the usual glazed expression. I love the fact that there are seven women in the room, but as far as he's concerned, they're men. And you know, I believe that he would think it was a compliment to them, as if being a woman in this job was an impediment.

Switch back on. He's taking a pause. His eyes settle on me for a moment and then move on. Not sure if he's trying to intimidate me, but I really really fucking hate him, so it's not happening.

'The release of this video footage is a serious matter, and one under which a line must be drawn with inordinate haste. If I find that anyone, regardless of rank or status, had anything to do with supplying the footage to this person, then they will be charged and dealt with as surely as if they had committed the murders themselves. Do I make myself clear?'

No one says anything, which is probably because we're all trying to work out what the fuck he's talking about. The footage was obviously taken by the killer while the victims died. It was never, at any stage, in the hands of the police. It wasn't police footage. Why even make that threat? Why even mention it?

That's how small a man he is. Needs to make up potential offences, just so that he can make up threats, just so that everyone can know he's a strong leader.

He has nothing else to add. He looks menacingly around the room, letting everyone know who's boss, and then walks quickly away, giving Taylor a filthy glance as he goes. Slams the door behind him.

What a complete arsehole. Really.

Taylor steps back to the head of the room and looks around us all. He probably wants to say something to show solidarity, to let us know that we're all in it together, not just against the killer. But against that level of stupidity from higher up, it would be unprofessional. So he does the sensible thing and acts as though the last minute and a half never happened.

'We're needing to check on all missing persons in the last couple of weeks. In particular we're interested in police, media, social services, but let's check every missing person that's out of the ordinary .'

He talks on for a while longer, divvying up the various tasks that have to be taken care of. Suddenly this has gone national – global – and there's going to be all sorts of shit hitting all sorts of fans. A lot of the work of the next few hours will be liaison with other authorities, as we try to get as much of the Plague of Crows stuff taken off the internet. The chances of getting it all removed seem incredibly slim.

Taylor, at least, looks keen to rise to the challenge.

Finally, after three months, there's something to do on this case, other than stare at the ceiling and think.

*

Sitting in his office twenty minutes later. He called me in for a quick chat, before I go and spend the next however long it takes searching through as much of the various online footage of the murders as I can find. There's a lot of it out there, on many different sites, although most of it is replicated.

'We don't have much time, Sergeant,' he says, 'so glean as much as you can, as quickly as you can.'

'You reckon the guy's already lined up his next victims?'

I'm dying to go out for a fag. We used to smoke in here quite happily, until Connor arrived. I don't think anyone's risked having a fag indoors since the minute he walked into the building. That first morning he stopped as soon as he walked into the office. He smelled the air, looked around the room. 'There's a no smoking policy in the building, I take it?' he asked. Someone nodded. 'Good,' he said.

That was all it took. None of us have smoked inside since, although all of us immediately thought, *wanker*...

'Well, yes, I do, but it's not that. We're not getting left with this much longer.'

'How d'you mean?'

He waves a dismissive hand out at the station.

'The shit's hitting the fan, Sergeant. This isn't just a national story. It'll be global. It'll be on the news in ... I don't know...everywhere. America, Brazil, fucking Vietnam... You think they're going to be happy about a no-name DCI from the arse end of Glasgow being in charge of a crime investigation that'll be in the New York Times?'

'You think Connor will take over?'

'Connor? No way. He was sent here to be a school

teacher. To impose discipline on you lot.'

'And you,' I throw in quickly, but we're not really in the place for any light banter.

'He's an authoritarian, pen-pushing arsehole, as we just witnessed first hand. He's not getting to investigate anything, and neither will he want to. He's the kind that'll only take on what he's confident he'll succeed at.'

'So, who d'you think?'

'I think they'll bring someone in from outside.'

'Fuck.'

'Yeah, fuck,' he says.

He rubs his hands over his face, but he's not tired, he's not stressed. He's in a good place these days. Determined, if nothing else.

'So, we need to get somewhere before they breeze in and take it off us. Best case scenario is that they leave us working on it too, under some sort of umbrella operation. It'd be stupid not to. But the new guy might want us to have nothing to do with it. It's not like we can claim any sort of resounding success the last few months.'

Nod. Move to the door. 'Right, I'll crack on.'

'Frame by frame. Flag up the slightest thing, no matter how trivial.'

And I'm out the door.

Almost bump into DI Gostkowski as I step back into the office. She hasn't mellowed towards me over the last three months. The only real change in our working relationship is that, as so often happens with me, familiarity has bred attraction, and I've decided that actually she's pretty fit. A few warm summer days with her jacket off and the top buttons of her blouse undone.

She's still too much of a grown-up, and unlikely to touch me with a stick, but what the hell. I can dream.

'Detective Inspector,' I say, with a polite nod.

'Sergeant,' she says back.

Then I smile. Always good to hit them with a smile. You know, it doesn't cost anything. It's polite, it's friendly. She, on the other hand, heads off without a second glance.

Work to do. Only the immature are going to bother with the slightest flirtatious smile at a time like this.

Well, there you have it. Time to address the issues at hand, not to be thinking about the endless search for the Holy Grail of convenient, fun and low maintenance office sex.

Mind on the job.

*

Some time later. Called back in to Taylor's office. Me and the boss and a constable from Strathclyde HQ in Pitt Street who's an expert in computer hackery and the like. Detective Constable MacGregor. Looks about twelve. Knows shit about computers, the way I know shit about types of fags and Bob Dylan. His thing is probably more useful than mine.

'You're not holding your breath, Sir, right?' he says.

Taylor shakes his head. 'Can we just try and trace this guy somewhere, even if it's to a cafe or a wi-fi network or something?'

'Not looking good,' he says.

'Fuck,' mutters Taylor, then he gives a small dismissive wave to indicate that the constable should continue. 'Talk me through it like I'm an idiot,' he adds.

'Yeah, me too,' I throw in from behind, which is mostly to let Taylor know that he shouldn't switch off on the basis that I'm going to be understanding what MacGregor's talking about.

'So, your dude's done everything through this e-mail account, PlagueOfCrows@freemail.jp. Now, you can only get a dot-jp e-mail address if you're in Japan. Or rather if your computer is in Japan. Or, and this is the thing, if your computer *seems* to be in Japan. So either he's now in Japan, which isn't completely impossible, as the crimes were three months ago and he could have, like, walked there by now, or he's sitting in Scotland somewhere and he used a proxy server… You know what a proxy server is?'

Well, do ya, punk? Taylor shakes his head, although it's not like he won't have some idea, because the clue's in the title. Our new friend the geek is trying to be dramatic and we're letting him.

'The proxy server is the thing that means we're fucked. Sure, we can get warrants and shit to track down the ISP and IP and the like, but if he created it while sitting in Starbucks, you're screwed. And if he created it while sitting in a library, then you're double screwed, with marshmallows and extra cream.'

'Just…' says Taylor, 'you know, just get to the good news.'

He laughs. 'You're kidding, right? This isn't a good news, bad news situation. You're probably thinking that we can get him when he uploads shit to Facebook, but you know, I can tell you now we're going to find the dude used a proxy server for that too. It's totally boss…'

'Is it?'

'Yep. Totally. He uses a proxy to upload shit and then it looks like he's been posting from Tokyo, from you know, like Fukushimi, some shit like that, and you're just like, wow, what the fuck?'

'We can force the proxy server to give up the info, though?' I throw in from the cheap seats.

He laughs again.

'No can do, compadre. You can't force the proxy dudes to do shit.'

No can do, compadre. Please…

'Listen, Sir, I'm not saying that I'm not going to try.'

'Good,' says Taylor with a bit of tone.

'I'm just letting you know that I doubt we're going to get anywhere. There are people who do this kind of shit, they have no idea of how easy it is for us to track 'em down. But this dude, he knows what he's doing. I'm about to spend the next several weeks on this, and I'm already pretty sure that every alleyway he leads me down is going to have a brick wall at the end. It's like, you know, there could be metadata and shit included in the film and JPEGs that he's uploaded, we often times catch out folks with that shit. Just got a feeling, though. Just got a feeling. This guy knows what he's doing. He's boss, man. I'm telling you, totally boss.'

Totally boss… Bloody hell.

9

Jesus, this sucks all kinds of shit, it really does. Sitting in an office at eleven-thirty in the evening watching video footage of three people getting their brains eaten out. Again. I'm watching it again. Not counting how often I've seen it now. Just keep playing it over and over. I want something to take to Taylor. He got me my job back, making sure I wasn't kicked into touch, for a reason. He finds me useful to work with.

Right at the moment, I'm not being very useful. The Plague of Crows might well have been everywhere on the internet, but it was the same shit all over. A lot of it's gone now, but we got copies of it and it was so widespread that there's still a fair amount up there.

As the evening has worn on, the thought has been getting stronger and stronger. This guy is in complete control. He was in control when he committed his crime, he was in control when he chose to release all this stuff to the media. It's not like he was going to have inadvertently included his name and address, or that he'll have accidentally walked in front of the camera and then not edited it out.

And, as predicted, so far the geeks have been unable to unearth any trail through the internet postings. It was beautifully worked. Knew what he was doing, knew how to cover his tracks.

I suddenly get the feeling that he knows I'm sitting here, right this minute, and he's laughing at me. I glance round the office. Most people are still here. Connor might be a total wanker, but he's managed to get us all to do his bidding. No one has dared leave yet, which is a fucking joke.

We're all getting the feel for this, same as we got the feel for it back in the summer. This guy is going to choose when and if he reveals himself. If we get lucky before that, well, it'll be just that. It'll be because we'll get lucky.

Need a fag. Morrow is across the desk, but he's a good lad. Whatever his vices are, and it's not as though he won't have any, they're much better hidden than mine. I've already got Bob and the cigarettes in my pocket. A ten-minute break out the back, will listen, I think, to *Positively 4th Street*, *Will You Please Crawl Out Your Window?* and one other yet to be decided.

My feelings on *Positively 4th Street* have changed over the years. There's really not a lot to it, but it's the feel of thing. I love the organ.

There's a place to smoke out near the front, but go that way and you'll get passed by anyone walking out, including Connor. He's still here, in a meeting with the Chief Constable of Strathclyde and, fucking get this, the Justice Minster from Holyrood and his minions. Ha! Wankers, the lot of them. The shit's hitting the fan so let's bring the politicians in, because obviously they'll know what they're doing.

Out the back, just digging the earphones out of my pocket, find that I'm not alone. DI Gostkowski, halfway through, at a guess, a Lambert & Butler. Like smoking a dog shit, but each to their own. I nod, she nods. Hesitate for no more than a second while I decide whether to engage, then decide not to. I'm knackered. I really want to go home and go to bed, and I need the break. I need the filthy smoke in my lungs, and I need Bob whining in my ear.

I get the music going, earphones in, light up the fag, deep draw, milky and smoky death filling my insides. Fuck, that tastes good. Breathe out slowly. It's a cold night, and I've only got a shirt and jacket on. Feel the cold, but don't care. It's fresh. Gostkowski, being possibly the most organised person on earth, is appropriately dressed.

Stand in classic pose, one hand in pocket, other with a

fag, eyes closed. I'm not even thinking about her.

'Dylan?' she says. As if she knows exactly how loud she'll need to speak for me to hear her above the music.

Earphones out and back in my pocket, don't fiddle about with the MP3 to turn it off.

'You like Dylan?'

'Some of it,' she says. 'Haven't listened to him in a while. You and the boss listen to nothing else?'

'Pretty much.'

She nods. That'll be it, then. She planned a four-sentence conversation. And some of them were pretty fucking short sentences. Now I'm stuck with the dilemma of whether or not to put the earphones back in.

What a stupid dilemma. It shouldn't even be a dilemma, but it is. I don't want to stand here in silence, I don't have anything to say to her. If I try to force conversation it'll be awkward and uncomfortable and just generally shit, but then I'm standing here thinking that if I put my earphones back in she might think I'm rude.

For God's sake.

'You ever see him in concert?' I ask.

The kind of small talk that normal people have.

'Is it true about you and DI Leander?' she asks. 'Well, Leander's wife.'

'You don't believe the stories?'

'People make things up,' she says. 'They exaggerate.'

Acknowledge that with slight head movement. Doesn't take much. She's got a nice voice. I like DI Gostkowski.

Jesus, and what are you basing that on? *Her voice, she's more organised than I am and she looks good in a coat.* Get a grip, Sergeant.

'It seems very cavalier,' she says. 'Once, maybe, because that's what happens. But an affair, a public affair that everyone knows about. Seems curious behaviour.'

She doesn't add, *for a grown-up*, but she might as well have done.

So I do that thing that ultimately proves very dangerous. I don't try to employ artifice of any kind, don't measure my words, don't try and sound something I'm not, to try to impress her. I'm just honest. Women have this weird view of honesty, as if it's a positive.

Start by shrugging, albeit a shrug that doesn't get any further then a casual movement of the cigarette.

'I thought the same thing too. Just once. Makes sense. You get a taste, you know what it was like, add her to the list, she can add me to her list, everybody's happy…'

'Except DI Leander…'

'Well, at that stage I guess he wouldn't have known. But, of course, you're lying to yourself, aren't you? Maybe if it was shit, if the sex was shit, then sure, once is going to be enough. But we're both in our 40s, we know what we're doing. The sex wasn't shit. It was fantastic. Loud, raucous, tender in places, fast and slow. When she went on top… man, you should have seen her… Jesus.'

Take another draw from the fag. Getting a little carried away. Happy days. Look at DI Gostkowski. She's staring at me, but there's nothing in her face.

Shake my head.

'What are you going to do? Once is never enough. And you know… you know if the first time is brilliant, if it's brilliant from the start, it's only going to get better. It always gets better. So you do it once, and you think, all right that'll do, enough already. But there's a voice, and the voice is saying, imagine what it's going to be like a month from now. Two months from now. You know there'll be a point where you've done it enough, when it stops getting better, when it's no longer fresh, but it ain't after the first time. Never is…'

I'm not looking at her. I've got her hooked though. And the reason she's hooked is because I wasn't trying to hook her. I look across the car park to the dull houses on the street. Some lights on, some people already in bed.

'Well, I had sex with PC Grant once. That was a relationship with a natural lifespan of one night.'

As soon as the words are out my mouth I kick myself. Fucking idiot. Really. For months now I've been priding myself on the fact that I've managed not to tell anyone about Grant, and quite liked the fact that I'd obviously surprised her. And now I just blurt it out. Fucking moron. Gostkowski looks like a safe pair of hands, but you never know, do you?

Look at the ground. Embrace self-loathing. And although it has nothing to do with it, although a glib throwaway comment about a night spent with PC Grant really ought to have no bearing on the past, self-loathing always takes me back to the same place. Takes me back far enough, to a warm night in a forest. A long time ago. A different world. A different me.

That's what I want to think. A different me.

'When are you stopping? Tonight I mean?' she asks, pressing the butt into the ground with her boot.

Dragged back. The chord to the past temporarily snapped. Although it'll never be broken. At least, not until I face up to it in some way other than the odd moment of darkness, staring into the night.

'Don't know,' I say. 'He's a fucking idiot if he thinks he's going to get anywhere with no one getting any rest...'

'Yes.'

There's a movement behind us. One of those young constables whose name I haven't managed to learn yet since I got back. He addresses Gostkowski. Maybe it's because she's the senior officer, maybe it's because he knows her. Maybe I'm invisible in my smoky, melancholic haze.

Shut up!

'The DCI says everyone not on the night shift has to go home, be back in for eight.'

'Thanks Graham,' she says, and the young fellow heads back inside, out of the cold.

She glances at me as she turns towards the door. I've not finished the smoke, and am in no rush. There's a moment while we stare at each other. One of those stares. You know the kind. The one where you both know that at some stage you're going to end up in bed together, but not tonight. The mood might have been heading in that direction, but it's been broken.

The seed has been planted, however, if only because neither of us was planting anything.

'Good night, Sergeant,' she says.

I nod, she breaks the look and heads inside.

The door closes and I'm left on my own looking across the car park. I'm knackered, but tonight will be one of those nights when I don't sleep.

There are too many of those nights.

10

Seven minutes past eight. Made it into work ahead of schedule, mainly because I didn't have time to get drunk last night, hardly slept, was wide awake from about six. Got up, already wearied and worn out. Shaved, showered, made myself some bacon and toast and coffee. Drank orange juice. Watched the news. The Plague of Crows was all over. They had the Justice Minster on, announcing that this would be the government's top priority and that a team of top Edinburgh detectives were being put on the case.

He actually said that, used that very phrase. Top Edinburgh detectives. He didn't say that it was because Glasgow detectives are obviously shit, what with them being so provincial, but then he didn't say it in such a way as he said it.

So I got into work not long after seven, and now it's seven minutes past eight and Taylor and I are sitting in Connor's office. Waiting to be informed, presumably, that we've been put back on traffic duty what with us being so shit, 'n' all. If only we'd received our training in Edinburgh. We're so disadvantaged.

I reckon, and I'm just saying, that if we ever get to be independent, the nation will quickly descend into the kind of ethnic violence and hatred that you get in all those countries in the middle of Africa the minute the sensible (or vicious imperialist) authority buggers off. Catholics versus Protestants, Edinburgh versus Glasgow, Highlands versus soft southern lowland bastards. Someone, somewhere, will want to make amends for Culloden. We hold a grudge. It'll be shit.

I'm still going to vote for it, though. Time to stand on our own two feet, rather than get a piggy back for the rest of eternity.

'What the fuck are you thinking about?' says Taylor.

I glance over. Uh-oh. Must have been doing that thing where I was having an internal discussion and was letting it show on my face.

'Politics.'

He looks at me with that wry paternal smile.

'Trying to decide whether you'd shag Sarah Palin or Aung San Suu Kyi?'

The door opens behind us before I can puke my stomach out laughing, and Connor walks crisply into the office. Sits down across the desk. First time I've been in here since the Leander incident. Still feel that vague discomfiture at being forced to sit in the presence of authority. Even, or maybe especially, when it's a total ball sack like this bloke.

'You'll have heard the news,' he says.

He's tired. Hasn't slept at all. Must give him credit for that, I suppose. When he'd first made his preposterous 24/7 speech, I kind of imagined him buggering off home at some time after six, spot of dinner, game of bridge down the club, early night, swan into work about nine. He's still wearing the same clothes as yesterday. Hasn't been home.

'There's a task force coming from Edinburgh,' said Taylor, who somehow manages to say the words *task force* without spitting.

'Yes,' says Connor.

He stares at us both for a moment, and I suddenly realise that he's pissed off. I'd been assuming he'd love it all, the attention, the murders on his patch, the meetings with senior constables and government ministers. But of course, of course he's pissed off. He loves being in charge, he's a micro-managing control freak. Needs everyone doing exactly as he wants. And this absurd task force of red-hot genius coppers who have solved every fucking crime they've ever stumbled across – which is why Edinburgh is such a shiny, beautiful, crime-free place to live – won't be coming in here under his charge. There'll be someone arriving to take over, leaving the Superintendent to do his usual thing, dealing with local crime and overseeing us bunch of shit Glasgow polis who are incapable of solving our way out of a paper fucking bag.

'It's understandable,' says Taylor. What the fuck? Connor gives him the imperious eyebrow, but Taylor never was one to be intimidated by authority. 'We thought we were looking for one guy who had committed a grotesque murder on our patch. Now... well, we know it was a pretty damned well-organised murder, and that level of organisation has continued. Maybe it wasn't just the one guy. The victims came from all round the city, and now we've got the internet thing. Presumably it's been done from within Britain, but we don't know if it's from Rutherglen and Cambuslang, do we? Could be anywhere. Indeed, anywhere in the world. I hate it as much as you, but it's understandable.'

'I'm glad you hate it,' says Connor glibly.

Taylor doesn't respond to that. He's said his bit. Makes sense, albeit it wasn't what I'd been thinking. I'm keeping my mouth shut. Not that I've got anything to say anyway.

'We've no option, of course,' adds Connor. 'They want a couple of local officers as liaison.'

He's looking at Taylor. I'm here, but I'm not entirely sure I need to be. Liaison. Taylor's going to be chewing my testicles off when we get out of here, as if it's my fault. Liaison, for fuck's sake.

'I've given them DI Gostkowski and Constable Grant. They've been involved before, they know everything... They do know everything?'

Taylor takes a moment to think about it. He's given the case far more time than anyone else. It's been his case, his priority. How much does he know, how many mental moves ahead has he made on the chess board of the investigation that he hasn't communicated to anyone else?

'Yes,' says Taylor. 'Gostkowski will do a good job.'

'She'd better,' says Connor. 'I'm going to ask her to play

both sides.'

Holy crap, now we're talking.

Oh. He didn't mean *that*, did he?

'Sir?' says Taylor.

He's genuinely curious, while I'm sitting here with an image in my head of DI Gostkowski playing both sides. Need to get a grip.

'I'm not letting this investigation get away from me,' says Connor. 'I'm not happy about it. I want you two to stay on it. You'll need to be discreet and you'll need to keep out of Edinburgh's way. You've been working it for three months now, Chief Inspector, so hopefully you'll be a few steps ahead. Should be, at any rate.'

He pauses, looks from one of us to the other. Office politics. Holy shit. They all condemn me for the office affair, but shit, that's nothing compared to office politics. That's a fucking battleground, plagued by all sorts of evil pitfalls.

'You will report to me, and Edinburgh will not know you're involved. DI Gostkowski will liaise with you. It will be one way. She'll let you know what's happening with their side, but will not reciprocate, unless I gauge that we should. I very much doubt that she will be given anything like full access to the investigation, but she'll be on the inside and we'll have to wait and see what she can generate.'

'PC Grant?' I ask.

'Will not be in on any of it. She'll be liaising with the task force as intended.'

Taylor sits back. Thinking it through. This has potential to be ugly. There are power games going on, and we're getting sucked into it. That's what he's thinking. Is there a way out? How can he avoid this? It is tempered, of course, by the thought that he'll want to do it too. He really does hate Edinburgh getting brought in.

'OK,' he says. 'How do you want us to work?'

'You do your own thing,' says Connor. 'I'm not a detective, I'm leaving you to it. It's… it's rogue, going rogue. I don't like it, but I like that lot coming here much less. And like I said...'

He hesitates then looks at me.

'... be discreet.'

He nods in the direction of the door.

Taylor rises and I follow him out. Not sure that I've taken a breath in the last minute or so, Connor built up such an air of tension.

We get out his office, the air clears and we stop for a second to look at each other.

'Fucking rogue,' is all that Taylor says, shaking his head.

'You be Danny Glover, I'll be Mel Gibson?'

He gives me the look then heads for his office, his discreet and obedient sergeant in tow.

11

When I say office… Twenty minutes later we're sitting in Starbucks in Hamilton. Just got off our patch, come for morning coffee. The place is jumping. Why make yourself a cup of instant at home, when you can give Starbucks a few quid plus some other stupid amount of money to eat something you didn't know you wanted until you got in here? This is the coal face of the recession. People with nothing better to do than drink over-priced coffee.

As we were walking out of the station, the cavalry were arriving. I wondered if they'd all be dressed in black suits, wearing shades, and have toothpicks sticking out the corners of their mouths. But they were just a bunch of guys. And women. The alpha male wasn't obvious as they walked by. Perhaps they're an autonomous collective.

'I don't know how this ends well,' I say, to break the long silence. Taylor has been drinking coffee and thinking. He shakes his head. In agreement. 'They catch him and we don't, we're wasting our time,' I continue. 'None of us catch him, we're all fucked. We catch him… then what do we do? We take him in there, throw him to the wolves and say, *Boom! In your face, you Edinburgh wankers…*'

'There is no end game,' says Taylor. 'Connor's not thinking that far ahead. His nose is out of joint and he's doing the first thing he thought of to fight back. Not a lot else he could do.'

'He could have sucked it up and accepted his place.'

'No one sucks anything up any more, Sergeant.'

We both drink. Neither of us bought anything to eat. Another customer arrives, but they won't find anywhere to sit. Cold morning again, feel the draught as the door opens and closes.

'He's coming again,' says Taylor. 'He has to be. Why start all this shit off unless that's what he's doing? And he's confident he's not going to get caught at it. He knows he's not going to get caught. How does he know he's not going to get caught?'

He looks earnestly at me. I've just been thinking that my coffee could be warmer.

'I'm thinking.'

Rubs his chin. We both find ourselves looking over at a kid in a pram agitating to be given more chocolate, which the father inevitably hands over.

Have barely seen my own kids this year, which is shit. Can't think about that now, although that appears to be what I usually think when I think of my own kids. No time.

'Maybe we need to start looking at woods, the woods around here, further afield. Work out where he strikes next.'

'That's a lot of woods,' I say. 'An unworkable amount of woods. And we're assuming he does the same the next time.'

'Exactly,' says Taylor. 'He may have called himself the Plague of Crows, but maybe next time he's going to be the Plague of Chainsaws and tuck his victims away in a disused warehouse.'

I laugh, but we both know that's not going to happen.

'He's established an instantly identifiable corporate image,' I say. 'I don't think he's changing that.'

'Which means, if he's coming back, chances are he's doing the same thing again. Multiple killings in a wood. So how does he know he won't get caught?'

'He doesn't do it around here,' I say. 'Unless he's already done it.'

'Yep.' Quick, unnecessary glance at his watch. 'We've known about this less than twenty-four hours. Not impossible that it's happened in a wood in central Scotland, or anywhere else in Scotland, and the victims haven't been discovered yet. For all his careful planning, that is one thing he must have left to chance. How could he know that someone wouldn't be out walking? A hiker, someone walking the dog, whatever.'

'He could take care of them. Add them to the list. A more regular murder.'

'But he wouldn't know that they hadn't told someone where they were going. That's chance again. They don't come home, odds are someone goes looking for them… Shit, we've been over this before... He knew he was safe, and whatever it was he put in place the last time, he could have done it again.'

'One thing's different,' I say. 'The trees.'

'Fuck, aye. Decent thought, Sergeant, he's not going to have the same level of cover.'

'Which reduces the number of woods or forests he's going to be able to use.'

'Hmm…' he mutters. Hand drawn over the face, more coffee, another look around the joint. The whining kid is demanding something else. The dad immediately capitulates and hands it over. We ought to be able to arrest people for that kind of thing. Sure, they'd object at the time, but they'd thank us in the long run.

'We're looking for an evergreen forest,' says Taylor. 'You think that's it? A pine forest, something like that?'

'Do crows like pine?' I ask. He doesn't answer, but he isn't likely to. How the fuck do we know if crows like pine?

'All right,' he continues, 'since we've picked up the ball… We've got our pine forest. Where the fuck is it? There's not a lot of pine around here, but one of the things he's done in the last twenty-four hours is take it global. Why Scotland? He could be anywhere. Hell of a lot of pine in the world.'

'And if he was somewhere else, it wouldn't necessarily be pine. Could be any kind of forest. Could be in the middle of the fucking desert.'

Taylor nods, drains his coffee.

'We can't go everywhere with this. We need to keep it

grounded. Small steps. We've got a wood or forest, we've got crows, and we've got crows' nests. He needs cover so he's likely to have to use an evergreen forest...'

'But not a densely populated one, not one of those they plant just so they can chop them down again a few years later...'

'Too dense for the crows, less likely to find a convenient, natural clearing in the middle of it.'

'Yes.'

'Yes, yes...' says Taylor, his mind going over the options, '...but there are still going to be woods with bare trees that just by their sheer volume or location provide cover, so we'll have to consider those too.'

Suddenly Taylor straightens, shoulders back, head up.

'You finished?'

He still drinks faster than me.

'No,' I say.

'Leave it then.'

'Where are we going?' I ask, as we make for the door.

'No point in us sitting around talking about trees. What do you know about trees?'

'Bugger all.'

'Same here. Let's go and find someone who knows about trees.'

'You know wh–'

'No, but we'll find someone who knows someone who knows about trees.'

There's probably a website for that.

12

In the office of the tree expert. Forestry Commission out at Aberfoyle. Forty-five minute journey. I drove. Might have been a waste of time for us both to come out here, but this is how Taylor works. He likes the time in the car. We can stick Bob on the CD player and think. Or we can stick Bob on the CD player, turn it down a little, and talk things through. Only in the most serious of circumstances is Bob sacrificed to the necessity of quiet.

Alice Whittaker is standing at the window looking out over the local woods. We can see the edge of the golf course. Played a round there once on a station day out. I think I shot a handy 136 or so. 70 over par. Not my best round, although sadly not my worst either.

Taylor is looking at maps on the walls, I'm standing with my bum against a ledge, arms folded. There's an informality about the whole thing that wouldn't be there if we were seated around a desk.

So far all we've had is general chitchat and a couple of questions about crows and trees. Nothing much. We didn't say why we were here, but it became pretty obvious the minute crows got a mention.

Taylor spoke to a crow expert last time. Maybe we'll go and see him again. What kind of job is that? Crow expert. I don't suppose it was his actual job title.

'You think your man is going to strike again?'

Taylor can do artifice and bullshit as much as the next man, happy to tell an interviewee as little as possible. He'll gauge the woman, make a call.

Alice Whittaker is all right. You can tell. She won't call a newspaper as soon as we walk out the door and let them know what the police are thinking. She probably won't even tell her husband over dinner tonight that the police called.

'Yes,' says Taylor.

'Which would explain why the man responsible has gone public with footage he's kept tucked away for several months.'

'Yes.'

We're on the first floor, allowing that view up to the woods and the golf course. Taylor, clutching the mug of tea we were given when we arrived, goes over and stands beside her and they look out at the view together. I'm a couple of yards away, feeling a bit left out.

No, really, I don't feel left out. Take a sip of tea. My mug has Arbroath FC written on the side, and I wonder why anyone would have an Arbroath FC mug.

'What are you looking for exactly?' she asks.

'I know this sounds absurdly far-fetched, but we need to know if there's any way we could narrow down his next kill site. You've seen the footage?'

She nods, making the appropriate expression of horror.

'We have to make some assumptions at this stage. So we assume he's doing the same again. But we also assume he's going to need cover to carry out his work. He's not going to be using a wooded area where the trees have shed.'

She's nodding. Thinking it through. Some people would already have laughed at him and told him not to be so fucking stupid. The notion is absurd. It's Scotland. There are trees all over the place. Not as many as there were a thousand years ago, but enough to make it needle-in-a-haystack territory.

'OK,' she says. 'We can lose the densely populated planted forests, as that won't suit his purposes. We can discount some of the deciduous woods, although I'm not sure you can dismiss them completely. Maybe not areas as close to suburbia as the one where the first murders were committed, but there are going to be woods in the middle of Perthshire, and further afield, where there's going to be the opportunity to carry out that kind of work. Around here even. Where it doesn't matter that the leaves have shed, because there are enough trees in the middle of nowhere to provide adequate protection.'

'This guy doesn't leave things to chance,' says Taylor. 'Every angle covered. Spare bit of ground in the country, someone's out walking their dog.'

Slight movement of the head. She doesn't completely agree. But we need to make some calls to narrow down the list. We need something.

'All right…'

'Do you have… is there some kind of reference work, easily referenced map, something like that, where we can look at it and say, right, it can be here or here or here? That's what we're getting at. If we did that, how many areas are we going to need to check out and how many are we likely to miss because we're looking at a map?'

She glances at him, then turns and takes a quick look at me. Making sure I'm still there. Or that I'm not stealing anything.

'Might as well start with Google Earth,' she says.

'What?' Taylor looks annoyed. 'I already looked at Google Earth. I was looking for…. I don't know, something that…'

'You were looking for something that showed all the wooded areas in Scotland, with an overview of the position of those woods in relation to urbanised areas?'

'Yes.'

'Well, let's look at Google Earth. To make you feel better, I'll do it with you, tell you what kinds of trees you're looking at and give you my opinion on whether or not any particular wood is a plausible place for your chap. Happy?'

Taylor makes a throwaway gesture. It is, despite himself, exactly what he was looking for.

'Will you scream if I say you're looking for a needle in a haystack?' she says.

He doesn't scream, but doesn't reply. Takes a step away

from the window, goes and looks at an ordnance survey map on the wall.

'That's south Devon,' she says. 'Won't help you.'

He shakes his head, glances round at me.

'How many men have you got?' she asks. 'Are you going to be able to put officers out in every town and every area? How long are you going to be able to do that? If this guy is smart, he's probably planned for you to be looking out for him.'

'There are two of us,' said Taylor.

She stares at him, and then back at me. Back to Taylor. There's a beautiful silence in the air. With the hills in the background it's taking me back to the summer. A long quiet summer without any of this shit.

'There are two of you on the whole investigation?' she says. 'You're kidding.'

'There are two of us on this part,' says Taylor. Not giving her any more, despite the look she gives him. 'Look, this is shit. It's shit that the guy's done what he's done, it's shit… whatever, it's all shit. We just need your help to try and get ahead of the game. I want to walk out of here with a list. That's all. An ordered list. If the list has a hundred thousand individual small areas of woodland on it I don't care, as long as there's a top and a bottom, a note of what kinds of trees they are, a most likely and a not really much of a chance, a list that we can check out. If there are crows' nests and the wood is in any way secluded, it stays on the list. This guy has given us nothing. We need to get lucky, and all we're trying to do is make our own. Can you help?'

It's obvious she likes the speech. She nods.

'Well, Chief Inspector, it's not like I've nothing else to be doing today, but what the hell. Might as well give it a go. Let's get to work. You can use separate computers, split up the country, and I'll move between the two of you letting you know what I think.'

She moves around her desk and logs onto a monitor that is yet to be activated today.

'We've only got an hour,' says Taylor. 'Don't want to lose too much daylight.'

'Dream on, sunshine,' she says, smiling and shaking her head.

*

Four-and-a-half hours later we're sitting in the car. We have a long list, hastily arranged into order of likelihood. Sadly the top of the list starts with pretty unlikely and then gets progressively more far-fetched.

'We starting around here since we're in the area?' I ask.

He shakes his head. We've been concentrating on the absurd task we've set ourselves, but I know he'll have been thinking ahead. Mentally, I realise that I've been playing the part of the subordinate, waiting to be instructed on what to do next. I'll catch up eventually.

'No,' he says. 'We're going back home, split up, start looking at potential areas as close to the previous. Really, if it turns out the next killings are in Dundee or Inverness or Perth then we are, as Corporal Hicks says in *Aliens*, fucking fucked, man. We look at the places around our patch and hope for the best.'

Start the car, head off, quickly onto the A95 back towards Glasgow. Look up the hill to my nemesis of a golf course.

'We're just wasting our time,' I say after a while, as the pale green countryside passes by. Sudden melancholy, feeling a little bit lost. Put on a hopeless mission, driving around being told what to do. A cold couple of hours ahead, checking on small clumps of trees. And for what? A man cementing chairs into the floor?

'If he never kills again, we're wasting our time,' says Taylor. 'If he kills again, but this time he's gone to Sweden or Normandy or somewhere, then we're wasting our time. But if he picks somewhere that happens to be on that list… even if we don't catch him, it doesn't matter. It means we're on the right track, and we'll have more to work with… next time. So, no…'

Feeling tired after a sleepless night. Would love to fall asleep, but then, I'm driving, so that would be bad. Nevertheless, there isn't any more talking to be done. There really hasn't been any talking to do since early August. It's all been about waiting, and now this rather desperate attempt to force the pace of the investigation.

Get back to the station at 2:43pm. Time to grab a sandwich, then take about 0.005% of the list and get going.

13

6.33pm. Trudge back into the office, stop in the middle of it all. No sign of the hired hands from out of town. Everything seems to be normal, the usual kind of shit and general level of activity for this time of day, midweek. Morrow looks up from his desk and nods. I nod back. Presumably, after one day on the job at all-out speed, he's been removed and put back onto the mundane day-to-day stuff of the Cambuslang/Rutherglen area.

Taylor's in his office so I wander through. Smoked enough fags during the afternoon not to be feeling deprived. Could use a coffee. Maybe some alcohol. Alcohol later, coffee first. Would have stopped off at the Costa on the way in, but thought I should report back. Had hoped that Taylor wouldn't be here yet.

Stand in the doorway. 'How'd you do?' I ask.

He's got one of the maps spread out in front of him, which he's been marking off.

'Looked at around twenty spots. Some of them are definitely out, some 50/50... found two, maybe three that would be good places for our man, nests in place, definite signs of crow activity. How about you?'

'You didn't catch him in the act then?'

'Sadly it's not an episode of Scooby Doo, Sergeant.'

I grunt and walk round behind him to look over his shoulder at the map.

'You make notes?' he asks.

'Yes.'

Annoyed at the suggestion that I might not have done, although generally my paperwork is so shit that I oughtn't to be.

'Right, grab a seat and mark them off.'

'Yes, boss.'

Pull up a seat across the desk from him, turn the map around and start to mark it up. He watches me for a few seconds and then turns back to the computer. Quick glance to see what he's looking at. Twitter. Ah yes, the modern way. That's how we'll find out.

For the moment Plague of Crows isn't trending, having been usurped by four tags related to Justin Beiber, two about John Terry and #replacemovietitleswithcock. Society knows what's important, and here's us worrying about this shit. But he's right to look. While we're running headlong down our tunnel-vision wild goose chase, and the boys from Edinburgh are throwing money and resources at every aspect of the investigation, you can guarantee that the next piece of information will first come to the attention of the police via social networking.

He's searching Plague of Crows, tracking the most recent stuff. A quick glance doesn't reveal anything new.

'I'm going to leave you to speak to DI Gostkowski,' he says.

'Sure.'

'We don't want any of that new mob asking questions. If they see you talking to her, it's just going to look like you're trying to get a shag. They might start questioning it if they think I'm sniffing around.'

'You think there are people on the Edinburgh police force who assume that I spend my entire life trying to get laid?'

'Sergeant, there are police officers in Bandar Seri Begawan who think you spend your entire life trying to get laid.'

Funny. Nice thought, though.

'So, do we have some sort of code?' I ask. 'Is she going to leave a flowerpot on the balcony?'

He turns away from the computer and looks at me like I'm some sort of ridiculous police freak with no clue. I get that look from him a lot, although it is at least contradicted by the fact that he wanted me here in the first place.

'You're meeting her in the Costa down the road at 7.'

'Oh. Right.'

'You'll be talking about work,' he says, giving me the look.

'She's way too serious for me,' I say.

'Bollocks,' he mutters, shaking his head and looking back at the monitor. 'Too serious... You'd have sex with a four-thousand-page essay on 17th century Scottish agriculture if it'd let you.'

*

I've got an Americano. I asked for space for extra milk and still had to give it back to them so they could tip some of it out to allow space for extra milk. It's like their mission statement is *We Will Burn Your Lips The Fuck Off*. DI Gostkowski is drinking mint tea with delicate little sips.

'What d'you do all day?' she asks.

'You're on our side, right?'

She smiles.

'Despite what all you strapping men think, it's not a competition. Nevertheless, I've been instructed by the Superintendent only to pass back the information that he authorises me to. So, your secrets are safe with me.'

'We went looking for possible woods that the killer might use the next time.'

She pauses, the cup at her lips, then sets it back down without taking anything from it.

'You looked for trees? In Scotland?'

'Yes.'

'Did you find any?'

'Funny.'

'Seriously? There have to be a million places that this guy could use...'

'We narrowed it down to around nine hundred or so... Well, you know, in the vicinity. And then, you know, some of them are going to have nests and very obvious crow communities, and those are the ones that we can concentrate on. Shouldn't be so many in the end.'

It seemed pretty lame as we went about our business this afternoon. Now, explaining it to another polis, it sounds flat out stupid, despite my best attempts at justification.

She takes her next sip, bit of a longer drink this time as it's cooled down enough. Finally makes some kind of 'well, I suppose you have to do something' expression with her face.

'What are the Bat-team up to?' I ask to get us off the subject. Don't want to loiter over the possibility that two senior detectives spent their day chasing their own bollocks.

'I don't suppose what they did amounted to much more. Spent the day familiarising themselves with the investigation. I can't say that they had anything new to add at this stage. Seem like a sharp enough bunch.'

'Full of themselves or aware that they're stepping on toes?'

'Oh…' she begins, and then thinks about it. At least, she's thinking about how to put it, rather than thinking about whether or not these people might actually be in danger of disappearing up the arsehole of their own self-importance.

'They're confident,' she says eventually.

'Good. Confidence is important.'

She smiles a little at that. We glance at each other, then let our eyes drift around the café. These places are just permanently busy nowadays. Everybody's drinking coffee. Even the people who are going to go and get pissed later, still have a coffee first.

Maybe I'm just making that shit up. What do I know?

'So, have you got anything for us?' I ask.

Quick shake of the head, and she looks slightly abashed. This will, presumably, become a nightly thing, and it's going to get a little awkward if she has nothing to say every day.

'Like I said, they were getting their feet under the desk. They spent the day asking questions. Tomorrow, I suppose, we'll find out if they've got anything new to bring to the table.'

We hold each other's eyes for a moment, then she looks at her watch.

'Gotta go,' she says and takes a last quick sip of tea. Her phone has been sitting unlooked at on the table, and she lifts it and puts it in her pocket as she stands. 'Same time tomorrow, Sergeant?'

'Sure,' I say, which doesn't sound like much, but is better than all the innuendo that immediately came to mind.

'Right. I'll be in touch if there's anything I think you should know before then,' she says, and then she's off, back out the door and onto the street, leaving me alone with a half-drunk Americano with a little too much milk.

I watch her across the street. Can't quite see the entrance to the station from where I'm sitting, but keep following her until she's out of sight. Then I turn back to my coffee and take a long drink.

Check my phone. No messages. 7:17. Ought to be getting back to work. Wonder how it went with Taylor explaining to Connor that we set out on a two-man mission to search every wood in Scotland.

Hopefully he lied. That's what I would have done.

14

Already dark.

The policeman, the journalist the social worker; the tailor, the baker, the candlestick maker.

The lucky three.

Police Constable Morgan. Lives on the outskirts of Dundee, works in Perth. Single, no kids. Has been friends with his killer online for nearly a year, although all this time has known the Plague of Crows as a twenty-seven-year-old woman named Dulcie.

Linette Grey. Lives in Bankfoot, works on the front line of social services in Perth. Single, no kids. Spends her days visiting families who hurt each other. Three-year-olds still in nappies who are never fed or changed, six-year-old children given alcohol and cigarettes and not much else, drug addicts, wife-beaters, husband abusers, child abusers. She deals with the police often; a couple of times it has been Constable Morgan. But just a couple, which isn't many, given the number of years she's been doing the job. The police, however, when it comes to looking for a connection between the victims, are at least going to be able to find one, and it will lead them off in entirely the wrong direction.

Malcolm Morrison. Lives in the centre of Perth in a modern, chic apartment. Small, but perfect for impressing women. Single, no kids. Works for the Dundee Courier & Advertiser. Fancies himself for a job on one of the big London tabloids, but there is plenty of time. For the moment he's compiling an interesting body of work. Some people might consider that they'd suffered by his hands along the way, but they could live with it. Or not. Has been friends with his killer online for nearly a year, although all this time has known the Plague of Crows as a twenty-seven-year-old woman named Dulcie.

Dulcie has a lot of friends. Dulcie knows how to cover her tracks.

Linette Grey awakens to find herself in a small clearing in the middle of a wood. She feels cold. It takes her some time to sort out all the sensations in her head. The cold. The fact that she can't move any part of her body. The low hills above the tree line. The two men strapped to chairs less than a couple of yards away. The fact that she recognises one of them but can't remember who it is. The fact that the one who isn't strapped down, the other person in the clearing doing something to the head of one of the men, she doesn't recognise at all. The fact that when she realises what's happening, and she tries to scream, no sound comes out.

From somewhere overhead comes the loud squawk of a crow. She can't compute that either. She tries to scream again.

They are in a small wood, about a mile from the A85 between Perth and Crieff. Even if she had been able to scream, no one would have heard, but the Plague of Crows doesn't like to take chances.

15

Worked until just after eleven, reviewing everything we have on the case, looking over all the potential murder sites trying to make some sort of informed guess about where we should check next, then home to a late supper and crawling into bed – on my own – about one. Started thinking about Gostkowski late in the evening and wondered if we might bump into each other at the cigarette hole, but it didn't happen.

Home alone, late, two nights in a row. Not about to end either, is it? We're no nearer catching this bloke or having even the faintest idea who it is. Long, late nights stretching immeasurably into the future. Jesus.

Slept all right, got to the station just before eight. Still have that feeling that I'm last to arrive. Feel everyone looking at me, like *where the fuck have you been, don't you know there's a war on?*

I stop, look around. I'm imagining it. Most of our lot aren't involved in the war, and they don't give a shit that I wasn't at my desk by 6 a.m. They're like soldiers, trained and armed to the teeth, dispatched into the war zone, and then told, *nah, don't bother, these other guys are going to do the fighting, you lot go and jerk off in the corner*.

Since the Leander business I've got it in my head that they're all wary of me, all looking at me. I'm thinking it's about me. The disease of conceit, as Bob says. Despite having been here for more years than I want to remember, I'm just not one of them. They don't give a shit about me, I don't give a shit about them.

Straight to Taylor's office. No point in even going to my desk. Ramsay at the front desk has been instructed not to send anything new my way. The endless piles of crap that are sitting there and have been waiting for weeks or months, can continue to sit and wait.

Shit day outside, low cloud, miserable. It's not been light for long, and it's one of those days when it'll never be anything other than gloomy as all fuck. The grey light of dawn will merge horribly into the grey light of morning and afternoon.

'Morning.'

Taylor glances up from a map and grunts.

'Made it in, then,' he says.

I'll ignore that.

'What's the plan?'

He waves a hand which I take to mean that he wants the door closed, then I pull up a seat across the desk.

'You go your way and I go mine?' I say.

He looks up. 'You're not going to start singing are you?'

He doesn't seem particularly chipper.

'Not get much sleep?' I ask.

He looks up again, the angry frown still on his face, then a moment of self-realisation kicks in and he shakes his head.

'No,' he says. 'Not much.'

He gets wrapped up in this shit. When he's given a job – I mean, a good job, an interesting job, one where peoples' lives are at stake – he throws himself into it. I'm still doing it because it's what I do, in the way that I breathe and eat and go to the bathroom. There's no option. Taylor has a social conscience, which frankly I find absurd. Most of the fucking public don't deserve to be watched over.

'Thought of anything else we could be doing?' he asks.

'What?'

'That'll be a no then.'

'You've been on this for three months,' I say.

'It changed two days ago,' he replies. 'And all we've thought of in those two days is this wild goose chase. Jesus.'

He shakes his head, sits back. Looks across the desk. I

get the feeling that it's the first time he's looked away from one of these maps in about fourteen hours. At least he's not wearing the same shirt he was wearing when I saw him last night, so he must have been home for a little while.

'You've been on this for three months,' I say again. 'The only thing that's changed is that we're pretty sure he's going to repeat. Apart from getting ahead of the game, what else can we do? We could try contacting every police officer, journalist and social services bod in Scotland to make sure they're not currently getting their brains eaten out by a bunch of ravenous birds, but holy fuck, you know we can't. Even if we weren't working under these preposterous circumstances.'

Hands across his face. The usual gesture. However much sleep he got, it wasn't enough.

'We need to spend at least one more day doing what we did yesterday,' I say. 'Get a feel for the places, the kind of area he might be inclined to use. You must be getting that already. Sure there are hundreds of wooded areas, but then you go to them, and you realise, he's never going to do the kind of thing he does right here. You realise that it must be somewhere else. Then, every now and again you think, wait a minute, this would be perfect.'

He's staring at me. You can see him almost fighting internally on whether or not he's going to allow himself to be dragged out of his moment of temporary despair.

'Coffee shop,' I say. 'Thirty minutes, chew the fat of the case, then head off. If nothing else, we get to sit in our respective cars and listen to Bob.'

Big sigh.

'Fuck,' he says.

I stand up.

'Come on, shift your arse,' I say.

Not terribly respectful, but you have to judge your moment.

'Fine,' he says, and he stands and grabs his coat from the back of his chair.

We walk out together. Since I'm in one of my rare

moments of not believing that the entire world revolves around me, I don't presume that everyone is looking at us, thinking, where the fuck are they going now?

'What you listening to at the moment?' I ask, as we head outside and start walking down the street. Light drizzle in the air. You know, the soaking, horrible kind.

He doesn't immediately reply.

'I'm still on a *Together Through Life* kick,' I say. 'Been listening to it all week.' Of course, he knows that, as he had to listen to it on the way out to Aberfoyle. And back.

He grunts. Give him a glance.

'Been listening to Adele,' he says, his voice low.

What the actual fuck?

I give him the appropriate look.

'What the actual fuck?' I say.

'You just hear it so much. Quite catchy. Thought I'd give it a go.'

Feel a weird, genuine sense of revulsion. Like cockroaches crawling over my skin. Like finding out your wife's a man. Like Scotland getting beaten 1-0 by Andorra.

'What? I mean, seriously? You can't listen to that. Jesus.'

'It's just... you know, bugger off, Sergeant, I can listen to something other than Bob for once. He won't mind.'

'Fine, listen to something other than Bob, but for God's sake, make it Leonard Cohen or, if you must be populist, Springsteen maybe. But fucking Adele? Seriously. What are you? You're like, fifty-something aren't you? And a man. You're a man in his 50s.'

'Fuck off, Sergeant.'

'She's a chav, 'n' all. We'd probably arrest her given the chance.'

'Sergeant, shut the fuck up,' he says as we reach the café. 'I've been listening to it for a few weeks, but out of respect to you, not when you've been in the car. But you're on warning. Some respect for your senior officer, or I'll play it every time you're in the fucking motor.'

Holy Jesus. He sits down and I head to the counter to

place the order. Don't think it's too much to say that my faith in my fellow man – which was already on a very shaky peg – has just been shafted that little bit more.

16

Headed up the Clyde valley, past the garden centres and the old people out for their morning cup of tea. Plenty of available spots out here for your demented killer to murder someone in the woods. This whole section is the kind of area that just makes our task look impossible.

There are, actually, huge chunks of the country that can be ignored. All those swathes of open farmland and moor with neatly planted forests stuck in the middle. Populated and built up areas. Lots of them. But areas like the Clyde valley, roads snaking up the length of the river, towns and villages and individual homes strung out, patches of wood all over the place. This is the kind of place I'd go for if it was me.

It happens to me the third patch of wood that I stop beside. Up past Larkhall, to the west of the river. Up a slight hill from the road. Park the car on the verge, still sticking out a little, so turn the hazards on.

Over the brow of the hill, the wood stretches away far enough that I can't see where it ends, although I've already got a decent idea from the map. Don't know enough about trees to know what we have here. Most of them have shed; there are a few conifers around. It's an old wood, a naturally occurring wood. Almost seems odd that it hasn't been turned into a turnip field or an extraordinary development of four-bedroomed homes for the young professional.

Head towards what I think will be the middle of it. Away from the noise of the road, a sound that dimmed naturally as soon as I got over the brow of the hill. Looking all around me. A few birds in the trees, a few nests up above, but not yet that cluster of large crows' nests that we're looking for.

I reach the heart of the forest. It might be further still to the other side, to the border with farmland, but I get to the point where I can't see my way out. The forest isn't too dense, but there's enough of it that the perimeter and what lies beyond is lost. And two things happen.

Firstly, I get an all-encompassing feeling of utter hopelessness and dejection. What is the point? So, I'm in a wood that the killer might use. There will be others. And even in this wood, I need to trawl through it for the next... what?... fifteen minutes?... half an hour?... working out the most likely spot for the guy to use.

Then it gets worse. The past comes back, and the past is so much worse than the hopeless present. I don't want to know the past. There should be enough in my life for me to be able to forget it. Enough police work, enough women, enough evenings lost in alcohol. But all those things are like taking ibuprofen for toothache. You can keep it at bay, maybe you can cover it up, but when the painkiller wears off, it's still there. Nagging. Waiting to eat into you, stab at you, to not let you forget that it exists until you've done something about it.

Except there's no dentist for the past. You can't go and sit in a small room, get an injection in your brain and undo the things that you've done.

Maybe all you have to do is face up to it. Look yourself in the mirror. Accept what you did. Maybe you have to look someone else in the face and tell them what you did.

It was me. That fucking awful thing. I didn't just see it. I was supposed to be an impartial observer, I was supposed to be working. But it was more than that. I wasn't just an observer. I became part of the story.

This wood, this old wood with trees that just happened to grow here for whatever reason, and not because some forestry manager decided they would, this wood takes me back. It shouldn't. It's really not that similar to the forest where it happened. Perhaps it's just because it's natural. Feels natural in a way that so many woods in Scotland don't. So many woods. So many trees. Planted by big companies, or natural woods close to populated areas that end up filled with crap, the detritus of all our lives. Crisp packets and needles and condoms and beer cans and fucking shit.

This feels natural, like all those woods that are all over Bosnia. Nobody planted them. Of course, worse has happened in those forests in recent years than has ever happened in a small wood up the Clyde valley.

I end up sitting at the base of a tree, resting my head back against it, staring straight up at the bare branches out at a damp, grey sky. Immediately feel the dampness soak through my trousers, soak my underwear. Just as quickly forget it, ignore it. It doesn't matter.

Close my eyes. Can feel spots of rain on my face, or drips from the branches above. But I'm lost. Eighteen years ago. Nineteen? A long time, not long enough. I can hear it, see every detail. Every detail. If I could apply that kind of memory and analysis to every other crime scene, I'd be a far better copper than I currently am.

Hands over my head, bring my head down between my knees. But it's not going away. It's here now, just like it comes every now and again.

Guilt. Fear. Self-hatred. Shame. What could I have done differently? That's always the question. What could I possibly have done that night that I wouldn't be sitting here now in this position?

Why can't he take me? The guy, this guy, the Plague of Crows guy, why can't he take *me*? If he's got something against the police, take me. I'd be no one's loss. And it's what I deserve. Strapped to a chair, my head sliced open, picked at by birds. Angry birds.

Hah! Angry fucking birds.

End up curled on the forest floor wishing I was dead. Wishing I was dead. Then it could all go away, unless there is a Hell. Unless my mother was right. There's a Hell. And I won't be going there because I used to keep magazines under my pillow when I was fourteen.

Don't want to do this anymore.
Not anymore.

17

Taylor had headed up over Eaglesham moor. He gets back to the office about ten minutes before me, so that when I get back, having answered the call, he's in position. YouTube on the computer, watching the murder scene. The latest murder scene, the one we've been expecting. Everyone out in the station is going mental, they're on the phone, they're shouting, they're clustered around computer screens. For the time being this will transcend the dicks from Edinburgh. They'll get to it on their own when all the shit has settled down. Or, more to the point, when we find out where these latest poor bastards are.

'Any chance they're still alive?' I say to Taylor's shoulder.

He answers with a slight wave of the hand, then points at one of them.

'This guy's dead already. The other two aren't, but they can't last too much longer.'

'You spoken to Baird?'

'No, not long in. Give him a call, will you? He's bound to have watched it.'

It comes to an end and he immediately clicks back to the start.

'Any clue to where it is?'

He snorts.

'There are trees, a few low hills in the background and the weather's miserable as shite...'

I watch it through, start to finish, for the first time. As before, there's absolutely no evidence of the person taking the film. They're doing it on a hand-held, walking around the scene, catching it quickly from all angles. Two minutes, thirty-seven seconds in length. One person dead, two people alive, awake and terrified. Wide eyes. The guy got a great shot of a crow pecking into the middle of an open eye, and then withdrawing quickly as if spooked by what it had just done. The last shot before the end of the film is blood running from the eye. An eye with the eyelid pinned back, an eye that can't be closed.

The noise is just the clamour of the birds. Wings flapping, the occasional squawk as they get in each other's way. There's no sound from the cameraman, not even a muffled footstep or a low breath. No cars to be heard in the distance.

It's real, but of course you watch it as if you're watching *Saw II* or the *Texas Chainsaw Massacre*. Just a film. Given that there's not that much blood, maybe it wouldn't even be an 18. Kids today. Played *Call of Duty* with Andy one day last year. Fucking hell. Having seen the real thing, I didn't last very long.

'He posted this from a new account?' I ask.

'Plague of Crows 2,' says Taylor, and he glances over his shoulder.

'Maybe he's a Hollywood executive.'

'You look fucking awful, what happened?'

In the middle of the woods, with one bar worth of reception, and me lying on the forest floor curled up in the mother of all foetal positions, the phone had rung and dragged me back. Answered in a daze. Got in the car and started driving back without really knowing what I was doing. Finally came out of it somewhere along the last part of the M74. It was only when I'd returned to the station that I noticed the passenger side mirror had been swiped off. There was a note inserted in the socket, squeezed in, so that it hadn't blown off when I'd been hitting eighty-five on the motorway. I had a fleeting moment of thinking that I wouldn't bother contacting the person who had left their name, address and an apology and that I'd just get it fixed myself – or, more than likely, never get it fixed, ever – and then I read the note.

You was parked in the middle of the fukkin road, you

wanker. I've got you're number.

And he's calling me the wanker. People wonder why the police beat the shit out of them sometimes, but really. Hopefully he'll come and find me. Well, I'm saying he, but who knows. All we're looking for is someone who doesn't know the arse end of an apostrophe, but that doesn't really narrow it down, does it?

'Fell over in the woods running back to the car.'

He looks at me and I look down the front of my jacket and trousers. Not that bad. I don't look like I was curled up in a ball like a fucked-up trauma victim. That wasn't what he meant.

He doesn't introduce any more awkwardness into proceedings by pushing me on it.

'Call Baird. Ask if he's got any opinion to offer. Don't bother trying to pin the bastard down. Anything'll do.'

Back out to my desk. Morrow's walking by.

'You seen it?' he says.

'Oh, yes.'

'Fuck.'

'Aye.'

All delivered without breaking stride, and he's off out the door. No idea what he's working on at the moment, but I presume it's not this. Maybe we're all on it until we at least find out where the victims sit, the soft parts of their bodies eaten away by birds.

As usual Baird answers the phone without actually saying anything. Hello is too many words.

'You've seen it,' I say.

'Yes,' he replies abruptly.

He and Balingol are the two pathologists for our part of town. Joint winners of last year's Miserable Cunt Of The Year award. That's a genuine award, I'm not making it up. And as you can imagine, there was some pretty stiff competition around these parts.

'Anything to tell us?'

'I thought you lot had been taken off the case, Sergeant,' he says.

'It's all hands at the moment.'

He grunts, then doesn't say anything. He's not one to fill a silence.

'Any idea how long those two might have lived after that footage was shot?'

'I knew you people were going to ask that,' he mutters.

'So you'll have an answer then.'

'And you know that I can't possibly say.'

'Ball park?'

He grunts again.

'Taking into consideration the level of deterioration you can see in the film, the activity of the birds, what do you think?' I ask.

'Sergeant, tell your boss... with the blood vessels in the brain, they could have bled to death in five minutes, and if one wasn't hit right away, maybe twenty minutes, half an hour.'

'Let's call it somewhere between five and twenty minutes, something like that,' I say.

He grunts. 'I don't think that was exactly what I said.'

'Thanks.'

I hang up, no doubt marginally before he does. He doesn't do goodbyes either. I think his dad must've walked out on him when he was a child.

Go back through to Taylor. He's still watching, leaning forward now, peering closely at the screen.

'What'd he say?' he asks without moving his eyes.

'Somewhere between five and twenty minutes.'

'He said that?'

I smile. God knows what my face looks like. Smiling. Not in the mood, not in the right place mentally to be smiling at anyone.

'That's what it boiled down to.'

'Well, at least we can presume the poor bastards are dead.'

'You're assuming this was recorded this morning?'

He shrugs.

'God knows. We might as well. Whoever these three

are, chances are they've not been reported missing yet. This must be recent. Let's not get carried away with the weather similarity, but it was a reasonably bright day yesterday, today it's been pishing down everywhere.'

'Fair enough.'

'Right, need you to get an enhancement of the footage. That is one clear-as-fuck, stone-cold beaut of a shot of the terror on that woman's face. Let's see if there's any reflection in her eye.'

'If there is, that would be a mistake,' I say.

'And he doesn't make mistakes. Check it anyway.'

Off back out the door, away to speak to a woman I know.

18

Ninety minutes later we're sitting in Taylor's car, heading up the M80 on our way to the murder site. A polis in Perth thought he recognised the hills and went for a look. Found the bodies where the killer had left them, still surrounded by birds. Birds which seemed reluctant to leave despite the presence of the police. In the end, apparently, they killed a couple of them. Better not let that get out to the press. *Bird-Killing Cops Disrespect Crime Scene* or some shit like that.

We're listening to Bob, thank God, although Taylor stuck on *Saved*, which he knows I don't like. Petty. Very petty.

The boys from Edinburgh have already headed on out to take charge. We oughtn't to be going at all, but Connor called Taylor in and told him to get his arse out there. He's expecting us to blag our way onto the crime scene. Hopefully it'll be the locals who are in charge of securing the perimeter and they won't know to tell us to bugger off. Next time it happens, if there is a next time, the guys from Edinburgh will be ready for us. They'll know that we're still working the case.

What we're doing now is starting a turf war over investigation rights, but we're not thinking about that at the moment. Just doing what we're told.

The one positive, and it's a pretty small positive but we're grasping, is that the area was one that we'd marked off as a potential spot when we saw the Whittaker woman in Aberfoyle. We'd been thinking along the right lines, just without the resources to do anything about it.

If we'd told the Edinburgh boys what we were thinking, would they have done anything? Would they have said *good idea chaps, let's crack on*? Probably not. Or maybe they've been thinking the same thing.

Taylor's not talking. Thinking the case through, likely wondering the same thing I am. Will he have left no trace and be gone on his way? Will it be three months before he strikes again? Longer, shorter, exactly to the day?

Phone goes, take the call. Sophie in the tech room.

'Yep?'

'Sergeant,' she says, 'we got a good look at your guy from the video. He was wearing a mask.'

That makes sense. Even though he was obviously confident his victims were not going to survive, he doesn't take chances.

'What kind?' I ask. Pointless question, but I feel like I need to say something to justify a conversation that has already pretty much given up all that it will.

'Well… a crow. It looks like the head of a crow… I'll send the images over.'

I stare straight ahead, don't immediately say anything.

'Can you see his eyes?' I eventually think to ask.

'No.'

'He knew we'd check…'

'Fuck, yeah. And given the precision of the scalping that everyone's talking about, it's hard to imagine he wore the mask while he was cutting. He hardly needed to care that his victims would see what he looked like. So, he just put the mask on for filming. He knew we'd see. That's why he waves.'

'What?'

'Oh yes. And you know he's not waving at that terrified woman. He's waving at you.'

'Us.'

'If that's how you want to see it, Sergeant.'

There's a short silence which Sophie in the tech room breaks by hanging up.

She watches movies. People don't say goodbye when they end phone calls in movies, they just hang up. That's because at some stage the writer will have been told to cut the script down, so he'll have scrapped pointless shit like people being pleasant to each other. Now it's seeped insidiously into society.

'Mask?' says Taylor.

'A crow's head.'

'Oh for crying out loud... What was the other thing?'

'He waves when he's filming her eyes 'cause he knows we're going to check that shit.'

'Jesus. He's taking the piss?'

'I think we knew that already.'

The conversation is over, and we're coming towards the end of the motorway, still twenty minutes or so to go and Bob is well into *In The Garden*.

*

The place is crawling with our lot, sealed off from the public at a good distance. Fortunately, as we'd been hoping, it's the local plods who are guarding the site and keeping the ghouls at bay. Bit of an out of the way place, as it was always likely to be, but there are still plenty of people who have driven out here to try to take a look. Really. What the actual fuck are these people thinking?

On the other hand, maybe we should sell them tickets, make a bit of money, put it back into the Force. No doubt some liberal somewhere would object to selling tickets to see murder victims.

Not just liberals, you reckon?

We walk through the woods like we're meant to be there, badges at the ready. We've had to flash them four times so far. Closer to the scene there are no uniforms. A few plain clothes detectives, a host of the white jump suits. Already we can see the bodies, still cemented in place, still strapped in. Taylor saw the same last time, but obviously they were gone by the time I got there.

Grotesque murder. Does that bring it all back, all that crap from the past that I don't want to think about? You'd think, but it doesn't. Not at all. I'm ready for it. Prepped.

With the exception of all that shit with the Keller case last year, it's not like we're used to a massive pile of brutalised dead – although it's getting bigger pretty quickly – but I'm ready for it when I see anything nasty in the course of my duties. It's the moments like this morning, when it creeps up out of the blue, grabs me by the testicles when I'm not expecting it, that's when it really hurts. That's when I go hurtling back and I can't stop it.

Taylor nods at a couple of feds as we enter the small clearing. There's not a lot of noise, other than that of some low conversation and the occasional footstep taken through fallen leaves.

It's a similar forest to the one I was in this morning. At least it makes it feel like we're on the right track. Maybe next time, with a little more chance to prepare, we'll be ready for him.

Ha! If detective work doesn't get you there, sheer bloody-minded burying your head in the sand will see you through.

Just as we get to the cadavers a crow squawks high in the trees. We both stop and look up. The others all do the same. Just for a moment. The real killers are all up there, watching over their victims, wondering if they're going to get another chance to pick at the bones.

Wonder if the public will start going bat-shit crazy for killing crows. That collective mentality is so fucked up sometimes. Someone will point out that yes, it was the crows that were committing the murders, the other bloke just facilitated it. The crows are the real killers. Let's get the bastards! And off they'll go, all Henry the fucking Fifth, and crows will be laid waste all over. Not like I give a shit, but there's nothing worse than crowd violence just for the hell of it. Even if it is against crows.

We get right up to them before anyone intervenes. Two feet away, as close as we want to get. Stand in silence over the three cadavers, each of them exposed to the elements.

One of them, the guy who looked like he was already dead in the video, has had the inside of his head almost completely cleaned out. Fuck, I've never seen anything like this. It's so grotesque, so absolutely horrible, that it's almost like standing over a waxwork, or playing one of those god-awful video games that Andy spends all his time on.

With the other two there's a little more brain matter left in the cavity. A munge of grey/red soup. Vichyssoise or some shit like that. Damned disgusting. The heads are supported so that they can't tip forward, the remains of the brain matter can't spill out. Hard to read the expressions on the faces, as they've all had their eyes picked. Carbon copy of last time.

The possibility that that's what it might be – a copy – flits through my head, but it's not that. This is the same guy.

'Detective Chief Inspector,' says a voice approaching quickly from four o'clock. Here we go. We both turn, although obviously I don't really answer to Detective Chief Inspector. Give it another few decades.

We are met by Detective Chief Inspector Montgomery. He's the same rank as Taylor but obviously, in ranking terms, being from Edinburgh is like an away goal in Europe.

'Why are you here?'

Straight to the point. It was always going to get down to some sort of bitch fight pretty quickly. Would have been nice to get a bit more of a look before we got tossed. I do the sensible thing, turn away from the awkward handbags situation, and start making a mental note of everything that I can see before we get ejected.

'I thought it would be instructive for two of the investigating officers who were at the first crime scene to visit the second one, so that there could be some sort of direct comparison.'

Which is, of course, a perfectly valid point. But let's not let common sense get in the way of some dick jousting.

Taylor stares it out for a moment, but then Montgomery probably realises that the longer we stand here like we're in a Steven Segal film on Channel 5 at 11pm on a Friday night, the longer we get to take in the crime scene. A situation like this would have been so much more fun back in Bogart's day. There would have been punches thrown, we'd have cracked open a bottle of whisky and all three of us would have nailed the blonde broad.

What with it not being Bogart's day, Montgomery pulls his phone from his pocket. He stares at us as he makes his call, it's just that I'm not looking. Start walking round the small triangle of the dead, examining their bonds.

Duct tape, largely, but tight. Unbreakable from inside the bond. Bare feet cemented in concrete as before. High-backed chairs, the neck bound to the wooden slats as is the forehead, or what's left of the forehead after he's superscalped them. Eyelids stapled open. Lovely touch.

'Glasgow are here,' he says. Crisp voice. Sharp. I've nothing against the guy, and Taylor won't have either. Just doing what he's been told. Might even be worthwhile trying to be nice to him for a minute or two. Might be. He hangs up without saying anything. He must have been watching the movies too.

Taylor breaks eye contact, turns and starts looking over the bodies. Face impassive. Jesus, what other kind of face can you have when confronted with this? Having seen it before, he quickly makes the assessment that it looks exactly as it did previously, then he looks round the clearing, up at the tree tops. A few crows visible. Watching. Not as many as we saw in the footage. Maybe the others have all gone off to another killing.

Taylor's phone rings. He glances at Montgomery as he takes it from his pocket. Can see him briefly curse himself for not having thought to turn it off.

Taylor answers and doesn't say anything at all. Nice. The movie people would love him. Listens for a moment, then clicks the phone off and puts it back in his pocket. He takes a last glance around the area then looks at me. That last call might as well have been on loudspeaker. We all know what was said.

'Where was the van parked?' he says, looking at Montgomery.

This is where we find out how much of a wanker we're dealing with. If Taylor had asked before the phone call, Montgomery would have been obliged to tell him to clear off. Now, however, he knows he's won. He can afford a moment of magnanimity.

'Need to know basis,' says Montgomery, nailing his colours high on the wanker mast, 'and you don't need to know. I'll trust you not to interfere any further in the investigation.'

He takes a step closer.

'Now fuck off,' he adds.

Take a quick glance around the clearing while the two bulls mentally wrestle over shagging rights. The logical thing would be for the van to have approached the same way as the rest of us, up the track that leads most quickly back to the A85. Logic doesn't enter into it though.

There's another track on the far side of the clearing, leading away in the opposite direction, and there are three of the white jump suit collective in the vicinity examining shit on the ground. That'll be it then.

'Come on, Sir,' I say, to break the Mexican stand-off. Although, to be honest, it's not really a Mexican stand-off, is it? These days Mexican stand-offs usually last about a second-and-a-half and then fifty innocent civilians get massacred. 'We parked our car over this way,' I say to Montgomery, and nod.

Start to walk off, Taylor alongside. He's staring at the ground, fighting the annoyance, trying to gather as much information as he can in the short time that we have.

The short time that we have... Fuck's sake. Sound like a pair of cancer patients. Bucket list: walk the Silk Road, sleep with Kate Beckinsale, climb Kilimanjaro, establish if the killer's tyre tracks were the same as the last time.

'Don't tread on anything, don't speak to anyone, don't tamper with any evidence, and keep on walking,' gets thrown after us.

Into the trees on the other side. Taylor glances back over his shoulder. The camera never looked this way, there was never a shot from the other side showing this part of the clearing. He kept the van behind him the whole time.

We stop behind the forensics fellows.

'Same tracks as the last time?' he asks.

Can feel Montgomery's bitter little eyes burrowing into the back of us, but Taylor has hardly slowed down.

'Think so, Sir,' comes the reply.

And on we go, without breaking stride. We walk on down the track up which the killer drove his van packed with prospective victims, and soon enough we come to the police cordon and walk once more out of the crime scene.

19

Long day. 11:32pm. Sitting in Taylor's office. This time last year we would have conducted this part of the discussion in the pub. Suddenly it all seems much more grown-up around here, and it all comes from Taylor.

He had a shit time of it while his wife left him and DCI Bloonsbury was flushing his life down the toilet, taking as much of the station with him as he could. Nevertheless, he came out of all that a much stronger man. He was already a good detective; that whole shambles made him a better man, and that filtered through to his work. The added responsibility hasn't weighed him down either, and now even at 11:32pm, when the investigation is going nowhere and the circumstances just got a hell of a lot worse, he still looks switched on and determined, rather than stressed and miserable and knackered.

One day that great attitude might rub off on me, but it hasn't happened yet. Most days I still feel like a twelve-year-old playing at being a policeman; and I reacted to the general tumult of the Bloonsbury business by sleeping with the new Detective Inspector's wife. Very mature.

We have some still-shot close-ups of the killer's mask, still-shots of the look on the faces of the victims. We've written up everything we can recall about the crime scene and cross-checked it with the previous one to see if he's given us anything else. So far, he hasn't.

Connor had Taylor in for an hour or so going over it all. Connor seems quite chipper. He feels that we have as much chance of solving the crime as the Edinburgh lot, but we have none of the responsibility. For months it's weighed on him, and he was worried that Edinburgh would come in and arrest someone in the first twenty-four hours. Now that they haven't, now that someone else has looked at it and not managed to discover the really obvious, glaring thing that we must have missed, he's relaxed a little. The pressure is off and suddenly he sees the chance of some one-upmanship.

That's the kind of man he is. Maybe they all are by the time they get to that pay grade.

'Fucking crow mask,' says Taylor. 'Really.'

'There was you saying we weren't in an episode of Scooby Doo.'

'It's like Batman, some shit like that. Holy crap, what is the matter with people? It's like they can't just commit crime anymore. They want to be seen committing the crime, they want their name in the newspaper, even if it's a false name. The next thing the guy'll do is get a TV camera crew lined up to record his thoughts before, during and after the crimes…'

'Plague of Crows Confidential…'

'And he'll burst into fucking tears when he's talking about his victims, then the camera will follow him to the gravesides as he pays his respects…'

'And when we ask the TV crew for his address they'll protest client confidentiality and make us out to be the bad guys.'

He sighs, shakes his head. 'We're always the fucking bad guys, Sergeant, no matter what happens.'

There's a knock at the door. In comes DI Gostkowski. She looks tired. Haven't seen her most of the day, and we missed our seven o'clock at the coffee shop.

'Sir,' she says, nodding at Taylor. Doesn't even look at me.

'Should you be in here?' asks Taylor. 'We already pissed them off once today.'

'I heard,' she said. 'Your name's mud.'

She glances over her shoulder then turns back.

'DCI Montgomery went home for the night about half an hour ago. There aren't many of them left, Sir. Thought it would be safe to come up. For a minute or two.'

'All right. Just stand in the doorway, like you're stopping for a passing chat. Nothing official. Be precise.'

I feel like I'm in another room, watching a tense and intimately shot detective drama on TV.

'A replica of the previous job. The van appears to be a Ford Transit. He has a team looking through footage of the nearest CCTV to see if there's any sign of Transits on the roads out of Perth. Not a lot of CCTV around there, however, once you're out of Perth. Time of death between six and eight this morning, the journalist the first to go, maybe an hour before the others. They presume it was when the skull was removed.'

'Sloppy,' I say, with my inability to go five minutes without saying something glib. To the credit of DI Gostkowski, she completely ignores me.

'They ended up killing seven crows at the scene, and this evening they got word back that all seven contained human brain matter in their stomachs, so there's added confirmation on the crows. The video isn't just some set up.'

'Jesus,' mutters Taylor.

'Everything else that's been gleaned from the site so far coincides with what we saw in August. The same goes for the victims. One police officer, one social worker – and this one was a door-to-door, dealing on the front line with all the fuck-ups social worker – and a journalist.'

'It wasn't a Glasgow policeman,' says Taylor, more a statement than a question, as the name of the officer is already on record.

'No, it's all Tayside, work and homes of the three split between Perth and Dundee and thereabouts.'

A moment while she tries to remember if she's missed anything.

'What are they working on?' asks Taylor.

'The CCTV thing's pretty big. They're working on the basis that he will strike more quickly this time, now that he's gone public. He's contacted all police forces, and from tomorrow they'll be instigating procedures whereby every police officer in Scotland will have to check in on a regular basis. That's going all the way to the Justice Minister to establish what they feel is practical.'

I look at Taylor, because that sounds unbelievably mental. We're supposed to check in? Like we're children off on a trip on our own for the first time and need to keep calling our dad? Holy all kinds of shit. How about, let's all be careful out there, or something?

'Hmm,' is pretty much all Taylor says.

'And they're speaking to local authorities and to the NUJ about implementing similar procedures across those professions.'

Taylor finally glances at me, a slightly troubled look on his face.

'Seems excessive,' he says eventually.

'They claim duty of care,' she says.

'Do you agree?'

She gives it a second, then says, 'Not paid to have opinions on policy, Sir.'

Taylor smiles unattractively and then glances back at the pictures he's been studying for the last half hour.

'Anything else, Stephanie?' he asks.

'Think I've covered it all.'

'OK, thanks. Go home and get some sleep.'

'Thank you, Sir.'

'Aim to do your seven o'clock thing with the sergeant tomorrow unless something comes up. Presumably, with the level of planning this guy puts in, even if he doesn't wait three months before the next time, he won't be trying anything again tomorrow.'

'Good night, Sir,' she says, then turns to leave.

I watch her go for a moment – in fact, until she's out of sight – and then turn to Taylor. Had a weird feeling there of not being in existence. Taylor glances back at me.

'She didn't seem to be aware that you were in the room, Sergeant. I presume you've slept with her at some point.'

'Stop saying that,' I reply, a bit testily. 'I haven't shagged everyone.'

He grunts, looks back at his photographs. I wait for some other throwaway insult, and when it doesn't come I get to my feet. Everyone's tired.

'Do I get to go home now too?' I ask.

And suddenly I do feel tired. Tired and melancholic. If it was a regular day I'd be heading to a bar, to be followed by a really bad headache with potential vomiting. But even I'm not going to try to find something to drink at this time of night. A long day, with far too much of it spent staring intently at screens trying to see something that more than likely isn't there. The morning, when I ended up curled in a ball, seems a very long time ago. Yet I haven't slept since then and the life had been taken out of me all those hours ago.

He looks at his watch and indicates with a dismissive movement of his hand. I turn to head off, then look back at him, getting over my general annoyance.

'You shouldn't work much longer either, Sir. Go home.'

He looks up, irritation on his face, but it immediately leaves him. He nods and waves me out.

20

Only kept in touch with one guy after Bosnia. A Canadian journalist. Eddie. By kept in touch, I mean that we saw each other one time maybe, and he'd leave me a message on the phone or something like that when he had a piece from some distant war-torn shit hole in one of the British papers. We'd just about hung on to each other by the time e-mail really got started, so that kept us going for a while. Always said that he'd end up living in London – as if that was something to look forward to – but he never made it.

He used to say that he was comforted by the thought of suicide, that the possibility of it cheered him up. The idea that he could just walk away, turn his back on the memories and the visions and the demons, turn his back on the horrors that played out in his head when he closed his eyes. Then, having been dragged from the depths by the thought of suicide, he no longer needed to do it. And he'd say that it was a vicious circle he needed to break. One way or the other.

He finally broke it. One night in a hotel in Dubai. He'd gone there for a break from Afghanistan some time in late 2002. Dubai killed him off, sitting alone in the bath with a razor blade, listening to Turin Brakes' *The Optimist*.

I found out some time during the summer of 2004.

*

Wake up at 4.37am. Sweating, like I've left the heating on full, but the room is cold as I sit up out of the sheets. Rest my head back against the wall, stare into the orange light of a room with the curtains open, illuminated by the streetlights. A car drives past, and then there's silence.

Listen to see if a noise in the house woke me up. A policeman's expectation that around every corner a guy in a mask is waiting to bean you over the napper with a crowbar. Nothing. The dead of night, but I'm wide awake now.

4:38. The chances of getting back to sleep before I need to get up for work are slim. Can feel it already. Brain in overdrive.

The forest. The crows with human remains in their stomach. That's what woke me up. Then I remember my brain freeze in the woods the previous morning, something that seems a long time ago, and suddenly a warm evening in a Bosnian forest is back in my head and there's nothing I can do about it.

Fuck it. Fuck all that shit. I'm not lying here thinking about it, and if I stay in bed that's all I'll be able to think about.

Instant decision, even more awake than I was two minutes ago. Swing my legs out the bed and stand up into the cold night. Map out the next two hours: shower, coffee, toast, get into the station, start going over the whole thing again and this time find something I've not been looking for.

*

Taylor sits at Morrow's desk, what with Morrow not being in yet, and looks at me suspiciously. Checks his watch.

'What time'd you get in?' he asks.

'5.30.'

'Couldn't sleep?' he says. It's not like he's never been in at 5.30. Nod. He drags his hand across his face and leans back, as if just the thought of my sleeplessness affects him.

'Find anything new?'

Pause, long sigh, in the end don't even bother answering. Nothing found, other than a few random thoughts.

'I did wonder if we should apply the same methodology

to each aspect of the case as we have to the woods, and then see if we get a convergence.'

He thinks about this for a second then indicates for me to go on.

'We only needed to speak to one person about the woods. That one person talked us through all the woods we need to look at. So, if we take other aspects of the case, we know there are crows. Now we spoke to a couple of guys about crows in the summer. Just a couple. Let's throw the net wide and talk to everyone we can find who might have some knowledge. Maybe we'll even stumble across the actual guy, given that there seems to be an innate understanding of how crows are going to act, or react. We already chased down every angle on the possible provenance of the bone-cutting tool, so let's revisit that and see if anything ties in with the woods and the crows. Same with the Ford Transit. It all seems so disparate, so unlikely that they could be drawn together, so – you know, in the case of the woods – so random, that it might be highly improbable. But let's start getting that together, and then if the Inspector brings us anything from the other lot, we feed that in too, and maybe we get a break.'

Pause. He's thinking about it. I've been thinking too. Need to think. Try to keep the rest of the shit out of my head.

'Pretty fucking lucky break,' I admit, 'but you never know.'

He's been looking at me, and now he's looking at the desk, computing it all. Let's face it, all I've suggested is *let's do basic police work*. What the fuck else are we going to be doing?

'And you've got to ask for more people,' I say. He glances up. 'If this was a regular case, a few definite leads, a specific area of inquiry, the two of us might be able to make some headway. But this... a thousand different strands, a thousand people to see or places to visit. It's nuts. In one way we were onto something with the woods. We had that place on our list, but it's so damned far-fetched, so many to choose from, we were never going to just stumble across it at the same time. At the very least, we need someone else doing the woods.'

He's thinking about it, contemplating taking it to Connor and how that will go.

'We don't know the bloke's time scale, whether this is an escalation, whether he'll wait another three months, whether he just does it when he's ready... but the leaves are gone until April or May. Any survey of possible woods that he could use will be extant until late spring. I say four guys on the job for a few days. If he's got any favours to call in with stations further afield, then go for it. Otherwise, get a team on to it. Split the country up, tell them to get going. We can concentrate on the other shit.'

He claps his hand down on the desk before I can get into my full dogs-of-war, up and at 'em speech, and stands up.

'You're right. If he wants us to make some headway, he's going to have to staff it properly. I'll ask for eight guys and hope we get four.' Glances at his watch. 'Right, you get us a list of bird experts. I'll put a submission together for Connor, and before we head out today you can get everything together on the cutting saw that we dug up last time.'

'Yep,' I say, and immediately turn back to the screen. Have already started work on the bird experts thing, and so I get back down to it, nine names already on my list. Taylor marches off to put together his submission for Connor. Connor likes submissions. Makes him feel like a government minister. Hates people to approach him with an idea that's not been thoroughly thought out, laid down under a variety of headings and fully costed.

You'd think all that FOI shit would have put him off having his people write ideas down – because let's face, there are a lot of people around here thinking all kinds of shit that would have the media pishing excitable anti-police diatribes all over the TV and newspapers if they ever found out it had been put in writing – but he's obviously not yet been burned. It'll happen one day.

*

9:15am. Left Taylor back at the station fighting his corner. He managed to finagle a few more staff out of Connor, and was gathering them together to give them their brief. Now I'm sitting in a small office at the University of Glasgow. Some part of me is attracted to the notion that we are likely to stumble across the killer completely by accident. The man is getting crows to apply the finishing touches to his sick death rite, and I have it in my head – in a way that I didn't in the summer – that he knows crows in some way. Not that he has a power over crows like someone might have in a superhero movie or some shit like that, but that he has some affinity with them, knows how to manipulate them, how to get them to do something.

The man sitting across from me, Professor Tolbet of the Zoology Department, is putting me right on that one.

'To me, they're the rats of the sky,' he says. 'They'll eat anything. I'm never like... *holy shit, a crow ate that?* The thing a crow won't touch, that's the thing that surprises me.'

You know that saying about police officers looking younger as you get older? Well, it's not like us older police officers don't think that about all the spotty barely post-pubescent kids who pitch up in uniform on a daily basis, but in reality it applies to every walk of life. Like university professors, for example. This guy looks about twenty-three, and you can tell by the way he talks he's priming himself to be on some fucking documentary about birds on BBC4; a documentary that ultimately will be about him. Like there, I asked him a question about crows, and in his brief answer he mentioned himself three times. That's what they're all like these days.

'So you think that if a crow is hanging around in a tree, and it looks down and sees exposed brain, it's just going to swoop on down there for breakfast?'

He smiles, as if he's smiling at the camera. He's going to use the word extraordinary in a moment.

'It's extraordinary,' he says. 'And I'll say this. To me crows are the most intelligent birds in Britain. Those guys are just shit-smart. If I'm walking along a street, a crow will make a determination about how threatening I am. Sure, at the last second, he'll get out my way just in case. But if I've got a gun, or anything that might look like a weapon, that sucker'll see it and it'll be off much faster. Now, they're animals, and like all animals they constantly want one thing. Food. That's all they're interested in, except obviously when they're trying to get laid. But food's their number one priority. I've seen crows peck at anything. Anything. They don't give a shit. If, after a peck, they don't like it, then sure, they'll move on. But in my experience, it's pretty rare that they move on.'

'So you're saying they'd eat brains?'

'Not only am I saying they'd eat brains, they'd recognise that there was no implicit threat in a human who was bound and gagged. And even if they were wary, we're talking about a flock of crows, man, and one of those suckers is going to get brave enough to come and have a look, and as soon as that happens, and he doesn't get nailed in some way, that's when the others follow.'

'You ever been on TV?' I ask.

That one came out of the blue for him but he takes it in his stride and smiles.

'I've got a show in development with the BBC,' he says. 'Not been green-lit yet though. I'm still waiting. Apparently with that lot you wait and wait and wait and then suddenly someone higher up says, yeah, we'll take this, can we have it in the schedule in eight months? And everyone starts running around in a panic.'

'Maybe now that everyone's talking about crows you'll have an in,' I say.

'Oh, my show's not about birds, it's me trying to survive on nothing but insects in the Amazon for two months. It'll be, like, my most amazing adventure ever.'

The younger generation, that lot you see on television all the time, I reckon they pick their career based on what they think is most likely to get them on television in the first place. Or else they elect to not have a career, other than a career based around trying to get into television. Rather chew my face off than be on TV.

The next chap is at least more traditional. Two offices along the corridor from Talbot. Older, not a professor. Dr Weinstein. Wearing a shirt, bow tie and waistcoat. That's the kind of thing you want from an old duffer at a university. Now this guy might well go on TV, but if he did, he'd talk with enthusiasm on the subject that the show was about, not My Part In The Evolution Of The Species, in the way that they all do now.

'Yes, pretty much,' he says eventually. I'd asked if crows would eat anything, as it appears to be the general consensus. He could have answered immediately, but likes to think things over before committing himself. I like this chap. Bet he's a Dylan fan. 'It's understandable where you must be going with this. Is it possible that some fellow might be in a position to manipulate these birds. Has he trained them or...' and he waves his hand in a dismissive manner '... is he able to control them? Maybe he keeps them in cages and lets them out beside the victims. Yes, it's understandable what you might be thinking, and I've given it a lot of thought since speaking to your colleague in the summer. But really... they are the vermin of the sky. They will, genuinely, eat anything. And once one of them has the courage to investigate a possible food source, and it proves successful, then that will just open up the floodgates.'

He stares across the desk. I left the station forty minutes ago, full of energy and bravado and sure that a positive attitude would help bring a positive development. But what had I been expecting at this stage? For one of these guys to say, *'Well, as a matter of fact, these crows are showing just the kind of exceptional behaviours learned through extensive training, and there's only one man in the whole of Europe capable of manipulating an avian species to that extent. You need Dr Hans Wankoff of the University of St Andrews. Here's his phone number.'*

I just need to keep going. Someone, somewhere, might have something to add. Something different. This guy, despite being all the more professional and a much easier person to talk to, is just saying the same stuff as the last guy. Perhaps they all will.

'You like Dylan?' I ask.

He stares blankly across the desk.

21

I have a list of eleven people to talk to in and around Glasgow. From the professors and the civil servants to the enthusiastic amateurs.

The opinion on crows appears to be fairly universal. They will eat any old shit. Including brains.

Make it back to the station just after one.

I'd left Taylor with the brain tools information, and he's spent the morning with that, making calls, trying to extend the little information that we have into something more meaningful.

'How we doing?' I ask.

'Nothing new. Got four officers, as we wanted, sent them out with instructions to find the perfect secluded woods, crows' nests combo. And to keep schtum. You?'

'Crows are as crows do,' I say.

'No one willing to go out on a limb and say that we're clearly in an Emma Peel type situation?'

'Not so far. The consensus is pretty much as we had in the summer. Give a crow something a bit shiny and gloopy looking and they'll be all over it.'

'People have started killing them,' says Taylor.

'What?'

'We've had a couple of reports this morning. Morrow called around a few other stations and they're getting the same kind of thing. It'll make the news by the end of the day.'

'People are killing crows?'

He nods.

'So they don't get their brains eaten?'

He nods.

'Jesus. People are so...'

'I know. First report was of a guy shooting them in the woods behind his garden.'

'Woods on our list?'

'No. Too small, too populated. Neighbours reported him, we show up, he's shooting crows with a hand gun. Missed more than he hit, but he appeared to have plenty of ammunition.'

'Did he have a licence for the gun?'

Shakes his head. 'Said he was doing a public service.'

'Didn't take to being arrested, I suppose.'

'Not at all. The fault appears to be ours. Then there were a couple of kids throwing rocks at crows. Didn't get any, but they did put in a few windows. They told Constable Forsyth to take a fuck to himself, that they were doing the police's job for them.'

Big sigh. Need food. Enthusiasm slips away at the thought of heading out to do more speculative interviews with crow experts afterwards. There are so many people not really worth saving.

'Lunch?' I ask.

Quick check of the watch.

'Sure, but just fifteen minutes across the road. If Connor sees us taking time to eat, he'll probably vomit indignation and outrage out his arsehole.'

*

Small soup-and-sandwich place. Been here for years. Most of our lot come in here at some point during the day, so we usually don't. Taylor likes to stand apart because he's the senior detective. I just like to stand apart.

Pea and ham soup and a roll for me. He's got a prawn mayonnaise with side salad. That, of course, would be a Glasgow side salad, which features half a tomato and some chips.

Taylor looks at his sandwich. A shadow crosses his face.

'I shouldn't be sitting here,' he mutters.

Typical. He'll be thinking that it's all right for me to take a break, and in fact, that I ought to take one, but that he doesn't have the time. I don't say anything. Spoon up some soup, yet his annoyance and hopelessness and need to keep banging his head against the brick wall of the investigation are infectious.

He crams some chips into his mouth and at that point DI Gostkowski, who has entered the building without either of us noticing, sits at the table. Taylor looks at her, his mouth bulging with food. She looks amused in an annoyingly superior way, as if she never crams food in her mouth. She probably doesn't.

'In a rush?'

'Yes,' he says, through his chips, then he swallows and takes a drink to wash them down. 'You shouldn't be sitting with us, Inspector, too much chance your Edinburgh lot will come in here.'

As he says it he lowers his voice and takes a quick glance around. He doesn't know who they all are, so they might already be here.

'They sent out for food,' she says. 'Anyway, I believe there's no point pretending we're not speaking to each other and ultimately, if the Sergeant and I are seen together a lot, the likelihood, given his reputation, is that people will believe we're sleeping together.'

'The Edinburgh lot aren't going to think that,' he says.

'They'll ask around. They've already been asking around the station about you two, trying to get the full inside information.'

'Did they ask *you*?' I say, to bring her attention to the fact that I'm at the table.

'Yes,' she says, still looking at Taylor.

Taylor lifts his sandwich from the plate and stands up.

'Very well, Inspector, you're the one at the coal face. I need to get on. You two enjoy yourselves. Maybe you want to hold hands, keep the cover going.'

He doesn't even smile at his own hilarious joke, and then he's off, leaving behind a small plate of chips and a bottle of freshly-squeezed hand-picked sun-ripened orange juice. Gostkowski pulls them over beside her and takes a chip.

'I get the feeling you're not talking to me,' I say. I sound like some monstrously high-maintenance woman of the kind that I generally think should be carted off to a mental institution. She enhances the feeling of self-hatred by glancing at me as if I'm monstrously high-maintenance, and doesn't even bother humouring me with an answer.

'The politics are picking up pace,' she says.

Take some soup, don't look at her. But suddenly I have masses of respect for the woman. Me. Respect for a woman. Must be some sign that I'm maturely growing into my forty-five-year-old brain. Or not.

'What's up?'

'They've detailed a guy to shadow the pair of you so they know what you're doing.'

Pause with the soup. Glance at her.

'They tell you they were doing that?'

'No, they didn't. The guy himself told me. Think he fancies me, thought he'd have some sort of in. Maybe thought that it would help get me on their side.'

'So where is he now?'

'Back at the office. He knows you came over here for lunch, so he'll have nipped back to grab a sandwich. He'll be hovering soon enough, waiting to see where you head off to.'

'And he followed me this morning?'

'Oh, yes.'

Jesus. How fucking stupid is that? If it's not bad enough that I'm wasting my time, there's someone following me noting down how I'm wasting it.

'Fuck,' is how I express my unease at that level of stupidity.

'Yes,' she says. 'Quite.'

'So, they're going to be aware of you and me seeing each other to talk over the case?'

'Yes.'

Glance at her – she's sitting next to me, a foot away, so it feels kind of weirdly uncomfortable to be looking at her, which is probably a sign that I'm not as mature as I thought I was a minute ago – then go back to my soup.

'So what did you say about me?'

'I said we were in a relationship, which would explain why we see each other at the Costa. And here.'

Pause, soup spoon halfway to mouth. Another glance. She's eating chips, seems matter of fact.

'Won't they be worried then about pillow talk?'

She nods.

'I expect so. Not a lot to be done. I didn't say to the DCI, but I wouldn't be surprised if they're phone tapping. I wanted to get all the facts before I took it to him.'

Keep eating soup. Wonder if there's someone standing across the road, behind me, watching us.

'Maybe they're tapping into this conversation through our mobiles,' I say.

'Possible, although they're not MI5, so I don't think we should get too paranoid.'

This is just too stupid. Too monumentally fucking stupid.

'So they're just going to exclude you,' I say.

She nods again. Nearly finished the chips. There hadn't been many left.

'I expect so. They were heading down that road anyway. They needed me right at the start...'

'The day before yesterday.'

'Yes. The day before yesterday. I was there to help them bed down, but now they've got their feet under the table and they've been apprised of everything they need to know about the investigation up to this point. I was always going to be pushed to the outside. The initial premise of the Superintendent was a little fanciful. But we might as well spin it out as far as we can.'

Another quick glance. She's wrapped up the chips and is dabbing at her lips with a paper napkin.

'Enjoy yourself in Edinburgh this afternoon,' she says.

She knows I'm going to Edinburgh. Of course. 'Unless we hear from each other, I'll see you at Costa at seven.'

I nod. She leans over and kisses me on the cheek, then gets up and walks out.

I look across the table, as if I'm in a sitcom and I'm staring at the camera. She just kissed me on the cheek. All part of the act, because we're apparently pretending that we're sleeping together.

I think I need to talk to her about the fact that it's not really working. We'll need to take it a bit further.

22

People are killing crows. By mid-afternoon they're not just killing crows, but all kinds of birds, and the Chief Constable of Strathclyde is on air telling people there's no need to panic, and no need to become involved in avian slaughter. And it's a crime, apparently. Not sure how much of a crime it is, but he's telling people they're getting nicked if they're caught.

People are such lemmings. I believe what we need is for the Justice Minister to introduce a bird protection, shoot-to-kill policy, wherein all police officers are armed and permitted to instantly gun down anyone caught shooting an unarmed bird.

Now, don't go thinking I'm a Daily Mail-reading right-wing wanker. I firmly believe there should be a law in place permitting the police to shoot anyone caught buying the Daily Mail. Call it natural selection.

Some part of me knows it's wrong to shoot someone just because of their newspaper choice.

Edinburgh has so far turned up the same level of information as Glasgow, except for this guy I'm meeting now in a café at Leith docks. Not far from Britannia. Said he couldn't meet me at his work place as it's not suitable. Works in a lab. This bloke is from the enthusiastic amateur cadre. I buy coffee. He has some shit with mocha in the title, I have an espresso because I don't want to drink too much and I don't want to be too long about it.

He has the look about him. You know, *the look*. The one that fires warning shots. If you try to put your finger on what it is about them that makes you think, *ah, wait a minute, this might be what we're looking for*, you can't do it. But there's something. Almost as if you can spot the imbalance.

He plays with his coffee as he tells me he's been studying crows as a hobby ever since he saw *The Omen*.

'Wasn't that a raven?' I say.

'I study all the corvids,' he says. 'But crows are my favourite. Fascinating birds. Much misunderstood.'

'Go on,' I say.

He looks around him as if gathering inspiration from the absurdly uniform surroundings of a café that could be any café in any town or city in the western world.

'Down through history people have misunderstood them,' he begins. 'They treat them as carrion, implicitly unpleasant. Evil even. The raven is often seen as a harbinger of ill times, and the crow is sucked along in its wake. And you know, the reason for it is simple. Extremely simple. They're black. All black. That's all it is.'

'Hooded crows aren't all black,' I say to stop him in his tracks. His intensity is annoying, although I ought to be letting him talk as he's the kind of bloke I'm looking for. An over-enthusiastic nutter.

'Yes, there are variations, Sergeant,' he says. 'In general, the genus corvus are black, and throughout history they have been discriminated against. It's avian racism.'

Holy Jesus fuck. I'd say those words to Taylor if he was here. People get wound up about the stupidest shit.

'You hear that people have started killing crows?' I say.

'Outrageous. I hope the police are going to clamp down on this with extreme prejudice.'

'Of course,' I say, ignoring the stupidity of anyone using the phrase *extreme prejudice*.

'Crows don't eat brains,' he says. 'Not unless, seriously, not unless someone taught them how to do it.'

'Most people I've spoken to don't agree.'

He smarts and shakes his head.

'That makes me very cross,' he says. He leans forward on his elbows. 'Very cross. If these crows really are eating human brains – and I very much doubt that they are – then…'

'We've found crows at the scene with human brain remains in their gullet.'

'Have you?'

'Yes.' Saying a bit too much there, but it just slipped out.

'Well, then, in that case it's definite. Someone is training those poor birds to do this. They would not automatically attack a human in this way.'

I suppose this is the kind of thing that I've come out looking for, but when presented with it, it's so opposed to everything else I've been told, and it sounds so absurd, this bloke sounds so absurd, I just stare at him. Waiting for the moment when he implicates his arch nemesis in the enthusiastic amateur bird world.

He never does.

Make it back to Glasgow not long before seven. Don't bother checking in with Taylor, assuming he's at his desk, and head straight for the coffee shop. Seem to be spending a lot of time drinking coffee, but from the amount of the bloody places that are now open, and the amount of people who are always in them, I'm not alone. The world of the west is now conducted in Starbucks.

Not sure that I want anything, so I buy a bottle of water – water, for fuck's sake, am in need of something much stronger – and wait at a table for her. She arrives with precision timing.

'Get you anything?' she asks, heading to the counter and barely stopping at the table.

'Large cappuccino, please,' I say for some reason, then immediately worry that it makes me look cheap, because I never bought it myself.

Better just not to think.

Elbows on table, stare straight ahead. People come and go. This place used to shut at six, then seven; now it's open until eight-thirty. It'll be twenty-four hours soon enough, then they'll invent some kind of weird time thing, so that there can be more than twenty-four hours in the day. They say that people are spending less money on alcohol, which is something. You're a lot less likely to chib some other bastard after a skinny latte, although people do talk just as much pish in here as they do in the pub.

'What are you thinking?'

She sits down opposite, placing my coffee in front of me.

Fuck's sake. 'I was thinking that I might have appeared cheap because obviously I could have got myself a coffee, but I genuinely didn't feel like one when I came in, and then you asked, so now I feel a bit bad about it, and I was wondering if I should offer you money, but then I thought, maybe that might offend you a bit since you'd offered, and maybe I ought to just let you buy it.'

She kind of smiles and shakes her head.

'Usually men just say 'nothing'.'

Yep, ain't that the truth? But start telling a woman what you're thinking and the next thing you know she's lying naked in bed. But don't keep telling her what you're thinking or she'll come to see you as marriage material, and that never ends well.

Obviously I speak for myself there. I knew someone once who was happily married for a long time.

'Thanks for the coffee.'

Now I naturally look introverted and slightly awkward, as if I've said too much, which is what I would do anyway, but just serves to make her think that I'm slightly more complex than your average bloke, but in a good way.

She's thinking, he knows when to talk and he knows when to shut up... more than likely he's also a very considerate lover.

'How d'you get on this afternoon?' she asks.

'Continued the bird quest,' I say. 'Found one guy who disagreed with everyone else and insisted that some evil genius must be training the crows.'

'Who're you going to go with?' she asks. 'The majority, or the one? Much more interesting sometimes to go for the one, don't you think?'

'Yes,' I say. Find myself smiling. 'Unfortunately he had

the credibility of a shouty man on a radio phone-in. Still, it all helps. How about you? They let you in on any inside information?'

'Quite the reverse,' she says. 'Montgomery told Connor they didn't need me anymore. Or PC Grant.'

'Ah.'

'Connor's pissed off, but it's not entirely unexpected. They got out of me what they could, they didn't tell me anything, and then they got rid of me. Should have seen it coming. Well, of course, I did see it coming.'

Nothing to say to that. I hadn't seen it coming, but then I hadn't been thinking about it. In fact I'd rather enjoyed the whole clandestine thing.

'What now?'

'I get to work with you guys,' she says.

For some stupid reason that information goes straight to my groin.

'Just for a couple of weeks, see how it goes. Well, I'll be working for the DCI, doing whatever he thinks it's best that I do. So, I've got a message from him.'

'For me…?'

'Get your arse over there.'

I look down at the cups. For the first time the great detective notices that instead of getting mugs of coffee, she got takeaway cardboard cups. With lids.

'We're leaving,' she says, getting to her feet.

It's only at this point that I realise I'd been presuming we'd sit there over cooling cups of coffee until they'd gone completely cold and the place closed for the night, then we'd go somewhere for dinner and then she'd come back to my place; and if that latter part didn't happen, it would only be because I went back to her place.

She heads off, presuming that I'll trail along obediently in her wake. And I'll bet she's the kind of woman who won't have sex with someone with whom she's working on a case.

January

23

Months pass. The Plague of Crows disappears, and we don't know if he'll ever come back. We must assume that he will, that's all.

Edinburgh is still here, but they have slimmed down. For a while, for a month or so, they threw more men at the crime, and with no more free space in our building for them to occupy, they rented rooms along the street. Resources flooded in. At some point they had the same idea as Taylor, of narrowing down the likely areas the Plague of Crows might use; when he heard that that's what they were looking at, Taylor offered them the information we'd gathered. All in it together, after all, and Taylor's not worried about credit. He doesn't want his name in the paper, or a framed photo of the First Minister presenting him with an award.

In mid-December the Scotsman did a nicely detailed study on the level of resources Edinburgh were committing to these crimes that had happened – in Scottish terms – nowhere near Edinburgh, with some dubious statistics and the usual absurd anecdotal evidence to indicate just how badly Edinburgh's policing had been disrupted by this redistribution of resources. The Edinburgh police and the Justice Minister fought their corner, then as soon as they thought no one was looking they withdrew eighty per cent of the officers they'd brought through, relinquishing the new offices at the same time, even though they'd paid a six-month lease in advance.

Montgomery is still here, with his runt force, chasing

down ever more fractured and implausible leads. Which is what Taylor has been doing since August. It would have made sense for Montgomery to go back to his office in Edinburgh and continue the investigation from there. The first lot of murders might have been on our patch, but the second was nowhere near. Who knows where the third will be? So there's no reason for Montgomery to stay in Glasgow, except he wants to. Argued his case and he's still here. His case was based on not interrupting the operation that he's established at the station; Taylor and I assume it's because he likes the expenses, or he's worried that if he takes the operation back to Edinburgh it'll get swallowed up and ultimately he won't be the one to break the back of it.

Gostkowski stayed on the case for a fortnight, and then Connor was forced to move her on. I lasted into December, but as the Christmas season approached, and there was the usual rise in drink, depression and desperation related crime, they had to shift me back on to regular duties.

Taylor has stayed on the Plague of Crows throughout. It's not been good to him. Too long with nothing to do and no progress to be made. Day after day searching through the same old stuff, an increasingly desperate search, knowing that the killer is coming again, at a time of his own choosing.

When someone plans a crime, before it's been committed, when only they know it's going to happen, they hold all the cards. The course of an investigation is the act of taking those cards away from them, transferring the cards until it's the police who are in charge.

It's just over five months since the first set of victims was discovered, and so far the Plague of Crows is still in full possession of all fifty-two. Taylor is gradually suffering, gradually being dragged downhill.

Not all police officers will have a nemesis in their career, indeed most won't. But sometimes it happens, and pity those that do.

*

Fortunately for me, my nemesis continues to be sleeping with women that I really ought to stay away from. Got to the Christmas night out and imagined that it might be the time to finally consummate all that electric sexual tension that had been going on with Gostkowski. Then I got slaughtered on vodka and ended up taking home one of the waitresses. Not my proudest moment.

Caught DI Gostkowski's eye as I was walking out, absurdly young woman draped around me. Not sure how to describe how she looked. Not judgemental. Sensible.

Anyway, the waitress – and for the life of me I can't remember her name – was old enough to know what she was doing, and I think it was pretty good fun. It's supposed to be, after all. No point in casual sex if you're not going to have fun with it. She was gone in the morning.

Maybe she nicked something, although I haven't noticed.

Slim pickings otherwise. Some other night in the pub I ended up alone at a table with Alison – ex-wife number three – and she wasn't sounding so happy about her recent marriage to Sergeant McGovern. McGovern, at the time, was off at Ibrox watching the Rangers embarrass themselves further in the Stygian depths of Scottish lower division football. Really it was just early days marriage blues, something that she and I crashed and burned at, our faithful union before God not surviving into the second month, and some mature ex-husbands at this point would have comforted her with reassuring words about the future and how everything would settle down.

Me, I hit on her, asking her if she wanted to come back to my place for a shag. I'd been drinking. And I did actually use the word shag. Classless wanker.

She left shortly afterwards, and when I say shortly afterwards, I mean she was putting her coat on before I got to the 'g' in shag.

Oh, there was another one, another crappy night in the

pub. Went to her place. Rubbish sex. One of those where you crawl out the door afterwards, struck low by the colossal weight of your own depression and self-loathing. Horrible night. Didn't drink for nearly two days after that, and then, because I'd sworn I wouldn't drink again, like ever, I was full of self-loathing again when I went back to the bar. Having never seen her before, seems like every time I'm in the bar now she's there, and we look at each other with ill-disguised contempt.

Saw the kids a couple of times over Christmas, but things have been pretty ropey since I nearly got back with their mother, screwed it up and then bailed without giving her any say in the matter. We're drifting into disinterest and the kids are getting more and more distrustful of me at the way I've treated her as they get older. I'm losing them.

No, I've already lost them. All I can do is try not to completely fuck it up during their teenage years and then hope for some sort of rapprochement once they reach adulthood.

Taylor's moved office, now in a smaller room at the far end of the station. This one has a window on the outside world, however, unlike the last office, which just had windows staring at the rest of the station open-plan. There's a new DCI been put in his place in that office. Dorritt. Newly promoted, brought in from South Lanarkshire. A junior DCI, he's no threat to Taylor. Even if he was, in some way, a nominal threat, I doubt Taylor would see him as such. He doesn't care, too wrapped up in the Plague of Crows. If anything, thankful that there's someone else filling the void, leaving him to concentrate on the task that consumes him.

His office walls are covered in photographs of woodland areas around the country. Potential murder sites. His hunch is that next time the Plague of Crows will be even bolder. There will be a natural progression. From much delayed video, to video filmed only hours earlier, to something altogether more sinister. Next time, he thinks, it will be a live webcam. Sure of it.

And he's right. After all this time, trying to get inside the head of this killer, a killer who has been calculatingly brilliant in everything he's done, it's the natural progression. Live webcam, taunting us, laughing at us, mocking the entire force, every station and unit in the country. That's what's coming.

Taylor spends his days getting to know these places. There's not enough space on his walls for the photos, so he rotates them. Studies the photographs as he takes them down and puts them up. Has them on his computer, so he can watch them flash by when he's sitting thinking. When the next piece of footage starts to circulate around the web, and has gone viral within minutes, he wants to know where it is. Right there, that first instant.

In this regard, he needs the killer to strike again before late spring, because once the leaves come back, the number of potential woodland sites increases exponentially and we're fucked.

It seemed preposterous to start with. Of course it does. Just look out your window or pay attention when you drive to work or sit on the bus. There are hundreds of potential sites. Thousands. How could one man learn them all? But he's taken the time, visited them all. Stood in the middle of them and worked out what the killer will have worked out. Natural clearing. No one, or at least no more than the occasional house, within close range. Crows' nests. Good cover, even in winter. Decent access to allow him to get a Transit in.

Taylor worked at it, he narrowed it down, which meant his list was just incredibly long, rather than ridiculously unworkable.

Some are going to think he's obsessing, but all he's doing is giving himself the best chance of success. Although, of course, what will it do for us? The killer would be incredibly bold, and taking the kind of chance he appears not to take, if he were to hang around while the murders were broadcasting. He would have to make the assumption that some police officer somewhere might know where it was and therefore be long gone by the time the webcam went live.

And Taylor has started drinking again. The Plague of Crows would love what this is doing to him. He's not an alcoholic, it's not getting in the way of his work, but for a while, for a long while, he became the job, he became the authority figure in the station, he became his work; stronger, fitter, healthier. So now that he's started going back to the pub, and is having a drink when he gets home after work, regardless of time, it shows on him. He's not coming into work drunk or reeking of it, he's not drinking any more than your average middle-aged, middle-class bloke, but you can tell on his face. And I can tell from the fact that he's started coming to the pub with me.

Walk into his office, catch him standing at the window looking out at the car park. The same view, from one storey up, that you get from the back door area where all us smokers congregate these days.

'How's it going?' I ask.

He shrugs without turning.

'Nothing to report, Sergeant,' he says.

I stand at the window beside him, looking down on a sea of Hondas and dull Fords and cars that were in their prime fifteen years ago.

'It's coming,' I say.

'Seventeen days,' he says.

We've been working to a calendar. The number of days it will be before the next killing, if the Plague of Crows waits the same number of days as the last time, as if there might have been a specific reason for choosing that precise time gap.

Neither of us believe it though. It'll be sooner than that. Or later. To do it on the exact day might not be to invite capture, but it would certainly put the police in a better position. Give them a few cards perhaps. So it won't happen.

'Feels like one of those war movies,' I say, 'when they're waiting at the airfield to see who's going to make it back from the bombing raid. Or they've sent Clint Eastwood and Richard Burton out on a mission and there's nothing they can do other than wait for the phone or radio to start going.'

'Broadsword to Danny Boy...' says Taylor humourlessly. 'Yes, I suppose it feels something like that. What've you got on this morning?' he asks, turning, his tone picking up, shaking off the maudlin feeling of hopelessness.

'Usual,' I say. 'Thirteen year-old kicked fuck out her mum... a child abuse case... couple of stabbings, gang-related probably... and there were a few leftovers out our way last night after the Celtic – United game.'

'What are you doing standing here then?' he asks.

'Everything seems to be in hand,' I say. 'Everyone who had to be brought in, has been. Questioning has been done or is in order. Mostly just the paperwork and the odd talking-to to be delivered. Thought we could have lunch.'

He glances over his shoulder.

'It's 9.47.'

'Yes,' I say, 'it is. I meant, I was coming in to ask if you wanted to have lunch today. Talk about the case.'

He looks at me. Wonderfully expressive, lugubrious eyes, like an orang-utan whose forest has just been burned down, killing all his relatives and destroying his collection of David Attenborough DVDs.

'Sure,' he says. 'Twelve will suit me.'

'Right.'

I stand beside him looking out on the car park for a while. Nothing happens. No cars come or go, barely a pedestrian in the street beyond. The day is grey and flat and perfectly befitting of the mood. Eventually I turn away without speaking, and head back to my desk.

24

Back in the pub after work. Getting to be a regular occurrence again. You can't change your spots etc., etc. For a while there, after I'd gone up the mountain, and Taylor was determinedly getting his feet under the desk of responsibility, we went months without coming here. Then we came once, and then without really thinking about it here we are, several nights a week. Two divorced, miserable, single men out on the lash. Boo-yah!

Inevitably we always end up talking about Taylor's obsession. Sometimes I manage to get the conversation around to the new Bob album, or whether Thistle are going to get relegated or which one of the women at the station I'd like to sleep with next – although weirdly I never mention Gostkowski – but those conversations always end up rather one-sided and so I give in to the inevitable and let him elucidate what he's thinking. Because he certainly ain't thinking about Bob, the Thistle or women.

Of course, at the moment we're not talking about anything. Two fat old wankers sitting in a pub in complete silence. Silence, that is, apart from the rest of the general chatter and the fact that they're playing an entire album by that noxious little shit Olly Murs. Fucking hate Olly Murs. He'll be doing the Eurovision Song Contest soon, just you wait and see. That's his level.

Although, you know, I can imagine Bob doing Eurovision one year. It's the kind of crazy, fucked-up, completely out of left field kind of shit he'd do. Pop up out of nowhere representing Armenia or Latvia, some shit like that. Wouldn't be that much weirder than singing *O! Little Town of Bethlehem*.

'How are you and Adele getting on?' I ask Taylor, to

break the near ten-minute silence.

He takes a moment, while he gets dragged back from whatever woods it is he's inhabiting, says, 'Who the fuck's Adele?'

'You know, the fat, chav, singing girl thing. Her.'

He grunts, looks disinterested. Well, of course he does. No grown man is going to want to be reminded of the fact that they like listening to Adele.

'Got bored,' he says. 'Threw it out, I think... Maybe it's still in the car.'

'Back onto Bob?' I say.

'Been listening to Bach's Christmas Oratorio.'

I believe there follows what many would call a stunned silence. He doesn't even look abashed. In fact, judging from the glazed look in his eyes he feels so comfortable with this information that he's already forgotten he said it and is back in amongst the trees, searching for his killer.

'But Bob did a Christmas album...' is all I can find to say.

'What?'

'Bob did Christmas. Why are you listening to someone else's Christmas? And Bach... I mean... what the fuck?'

He shrugs.

'It's different. Heard it on Radio 3, quite liked it. Lasts just over eight minutes, which on most days takes up the entire drive to work.'

He shrugs again. Jesus. How can you casually say things like 'I heard it on Radio 3' and just shrug as if nothing's wrong.

'You were listening to Radio 3?'

'Aye. I do sometimes. At home. When I'm making dinner. Or breakfast. Have it on in the kitchen.'

'That's... that's...'

He's looking at me like I'm the weird person.

'Grow up, Sergeant. There are worse fucking betrayals than that in life.'

Suppose. Like listening to Guns 'N' Roses' version of *Knocking On Heaven's Door*.

'But you could listen to '*Cross The Green Mountain*. That's just over eight minutes.'

'You know how many times I've listened to that song in the last ten years?'

Continue to stare at him. 'It's like you've suddenly become bipolar.'

'Fuck off, Sergeant.'

'You're implying that there's a finite number of times somebody can listen to any one of Bob's songs before they need to listen to…. Bach.'

He shakes his head then drains his pint. Settles the glass down on the table and stares at it for a moment.

'I'm leaving,' he says.

Glance at my own drink, my third vodka tonic, nearly empty.

'We haven't done the Plague of Crows,' I say. Pointless really. He's too bloody maudlin even for that.

'No, we haven't.'

He looks at me. Nothing to say. The time for talking ended about two months ago, since when there's been nothing new to talk about. We need something else to happen, and when it does, then the shit can hit the fan, the politicians can take charge, the media can fly in ferment, and we can talk again.

'See you in the morning, Sergeant. You probably shouldn't stay too late. The drink's starting to show on your face.'

He leaves. I don't watch him go. That's ironic.

Is it ironic? I think it's showing on his face and don't see it on my own, and he's seeing the same thing with me. Or is that only ironic in an Alanis Morissette type of way?

And do I care?

Drain the glass, head to the bar. A quiet night. The girl behind the bar seems happy with something to do.

'What can I get you?' she asks.

I try not to stare at her breasts while contemplating an all out shock & awe offensive.

Boo-yah!

*

There are crows high in the trees. None of them are sleeping, all awoken by the noise from below. A grey early morning. They look down and watch what is happening in the forest. Three people tied to chairs, another walking between the three. Extracting information.

There is a light attached to the head of the person who's moving around. The light bobs, here and there, up and down. Something glints in the light.

Crows like things that glint. One of them wonders if it might be food.

25

Interview Room 3. A man with a baseball bat. Well, he no longer has the baseball bat. When you're interviewing a suspect it's best to relieve them of all weapons. Learned that from CSI.

Have no sense of impending action. The room springing to life. No sense that everything is about to change. Sometimes that happens. Not today. Not so far.

The guy in front of me, who would be defined in any statistical analysis as a nineteen-year-old fuckwit, is not being given quite as hard a time as he ought to be by the interviewing officer – me – because he quoted Bob Dylan right at the start.

'Let me die in my footsteps.'

He said that. Let me die in my footsteps. People generally don't say *let me die in my footsteps* because it doesn't really make much sense. Although it makes sense in Bob's terms, when he was writing it in the early 60s about not wanting to spend his life hiding in an atomic bomb shelter. So, in that sense, the clown was being a bit over-dramatic, but all the same, he'd nailed his target audience.

For his part, I could immediately see that he had a bit more respect for the arresting officer when he discovered that he was a Dylan freak. Now we're almost mates, and the only thing standing between us is that this idiot banjoed some bloke in the pub over the head with a bat because he made some comment about the length of his girlfriend's skirt. That, and the fact that the Bob thing was only ever going to get him so far.

'That's how it is, man,' he says, when we finally move on from Bob and get around to addressing the issue of assault.

'What do you think Bob would have done?' I say. Even I'm aware of how stupid that question is as it leaves my mouth. Wonder what PC Corrigan is thinking as she stares vacantly across the room.

'What the fuck?' he says. 'I don't fucking know, do I?'

Hah. You may have seventeen Bob albums on your iPod, you little shit, but you're no fan. He just likes Bob Dylan because he thinks it makes him look cool and it sets him apart from his contemporaries who are all listening to God knows what. And really, I don't know. What are nineteen-year-olds listening to?

'You admit that you hit Stewart Addleston over the head with the bat in an unprovoked attack in the King's Head last night at just after 10.30pm?'

He looks across the table then shrugs.

'I'm not admitting anything.'

'You'll be waiting for your lawyer…'

'Of course I want a fucking lawyer.'

Hold my hand up. Waste of time. Well, it's a waste of time for me to be doing this. And guys like this should be banned from listening to Bob.

'Anything else you want to say before I end the interview?'

He shrugs.

'It is what it is,' he says.

Oh for fuck's sake. The stupid little prick. All right, he threw me off my game with the initial Bob quote, but now I think I might need to find an opportunity to get his baseball bat and whack the bastard around the head with it.

All in all a very unprofessional interview, something mercifully brought to a halt when the door flies open. Which is unusual. Often enough you get interrupted in the middle of these things, but usually you're going to get a gentle knock and then a wait for an invitation.

It's Morrow. He's flying, right enough.

'Sergeant, we're on again. Taylor's office.'

He disappears. Heart in mouth.

'Interview suspended, 8:17,' I say to the room, and then, with a quick glance at Corrigan, intended to indicate to her that she should deal with the suspect, I charge out of the room after Morrow. Up the stairs three at a time. Into the main open plan. Everyone is standing around looking at monitors. Some hands are at mouths. Some mouths are hanging open. A couple of people are looking squeamish. Just as I get to Taylor's office, he's flying out in the other direction.

'Come on, Sergeant,' he says. 'Think we've got it.'

'You're fucking kidding?' is all I venture in return, as I fall in behind him.

'Been waiting for this for two and a half months,' he barks, careering down the stairs.

I'm out after him, into the car. Straight away he lights it up and we zip out of the car park, wheels spinning, siren wailing. On the charge.

*

A large wood out past Shotts. There would be some officers, seriously, there would be some who would have said nothing. Wouldn't have put the siren on, wouldn't have called in the local plods. Would have wanted to be first on the scene, would have wanted to be the one with the glory.

Taylor, however, ain't one of them. All he's interested in is getting to these people before they die. As soon as we're in the car, I'm calling it in. The local station, the guys from Edinburgh, letting everyone know.

He knows the Plague of Crows won't still be there. It's possible he's wrong in thinking that the footage currently playing online is being broadcast live, but even if it is, it's not going to make any difference. The guy isn't going to have taken any kind of chance. We're not going to find him standing there camera in hand, asking the players in the piece to give him more desperation and inner angst.

This is all about getting to these people before they die

to a) save their lives and b) hopefully get some information from them about how they came to be tied to a chair, their feet in concrete and their brain under attack.

'Same setup as last time?' I ask. Heading along the M8, touching a hundred. Could be going faster, but it's just not that great a motorway. Two fucking lanes, for crying out loud. Why improve that when you can flush fifty gazillion down the stank for a tram system in a wee bit of the capital? Bastards.

'Exactly,' he says. 'All three are women this time.'

'You think it's live? Live footage?'

'It's been taken on a grim, cold morning in central Scotland. Could be any morning. We might well find them completely decomposed, but I don't think so. And the last couple were filmed as he circled around them. This one's stationary, implying it's on a tripod, implying that it's happening now and he was making sure he'd be nowhere near it.'

There's another police car away ahead of us, lights on, siren blaring. Presumably going in the same direction. Wonder if Taylor has any fear of everybody turning up at the wrong place? Probably not. He had those trees emblazoned in his head.

Are they already showing it on the news channels? Jesus, they must be dying to, but really, it's nine in the morning. You can't go showing people getting their brains eaten out live on air, even with one of those messages that they have to put in front of everything nowadays. *You should be warned that the following clip contains scenes of a somewhat unsavoury nature.*

Lurch back into silence. Aware that there are sirens behind us as well. Could be more locals, or could be the Edinburgh guys. We weren't looking to steal a march on them, Taylor just didn't want to take the time to slow down, didn't want to lose the half minute it would have involved, along with the possibility of a bunfight with Montgomery.

That can come after the victims have been saved.

Off the motorway, nearly loses it as he flies onto the Shotts Road, then skids spectacularly as he takes a ninety degree turnoff before we come to the golf course, and he starts gunning it down a small road. See the feds up ahead, and wonder if they're the first on the scene. Must be others here by now, it's taken us nearly twenty minutes.

In the last few months he's visited all the potential places. All of them, all over the country. That's what he's been doing. Driving and thinking. Listening to Adele and Bach... He knows every one off by heart, knows exactly where he's going.

Can see it up ahead, through the trees. Three of our cars are there already and an ambulance. That's good. In my rush I never said ambulance, and just because it's obvious doesn't mean that someone would have thought to do it.

He skids to a halt having slithered along a final stretch of damp muddy track, nearly hitting one of the other police cars and coming up just an inch or two short. Out the car, quick dash into the clearing. There are seven feds and two paramedics. And crows. In the trees, in the air. Still lurking, upset at being interrupted in the middle of breakfast.

There's a sergeant, who appears to be in charge, although he seems as out of his depth as most people are going to be at a scene like this. A couple of the others are looking around the perimeter of the small clearing. There's an officer each beside two of the victims. The ones who are already dead. The paramedics are attending to the survivor. If you can call her that.

The video camera set a little to the side on a tripod has been turned away, and presumably turned off. All those fucking ghouls who've been watching it on their computers are going to be disappointed. The TV networks will now be able to switch to comfortable edited footage that was recorded earlier, footage they've already seen and so know what's coming.

As Taylor and I approach the officers move back to let us have access. The woman, a strange half-head of long blonde hair in thick curls, is sitting bolt upright, still strapped in the position in which she was left. Her mouth is gagged, her eyes stare blankly ahead. There's a little blood running down from one of them. Her whole body seems to be tugging against the bonds, but as we get closer we can see that she's not making it tug. There's no thought involved. She's spasming constantly, violently, her body unnaturally pushing against the restraints.

We both stand and look for a second. A crow flutters past.

'Anyone got a gun?' asks Taylor.

For a second I presume he means for the woman rather than the crows, but that probably says more about me.

'Didn't want to let it off, Sir,' says the Sergeant, 'in case we disturbed her.'

Taylor glances at her again. Another crow swoops in and tries to grab a piece of one of the other two cadavers, is waved away by the attending officer.

'Kill a couple of them, Sergeant,' says Taylor. 'If that's not enough, kill another couple.'

He steps closer to the blonde.

'She gone?' he asks of the paramedics.

They've been working either side of her head, trying to stem the bleeding, and they take their hands away so that we can see the damage.

Jesus fuck. Feel the vomit start to rise, but I can't go throwing up, not in front of all this lot. At that moment I get the smell of it and realise that others have already heaved a couple of times.

Her brain is eaten away, the light grey matter mixed with blood. It's not so different from the ones we saw last time, and yet it is much, much worse. She's still alive. A twitching, quarter of a life.

The gun goes off and I, at least, flinch. Maybe the others do too. Another quick couple of shots, accompanied by the fleeing of crows and the frantic flutter of wings and the crowing and squawking.

I step away – nothing more to see here – and walk into

the middle of the clearing. Montgomery is approaching, large strides through small trees. I hear Taylor say, 'What are the chances I'm going to be able to talk to her?' and one of the medics snorts in reply.

I step further away, to the edge of the clearing, looking around. A couple of constables are already doing the same thing, and I wonder if they've been told to or whether they just want to get away from the murder scene. Is that what I'm doing? Do I think there's worth in looking around the area, or do I just not want to look at a grisly murder site in the middle of a wood?

Too many times grisly murder scenes in woods play out in my dreams. Can't stand to look.

But has the killer waited in the undergrowth to watch? Or does he have another camera hidden somewhere in the trees? That would make sense. A camera. Maybe he did that before, although the surrounding areas were thoroughly searched. Yet there are changes each time to the way he operates, and those changes have been related to filming and release of video.

Is there another camera, which is already relaying details of the investigation live onto the web? Not so likely, because then we'd get to hear about it, and would be able to take the camera down before we'd finished. He might want to see the whole thing play out.

Montgomery and Taylor are talking, but I've walked out of earshot. Low voices. They're not arguing though, which is good. Back in November, Montgomery came in like he was General Haig, expecting to have everything solved and wrapped up long before Christmas, but as time's gone on he's likely grown just as desperate as Taylor. Doesn't want stuck with this for the rest of his life.

Walk over to the two constables, who have now been joined by a third.

'Looking for anything in particular?' I say.

'Just anything out of the ordinary,' says one, as the other two shake heads.

'Listen, the guy obviously knows what he's doing with

a webcam. Let's check around, look to see if we can find a camera. And let's be aware, he has some resources going on here. He may well have access to some cool-as-shit, microscopic little fucker that'll be easy to miss. So, check trees, bushes, at a decent level off the ground.'

We get to work in the trees. As soon as I've had the thought I know we're going to find something. I throw a 'Don't touch anything that you find,' over my shoulder at them.

Like the boss, I don't care who does the business that works out, as long as it gets done. The call goes up a few minutes later. In the meantime, Taylor has already been over to ask what we're doing, leaving the horrible twitching victim to the paramedics. They haven't even taken the gag out of her mouth yet, worried that the second the bonds get loosened she'll become a spasming horror. They're trying to sedate her, but so far her brain isn't recognising whatever it is they're pumping into her.

Taylor liked the sound of the camera search and left us to it. Wandered around the small clearing, breathing the place in. Won't be happy that all we found were two dead bodies and a convulsing wreck.

The camera is near the top of a bush, tucked in behind some leaves in the middle, but with a clear view through the foliage to the scene. It's one of the local guys who finds it, and it was me who sent them out on their task, but there's no doubt that this is in Montgomery's hands the second the cry goes up.

He walks over, doesn't immediately grab it and put it in his pocket. There's nothing to be gained from bringing the filming to an end the second we have confirmation of another camera, and he'll take a moment to consider whether there's anything to be gained by letting it run.

We can speak to him. The killer.

Do we want to speak to him? Have a one-way conversation, where we don't even know if he's listening? We don't know yet if there's a microphone.

While I stand to the side of the discussion between

Montgomery and one of his sidekick Inspectors – Marqueson I think – I realise that I'm in the camera's line of vision.

I stare into it for a moment. Wonder if he's somewhere watching right at this moment. Calls back to the station have indicated that he's not broadcasting this anywhere online just now, not that we can find – and he's been pretty adept at advertising himself to the world – so I'm not worried that at that moment I'm being ogled by millions of people around the planet. But maybe I'm being ogled by the one guy. The Plague of Crows. And if not right at this minute, later, when he's looking at the footage in the comfort of his own bedroom or his own basement, whichever hovel it is that he inhabits.

I feel no fear. Indeed, as I stand in his line of sight, I suddenly think that maybe this is what I'm waiting for. The brutal, unpleasant death. The death that makes people feel sorry for me, a death that makes people regret I'm gone, and forget why it is they want nothing to do with me at the moment.

Of course, I also believe that I wouldn't be sucked so easily into his trap, in the way that these others were. The police officers in particular, assuming that one of these three women is one of us. They know what's out there, they know we're being targeted. How in the name of fuck are they allowing themselves to be taken?

Not me. I have a moment, not of invincibility, but of knowing that this guy, currently watching me in the stinking depths of his festering fleapit, would not be able to get to me. I'll see him coming. Or her coming. Whichever, it won't matter. Maybe he'll take me down, maybe I'll die trying to take him down, maybe we'll go together, Holmes and Moriarty plunging hand-in-hand into the waterfall, but he won't get me out here, he won't get me bound and gagged, the top of my head removed.

I stare into the camera. Don't speak, but he can read my face. I know what he's thinking, I know he understands.

Come and fucking get me, you prick.

One of those moments when I don't care. I've lived long enough. Done enough. Seen enough. Had enough women, drunk enough vodka. And, more than anything, I've done things I deserve to die for. Or not done things.

Come and fucking get me, you prick. I know my lips aren't moving, but fucking read them anyway. Come on.

Marqueson moves in front of me and blocks out the camera. By the time the view is clear again I've moved out of sight.

26

Mostar, in the middle of Bosnia, was a bunfight in the war. Centre of the whole thing. The Bosnian Serbs bombed it, took it. The Bosniaks took it back. The Bosnian-Croats fought them for it. Back and forth, a shitstorm of war, death and destruction.

When I arrived in the early autumn of '93 the Serbs had moved on and the Croatians were laying siege. They held the city to the west, had ethnically cleansed, raped and murdered the Bosniaks out of that part of town, back over the main road and the Neretva river to the east of the city, and were shelling all kinds of shit out the joint. It was war, that's what happens.

Of the ancient architecture in Mostar, the shining light was the Stari Most, the old bridge. The Croatians shelled it to destruction in November that year. I watched it happen. It wasn't strategic in any way, wasn't like you could get a tank across it. They just did it for the Hell of it, for the effect on the morale of the besieged population. They did it because they could.

I arrived in town thinking that the Serbs were the bad guys, because that's what I'd been told, only to discover that everyone was a bad guy. Yep, the Serbs had already destroyed the Franciscan monastery and the Catholic cathedral and fourteen mosques and the library with 50,000 books, they just hadn't waited for me to turn up to see it. Weirdly it wasn't shocking, because I already knew that was the kind of thing they did. But I arrived to find the Bosniaks and Croatians doing the same to each other. For some reason I was surprised. Must have been young and innocent.

The Croatians, so innocent themselves, who would

later be so offended when the Serbs dared to lay siege to Dubrovnik. How could the Serbs shell an ancient walled city? How could they damage an historically important site, the heartless fuckers? Poor Croatia, they would never do such a thing. They were the victims. *Look at us world, we're the victims.* Victims. The world agreed.

Some say they set tyres on fire in Dubrovnik to make it look worse, that when foreign journalists drove into the city after the siege was lifted, there wasn't as much damage as they'd been expecting. I wasn't there then. I was in Bosnia, in the middle of the forest. Maybe it's not true. Maybe rather than the burning tyres being propaganda, it's the story of the burning tyres that's propaganda.

Who knows any of that shit? That's what happens in war. Everyone leaps up and down saying they're innocent, and if their absolute guilt is established, then they leap up and down justifying why they were just doing what they had to do.

No one wins.

There were crows in the forest. Were there crows in the forest? Probably. Once. Sometimes when I wake up, now that the Plague of Crows is in all our heads, I see the crows in the forest in Bosnia, even though I know there were no crows. No birds at all. Birds are smart. They may not be so smart that they can play chess or solve mathematical puzzles or design an iPad, but they're smart enough to get the fuck out of Dodge when the bullets start flying.

Maybe people are smart too, they've just got nowhere to go.

They destroyed the bridge at Mostar. The Croatian Army. I was there. I saw it. They say it's been rebuilt, but I'm never going back. I'm never going to see it again.

They destroyed the ancient bridge. Mortar attack. 9th November 1993. The bridge at Mostar. The ancient bridge. Yet they were the good guys. That's what we were told.

Good guys don't blow up bridges just for the hell of it.

Now isn't that a fucking joke?

*

It happens that night. Me and Stephanie. Gostkowski, the Detective Inspector. We work late. All of us. No one leaves before eleven. A long day. Some stay until two or three in the morning, but in general we're told to leave, go home and get some rest, come in again early the following day. Clear heads.

We meet where I first really talked to her, last August, which already seems a long, long time ago. Like that time, she's already out there, smoking, coming to the end of her cigarette when I walk out.

We nod, not a lot to say. Think I know right there and then. She stubs her cigarette under her foot and says, 'Let me try one of them.'

I light it for her and hand it over. Lighting a cigarette for a woman and then handing it to her is one of those things that's just innately erotic. Don't know why, it just is. You're passing her death on a stick, but it doesn't matter. Still laced with tension.

'It's all right,' she says after a while.

I smile, sort of, but there's not much smiling tonight. This has been too long a day, too shit a day. A really, really shit day.

I'm tired, but I need something else before I go to sleep. I don't want to spend the day buried up to my eyes in this grotesque murder enquiry, be unconscious for six hours, and then get back to it. I need distraction, and it's going to have to be a pretty fucking mental one. No use watching a documentary on BBC4 or eating a fish supper.

This is why people in war zones, all the soldiers and the NGOs and the paper pushers that are sent to places like Baghdad and Kandahar, just fuck, bonk, bang and shag their way through their time out there. The working environment is too stressful, so that when they do get some down time, it needs to be high quality, needs to be an experience. So they shag their way around the compound, or wherever the hell they're living.

I'm about to bluntly suggest that she comes back with me to my house, and I know she'll say yes, and I also know that we likely won't be the only two doing it at the station this evening.

'You want to sleep with me tonight?' I say. I think when I started the sentence I'd intended asking if she wanted to stay over, or some shit like that, but out-and-out honesty just took over.

'Of course,' she says, as if we'd been fucking for years. Or like she was some blunt non-native English speaker. Dutch or German. For sure.

*

We don't speak. I walk into the bathroom and turn on the shower. She follows behind me, and stands unmoving as I undress her. Slip the blouse off her shoulders. Walk round behind her to undo the bra strap. Kiss the middle of her back. Let my hands rest lightly on her shoulders. Even at that she lets out a small gasp, the gentleness of touch, the caressing of the skin. Then I unbutton her skirt and let it fall to the floor.

The naked DI Gostkowski is as I'd imagined. Slim, not skinny. Deliciously proportioned breasts, great butt. I bend down, my hands holding tightly onto her hips, and bite her butt cheeks. Two, three times. Then I start working my way up, kissing and nibbling at her back. Standing behind her, I continue to kiss while I quickly undress, so that by the time I'm kissing her neck, I'm naked. I reach round and take her breasts into my hands and press against her, my erect cock thrusting hard against her buttocks. She gasps again, and now I turn her round so that we're facing each other.

As usual at this point I want to do everything at once. I want to kiss her all over, I want her lips on mine, I want her tongue all over me, I want her breasts in my mouth, I want to sink my cock deep inside her.

I kiss her gently, teasing her, biting at her lips, she

seems to gasp with every enticement, and then I press against her, take her into my arms and kiss her fully and passionately and she gives in to it and I love the feel of her hands as they grab my back, and of her breasts pressed against my chest.

I step into the shower and take her with me, and then wonderfully, she takes over. Presses me against the wall, her hand immediately grabbing at my erection, squeezing my balls. Holy fuck, that glorious mixture of pain and pleasure.

She pulls away, grabs the nearest bottle of shower gel and squirts it over my chest, then starts rubbing it in, as the water – just a little bit too hot – cascades over us. She's not really concerned with washing my chest, as she massages the soap over my aching cock and testicles. She looks intoxicating, the water bouncing off her shoulders and her hair, the soap splashing onto her breasts.

Her hands are all over me, massaging my cock and my buttocks, and now she starts biting at my stomach, quickly getting lower. And then she pushes me slightly to the side so that the warm water is landing directly on my cock and she rinses off the soap, and then suddenly grabs the base of my erection, runs her tongue along the length, and then plunges onto it and starts fucking me gloriously with her mouth.

This is what I'm talking about. Who on earth is going to be thinking about work at this moment? I'm standing in the shower, hot water all over me, and a woman on her knees in front of me, gloriously sucking my cock. Holy shit. Start thrusting, and she takes it, takes every thrust of my hips, and now it's hard to know who's in charge, if she's fucking me with her mouth or I'm fucking her mouth with my desperate, inflamed cock.

Thirty minutes later we're dried off and lying in bed. Well, I'm lying in bed, she's on top of me. Stopped myself coming in the shower, because I didn't want it to end there. She didn't stop herself coming, as I pressed her against the wall, my tongue probing inside her, my lips and teeth massaging and nibbling her clitoris. And now she's sitting on top of me, her shoulders straight, almost leaning back, fucking me desperately, crying out with every thrust.

I've got my hands on her hips, watching the movement of her breasts. I love just watching them, but I want to reach up and touch them, hold them, grope them and squeeze them, those fucking glorious breasts, the nipples protruding and desperate for my touch. Finally I give in to it, and as she's moaning and thrusting and driving her cunt onto me, I take her breasts into my hands, and there's nothing tender or romantic, it's all wonderful, desperate sex, and then I lean up and take her right breast into my mouth, biting and sucking, my tongue desperate for her, and at the same time I'm driving my cock into her as hard as I can...

*

There were rights and there were wrongs, and there was very little truth. That was the Balkan war. That's every war. Generally there aren't good guys. There are just a bunch of people doing whatever it is they can to try and win. Maybe the guys who start it are always the bad guys, but then that would depend on why they started it in the first place.

That's why we're still talking about WWII in the UK, that's why it's nearly impossible to turn on the television without finding something on there about it, a documentary or a commemoration or a TV drama. We were the undisputed good guys. The other lot were stomping across Europe, murdering people for not being blond enough. We stood up to them. We were the good guys, so good that in general we can ignore the questionable stuff, like when we slaughtered tens of thousands of civilians in bombing raids. The overall cause was so indisputably right that we're still happy to talk about it. Over and over and over, long after everyone else has moved on.

There were bad guys on every side in the Balkans. But there's no ignoring some things. There's no ignoring Srebrenica, for example. There was no other side did anything else on that scale. No other side lined up thousands of men and boys and slaughtered them all. They all did some fucking horrible shit, but no one else did that. Just the Serbs. The Bosnian Serbs.

The side that I took.

27

Get into work for 6:53am. Not bad, under the circumstances, but I'm pretty wired as soon as the alarm goes at six. Very commendably, DI Gostkowski did not stay over, barely even lay in bed, me with my arm draped around her, after we'd finished. She came, she fucked, she came, she left.

Thinking about her as I sit at my desk, but not in any proactively vomit-inducing romantic way. Would be nice if we quickly developed into fuck buddies. Been a while since I had an out-and-out fuck buddy. Such a rare thing to find. There's usually one of you, if not both, ends up thinking romantic thoughts, and before you know it something's said, and there goes the fuck buddy relationship and then not long afterwards, there goes any kind of relationship.

Enjoy it while you can, as much as you can, in the sure and certain knowledge that it won't last.

Grabbed a look at the newspaper headlines on the way in. The Sun led with *The Crow Must Go On*, which was my favourite, although the Mirror's *Let It Crow, Let It Crow, Let It Crow* ran it a close second. Plenty of them happy to potentially offend their readers, or anyone who happens to notice the front page, with large graphic pictures of the dead and dying. At least three of them promise even more graphic pictures inside, promoted with the usual warning about not looking if you're squeamish which is just aimed at attracting as many readers as possible.

The victim who managed to last until the cavalry arrived – although it's doubtful she knew anything about it – didn't make it through the night. Heard the news on the radio as I was getting breakfast. Extraordinary that she lasted that long. She remained sedated once the paramedics had finally done the job, and had never had anywhere to go. There was never a chance of recovery. If she died because someone decided to pull the plug in the middle of night, then you couldn't blame them.

Taylor arrives just after seven. Stops at the desk, acknowledges my presence with a nod. I read into it that he's desperately impressed that I'm here, what with me having previous.

'Can you spend some time looking at the three dates?' he says.

'What am I looking for?'

'Whatever you can find. See if there's a connection. And I don't mean, you know, anything big, anything that would be obviously flagged up as happening on those dates, the This Day in History section. Check newspapers for the day after each of those three dates, note down every story that might be of worth, see if there's anything that recurs, any theme, any name. Anything.'

'You have a hunch or something specific?' I ask.

He stops. He'd been slowly edging towards his office as he spoke, as if he didn't even have time to get the words out.

'Neither,' he says, and suddenly, just for a moment, seems a lot less dynamic than a few seconds ago. Gives himself a shake, snaps out of it. 'Just a thought, nothing more. Clutching at straws. I assume...' He pauses at the use of the word. Never assume anything in this game, and he knows it. 'I'm thinking that he does it when he's ready, and the fact that there's less of a gap between the second and third than between the first and second, is an indicator that he's getting better, able to put his plans together more quickly. That's what I think. Nevertheless, it's no reason not to consider other angles. Let's give it a go.'

He looks around the office, maybe making a note of those already at work, but more than likely just collecting his thoughts, then turns back.

'The downside is that, even if you don't find anything, it doesn't rule it out. He could be committing the crimes on specific dates, but there's no public record of what those dates are. So...'

And he just lets the sentence drift off, waves a haphazard hand then walks to his office.

Turn back to my computer screen and start looking through the newspaper archives. Might as well begin with the Evening Times. My heart isn't exactly singing at the prospect, but at least it's something constructive.

Suddenly DI Gostkowski is standing beside my desk. Not sure what she's working on at the moment, how many of us are being placed under Edinburgh command and control. I'm very happily staying out of the office politics, leaving it all to Taylor. From the general lack of grown men shouting, throwing teddies in the corner and behaving like football supporters, I'm guessing that some sort of mutually beneficial agreement has been reached between the two forces – and let's not pretend that that would have been reached by anything other than total desperation – and we are all, like the High School Musical kids and George fucking Osborne, in it together.

She looks fresh. I'm guessing – although it's not a word I would usually use to describe a forty-five-year-old, marginally overweight bloke who smokes too much – that I probably look reasonably fresh as well. Rather than go home and lie awake in bed thinking too much about the day gone by, we banged each other's brains out and sleep came very easily.

'Fuck buddy,' she says, and a small smile comes to her face.

Interesting etiquette. Some would say that just the acknowledgement of the notion that you might be fuck buddies is overstepping the mark, that the person saying it is laying down some sort of rule and talking about the situation, which in itself is denying the very nature of one's fuck buddy role. You have sex, you don't talk, you don't acknowledge. So this is a bold move, early on in the fuck buddy relationship. I'd never make the move myself, but it probably is the case that if anyone's going to do it successfully, it has to be the woman.

And that smile. Intriguing. Beautiful. Almost not even there before it's completely gone. I attempt what I hope will be an equally small and intriguing smile in return and nod. She taps her closed fist on the desk, as if asking to come in, and then walks on her way. I watch her go, and I'm pleased to say that as I look at her, all I think is how great she looks naked and that I can't wait to sleep with her again tonight, and barely a romantic thought crosses my mind.

*

I never thought the dates idea was up to much. If that was what the Plague of Crows has done, then he was leaving something to chance. Using specific dates might have been a tricky one for us to work out perhaps, but if we did it, then we might have an in. So it was a long shot, like Taylor said. Something that he probably thought of while lying awake in the middle of the night, because he didn't have a fuck buddy.

Anyway. Four-and-a-half hours later – and I realise that this is something I could spend much longer on, but four and a half hours somehow seems enough – I'm standing at the door of his office.

'Nothing,' he says, without looking up. Not even a question. He knows.

'Nothing,' I say.

He sits back. Stares out the window. Another grey, cold day in January. There's a guy snooping around the car park, looking in windows. It could be someone hoping to nick a car – it's not like there aren't people around here with the sheer balls to nick a car from outside a police station – but we both know it's a journalist.

He lifts up the phone.

'Sergeant,' he says, to Ramsay at the front desk, 'there's

an intruder in the car park. Send a couple of guys out to put the wind up him, eh?'

He hangs up. Looks tired again. Indicates for me to come in and sit down. The walls are still lined with the photographs of the woods of central Scotland. Now they seem pointless. Now they're taunting him. How was it ever going to be any different? They told him where to go, but it was no use. It hadn't allowed him to save anyone, and neither had they ever been going to. Not unless the Plague of Crows chose a patch of wood within a couple of miles of here.

He lifts the phone again, says, 'Can you come in here, Stephanie, please?' and hangs up.

Neither of us speaks. He's vaguely looking at a couple of pieces of paper on his desk, but in such a way that I can tell he's not actually looking. I watch him for a second, then look away. Outside, the bloke in the car park has been confronted by Constable Carr. They're arguing. No doubt the journalist is stating his case that his human rights are being infringed and that this is undoubtedly just another example of a thuggish police force cracking down on innocent civilians engaged in perfectly innocent activity.

The police. Never the good guys.

DI Gostkowski walks into the room, stands for a second, then closes the door unbidden and pulls up the other seat. And in an instant we have the feel of a war room. The cabinet come to establish the strategic overview and map out the way forward. I prefer war rooms conducted in pubs, and it is lunch time. I'd probably suggest it, but somehow the very presence of Gostkowski puts everything onto a higher plain of maturity.

'All right, we've finally come to an agreement with Montgomery, although to be honest we've been working fine without it for some time. The three of us are going to be… I don't know…'

'Special Forces,' I chip in. 'Working to the same end, sharing information, but not actually part of the main force.'

He looks at me for a second. So much for the presence of DI Gostkowski. She says nothing.

'So the three of us are going to sit here until we decide what we do next. Look at dates, times, methods, places, woods, crows, brain-cutting equipment. We're going to do what we've been doing since last August, and at the end of it... I know we're not going to have solved anything, but we're going to have some direction we're heading in and we're going to be working together. And, despite the accommodation that's been reached with Montgomery, I don't give a flying fuck what they do or what they think. We're not relying on them for anything. If they work it out, then good for them, and we can all move on. But until that happens, we forget about them as much as we can. All this rests on our shoulders.'

He stops, looks between the two of us. Check my watch.

'Can we get sandwiches?'

'No,' he replies, then leans forward and turns the piece of paper that was on the desk in front of him. He's noted down six or seven points and listed off several strands from each of the central themes. I believe this is what is known these days as a mind map.

'Read through that, give me your comments,' he says.

Gostkowski automatically picks it up, and I find myself leaning towards her trying to see.

28

I'm standing in front of the press. Can see a couple of guys that I recognise, but most of these people aren't from Scotland. Sure, all the Scottish lot are here, but now they're outnumbered by the collective from England and Europe and the States. We've even got representatives from those weird news channels that no one watches like Russia Today and China Now and Al Jazeera in English and Breaking News Moldova. There are a tonne of them, and I ain't in my element.

I wasn't sure about it, but the thought started off early in the meeting and wouldn't go away. Maybe the thought had started standing in a wood, not really knowing what was happening, feeling helpless and stupid, knowing that this guy was giving us the runaround, knowing that he still held all the cards, all fifty-fucking-two, despite Taylor putting in the hours so that he knew exactly where to go the second the latest killings went viral. That wasn't us taking any of the cards from him, that was him showing us a card or two and then saying, 'Here's what they look like, now fuck off because you ain't getting 'em.'

If anything, it helped him for the next time. It let him know that there were police officers out there who knew, who had absurdly checked the woods and who had some idea where to go. And the next time – for none of us doubt there will be a next time – he'll know to be more careful, or he'll know which boundaries to push, which to rein in. He'll know how much he can toy with us.

And I looked at that camera, and I knew he was looking back, and I thought, fuck you, you arrogant prick. You don't scare me. You can't do anything to me. What can you do? Seriously. Cut off the top of my head? You think I give a flying fuck if you cut off the top of my head? You think a few crows sticking their beaks in there is going to make the mess that constantly fucks up my mind any worse? I'm not scared. Really, I'm not scared. Come and get me. Get me, you fuck. I don't know these people you're picking up, but I bet you're going for the soft ones, the easy targets. That's all part of your plan. The soft targets. The ones who won't fight back, the ones who'll be straightforward. Kill the easy ones, strike fear into the hearts of the nation.

Well, fuck you. Come and get me. Come on. Man up and come and get someone who isn't going to cry, who isn't going to be scared.

I'm not hard, not especially tough, I'm not fearless. I just can't care any more. About life. You can't do what I did and move on. I've tried. I've been trying for over eighteen years. It's always there, and that's why this guy doesn't scare me, and that's why I looked into the camera yesterday morning, with a look that said come and get me. Come, you cowardly little fucker, and get me.

And at some point this afternoon, after many hours sitting in that room with Taylor and Gostkowski, long enough that he'd even allowed me to go and bring lunch in, I suggested that I do what I'm doing now. Stand before the press and taunt the fucker who's been taunting us.

He's seen me already. He saw me yesterday. And there's no way he's not watching the press conferences. He loves the press conferences. He loves being in control, loves watching us being dominated.

I use the cards line. People like clichés. The press like clichés. Society likes cliché and shuns the original. That's how things like *Ice Age 4* happen.

'We're not going to promise the public anything we can't back up,' I'm saying. Got the prepared statement in front of me. Agreed with Taylor and Montgomery. Montgomery didn't look too desperate about putting me out front, probably just because I'm not one of his men, but then neither was Taylor, for different reasons. One side effect of saying 'Come and get me, yes me' might just be that he comes and gets me, dealing with me just as ruthlessly as he's dealt with three other police officers. I might well not care, but Taylor does. 'Nevertheless, with every crime this man commits, we are getting closer. With every crime he commits he makes mistakes. When he started he had all fifty-two cards, and with every crime he commits he hands some of those cards to us, so that he no longer holds anything like all of them. It is clear that the public at large do not need to worry about this man. His attacks have been profession specific, and...'

The Evening Times will lead its later editions with *One Last Crow Of The Dice*.

I burble on, saying all that shit that you have to say. The press conference. None of the rest of it is important. It's for the press, for the public.

But that first bit. That shit about the cards. That was for the Plague of Crows.

*

Back to the office afterwards. One or two looks from the rest of the brigade not used to seeing one of their sergeants on the TV, not used to that level of bravado. And all that shit about holding the cards... well, they know it's just that. Shit. We're holding nothing other than each other's impotent knobs.

Taylor and Gostkowski are still in his office. They barely look up when I re-enter and sit down. It's cold in here, since he opened the window some time during the afternoon and hasn't closed it yet. January seeps in.

'Nice job, sergeant,' he says. 'Might get you some work on The Bill, something like that.'

'They don't make that any more,' I say, pedantically.

He grunts.

'Long night ahead of us,' he says. 'You better get on.' Checks his watch. 'Don't work any later than eleven. Get some rest, back here before seven tomorrow.'

Since August, and even more so after November, we've been concentrating on people who might have had a grudge against the media, the police and the social services. There were more than you'd think. Well, perhaps not. Perhaps you might realise there are a lot of people with that kind of grudge. Given that the majority of the population are happy to blame everything that's wrong in their lives on someone else, there are probably many thousands with such a grudge.

All we could do was look for someone with an obvious chip on their shoulder. A documented case, something that we were going to be able to read about, and hopefully in the newspapers, rather than just in social services files, given the inclusion of journalists among the victims.

We identified about ten people who looked perfect for it, another fifty or so who weren't so perfect, another couple of hundred who were real outside shots. None of them fitted. It wasn't like they all had alibis for each of the murders, but we knew. These weren't people who were capable of doing this kind of shit.

So now, given the general air of desperation that hangs over the investigation, we've decided to expand the search by taking one of the three variables out of the equation, which we'd done a little of previously, but now adding in a broader scope and a more expanded timescale. Which one of the three – the police, the newspapers, the social services – is not obvious, not documented in any way. With someone like this, with this fantastic level of grudge, resentment and hatred, it might well be that the grudge is buried where only he can go, deep inside his head.

So we're spending the evening splitting it up, each of the three of us taking one of the variables out and searching for someone with obvious resentment against the other two. I get to look for someone who's mad at the police and the media. Holy shit. And I'm stopping at eleven, doing a little more first thing tomorrow morning, and then heading out to interview people.

Where am I ever going to find someone who distrusts

the police and the media? Apart from on every street corner, in every pub, in every work place and in every house.

Ultimately it's not about finding a list of names, it's about prioritising and guesswork and hoping that the combination of the two pays off. And, of course, we're going to be covering much of the same ground as the Edinburgh lads. Trying to identify potential suspects working from no clues whatsoever was one of the mainstays of their investigation. They, very obviously, got nowhere. So with every name we pull out of a hat, there's a reasonable chance that they got there first and already crossed them off a list.

Maybe this new spirit of cooperation will allow us to talk to each other about it. I'll just hold my breath for that one, then see you in Hell.

*

We finish work just after 11:30. Taylor goes first, and then Gostkowski and me. We barely speak to each other, my buddy and me, and she follows me back to my place again. We do the same as the previous night, shower then bed, although this time we start in the hallway before we get to the shower.

And at the end of it she kisses me on the cheek, goes to the bathroom, then leaves with a nod and a slightly crooked smile.

I might allow myself the thought that she's almost the perfect woman, except that would be outwith the terms and conditions of the relationship. Instead, I don't think about anything, not even crows and trees, dark and foul deeds, before I fall asleep and dream of nothing.

29

'That was ballsy.'

Seventh interview of the morning. Decided to take a cup of coffee from this guy, because I was desperate. Six brief interviews, the time taken driving around, as usual.

I start off every interview with the same view. This is the guy. This guy sitting right in front of me. It's him. Guilty until he persuades me otherwise. Might as well. I'm not wandering around presuming innocence; where did that ever get anyone? We're not randomly interviewing people off the street, we're talking to people who are at least in the ballpark of suspicion, and although there's still going to be an element of stumbling across the right person by accident, it's not as much of an accident than if we bumbled around Buchanan Street bus station testing people to see if they were handy with a bone saw.

Of course, I usually change my mind in about five seconds. Most people have *I Didn't Do It* written on their forehead, whether they know it or not. Today, for some reason, I'm not feeling so forgiving. This bloke is the third I've not yet crossed off the list, the third name to take away and do a little more research on.

Started with the first guy on the list. It's not going to be him, though, is it? Not the first guy you speak to after having come up with a new line of enquiry. He was arrested for the rape of a young girl outside a night club. And when I say young, she was seventeen and pished out her face. Nevertheless, there was no question she was raped. The newspapers picked it up because his dad's been on the telly a bit. Nothing major, but it doesn't take much for a tabloid to decide you're worth putting on the front page. So overnight the whole country thinks he's a rapist.

Then the DNA test falls flat on its face. It wasn't him. Some other fucker with short hair, a tattoo and his jeans round his ankles. He wasn't charged, off he goes.

The following day the newspapers carry banner headlines about how he's not a rapist.

Ha! As if. The following day the newspapers have moved on. Most of them don't even mention his release, and if they do, it's buried somewhere beside an advert for 2-for-1 at Iceland on page 57.

At some stage he picks up meagre compensation from a variety of sources, but the damage is done. Everyone thinks he's a rapist, and he has to live with it.

I spoke to him for ten minutes. Still wore the chip on his shoulder, still blamed everyone else. The girl, the police, the media, his parents. At no point had he ever asked himself whether he could have avoided any of it. Living in a reasonable house, with a reasonable car out front, and a wife and kids that he managed to hang on to despite the rape allegation, you'd think that maybe he would just move on. But he hadn't.

He stayed on the list.

Then there was the ex-footballer whose career frittered to a halt after being done for drink driving three times. Of course, it would be the police's fault he was done for that, and for driving without a licence. Perfectly reasonable for him to hate us, and not to blame himself in any way. His slow walk into the arms of disgrace, despite the fact that he played for a shitty wee team that was neither Rangers nor Celtic, nor even the great Partick Thistle, was well documented by the newspapers.

He lived in a squalid basement apartment in Dalmarnock. Miserable little shit more or less ranted the entire time at me for my part in his downfall.

He stayed on the list.

And now this guy. Comfortably middle class, living in a large house on the north side of the city. A Lexus in the driveway. No more than ten minutes drive from the hills and trees and the great outdoors. Similar to the first bloke.

Wrongly accused by the police, wrongly arrested, name in all the papers. This one for the murder of a schoolgirl who lived on the same street as him. Several years ago now, but people hold grudges all their lives.

Unlike the earlier guy, this one was on the front pages for days. You know the thing they do, where they get the creepiest photograph they can find and splash it as big as possible? They can't say he's guilty, they can't say, *this is the guy who did it*, but they're saying it anyway even if they're not using the actual words.

And worse for this bloke, even though he was ultimately released, even though it was proven that he hadn't killed her, the real killer was never caught. There was never anyone else splashed all over the front pages. The story was celebrated enough that the guy did get front pages to announce he'd been released, but you know what the public are like. No one believed it.

'What?' I ask.

'The press conference you gave yesterday afternoon.'

'You saw that, did you?'

This bloke reminds me of a businessman who's all smiles, and who you know is going to ram you up the arse just as hard as he can. As soon as your back is turned, obviously.

'You seemed to be offering yourself up as his next victim.'

'I don't think I was doing that,' I say, despite the fact that that's exactly what I was doing.

'Clearly you were,' he says, leaning forward and popping two sugar cubes into his cup. 'I wonder if you have some great plan to fall back on, or whether you think you're just going to be too strong for him. Was it intelligence of some sort, Sergeant, or were your words dictated by some misplaced bravado?'

'Tell me about your arrest,' I say. I'm not here to talk about me. And even if he hadn't come across as some dodgy fucker, turning the conversation away from himself is exactly the kind of thing that's going to make me suspicious.

'Are you looking for people with a grudge, Sergeant?'

They all ask that. It's fair enough. We can hardly sneak up on them.

'Tell me about your arrest,' I repeat.

He smiles, slurps at his coffee in an almost affected manner. I'd say he was gay, except for the photographs of the two children all over the place and the wife he's mentioned about four times. Maybe he's in denial. Maybe I haven't a clue.

'It was a long time ago, Sergeant. 2001. You must be really scraping the barrel. Desperate, are we?'

'The killer is working meticulously. So are we.'

'Well, you have to, yes. That'll be why your colleagues were here two months ago.'

Fuck. Inevitable. Bloody Edinburgh. I immediately want to ask him who he spoke to but I don't want him to know that I'm in a left-hand-knows-fuck-all-about-the-right-hand situation.

'As I said previously, and as I've said to you people many, many times in the past... I was arrested for a crime I didn't commit. What can I say? I was paid, in the end, just over two hundred thousand pounds compensation. Bought this place with the money. Can you imagine?'

He looks around. I don't follow his gaze. It's an old Victorian gaffe that would go for well over half a million now. Not that the price would have risen in the last four years. Just shows you how mental things were for a few years there at the start of the decade.

'Why would I be bitter?' he says. 'I understand totally what you're doing, and why you need to do it, but seriously? I've got all this, I met my wife, a fellow victim. I have two beautiful children.'

Can't help glancing again at one of the photos when he says that. They look like regular children to me. You know, fuck ugly.

'What d'you mean your wife's a fellow victim?'

He snorts.

'Used to be on *High Road*, you know, years back. They accused her of turning up drunk on set. Big scandal. Huge. All over the papers. Ruined her career. You must remember it?'

I don't read those kinds of papers. I shake my head.

'Mid-90s,' he says. 'Crazy times. I didn't know her then, of course. She was still fighting the press years later when I was doing the same. That's how we met. We had the same lawyer.'

'Who gets the lawyer in the divorce?' I ask glibly.

For some reason he doesn't seem to think that's funny.

I leave seven-and-a-half minutes later, and his name stays on the list.

*

Back in the office just after six. Maybe subconsciously I thought I'd had enough, and I didn't leave any more on the list throughout the afternoon. Three people to check up on seems enough. Neither Taylor nor Gostkowski is there when I get back, so I grab a coffee and a Danish and settle down at my computer to do some more reading on the back story of the three blokes who stayed on the list.

Gostkowski returns a few minutes later, gets to work, doesn't speak to me. Taylor comes in just before seven. He whistles at the two of us like we're dogs. Seriously. The whistle that's all teeth and lips and sounds like a referee. I've never been able to do that. Naturally, like obedient police puppies, we follow him into the office. He's already sitting behind his desk. He doesn't indicate that he wants the door closed, and somehow we know that we shouldn't.

'Sir,' says Gostkowski, just as he's about to launch. He raises his eyebrows. 'You just whistled at us,' she says. 'Like we were sheep. Can I ask you not to do that again, please?'

God, she's bold, isn't she? I just take that shit. I don't think you whistle at sheep though. You whistle at the dogs that are rounding up the sheep.

He looks slightly taken aback – too used to pishing all over me and having me accept it – and then nods. 'Of course, Stephanie, I'm sorry.'

She nods. We can move on now, as I choose not to push for my own personal apology.

'First of all, nice job, Sergeant, we've had a lawyer on the phone, pretty much before you even made it back to the office.'

Jesus. I hate people. I hate all people. Literally. I hate fucking everybody. I need to go and live in a fucking yurt. Or die. I've had enough. I'm just trying to do my fucking job here. Can't I do a job?

'Hazelgrove,' he says. The rapist. Who wasn't a rapist. But whose life was ruined by the combination of the police and the media.

'Suing us, is he?'

'Not yet, but he will do if word gets into the newspapers that he's been questioned by the police in connection with the Plague of Crows.'

'Do we suppose that the next call Hazelgrove's lawyer made was to the Evening Times or the Sun to tell them that they would sue the police if it became public knowledge that they'd interviewed his client?'

Taylor smiles ruefully.

'If it wasn't, it was only because he'd called them first. I hope you were a little more circumspect with the rest of your interviews.'

He looks at me. I'm going to ignore that.

'Right, I'm not going to ask how you got on. Like me, I expect you came back with a few people on whom to make further background checks. Get to it, bring me something when you have it. There are, however, a couple of things that are going to shit on our parade…'

That's a nice analogy. Police work as a parade. Marching along the street while the crowds cheer us on, fully supportive and desperate for us to do well.

'One of the things that separates the human race from the rest of their fellow fucking awful species on planet earth, is the ability to see an opportunity and make the most of it. Consequently, the criminal collective, on realising that the police are going to be occupied with the latest serial killer on the block, are using the occasion to steal more shit, beat up more people and trash more shops and businesses.'

Actually, those wildlife shows would indicate that there are a lot of opportunistic species, but it seems pedantic to mention it.

'Maybe we could bring the army in and put the city in lockdown.'

We both look at Gostkowski with slight surprise. Sounds like she's been spending too much time with me.

'It might well come to that,' says Taylor, and he's almost smiling.

'What's the other thing?' I ask.

'Birds,' he says. 'There are just hundreds – literally hundreds – of reports of people killing birds, then inadvertently hitting buildings and people and all kinds of shit that isn't a bird. Then, inevitably, they're getting into fights because they think they're justified in going after the birds and that other people should be understanding of the fact there might be a little collateral damage. And of course, the folk going after the birds in the first place are already armed. Getting ugly out there.'

'Any deaths?' asks Gostkowski.

I hadn't even thought that. Was just assuming a bit of a bunfight.

'One so far. Who knows how many it'll end up with.'

That thing I was saying about hating people. Double it.

'I saw a couple of guys fighting not that far from here on my way back this evening,' I say. 'Didn't think anything about it at the time.'

Neither of them make the observation that I might have stopped to do something about the fight. Life's too short. Even for your average police officer.

'Well,' says Taylor, 'the suspects are piling up in the cells. Fullest they've been since last summer.'

'Jesus.'

'Yes. So, I'm afraid you're both getting some work divvied up to you. How many guys you got to follow up after today?'

'Three.'

'Ditto,' says Gostkowski.

'Well, whatever you were going to do this evening on those, I'd like you to try to fit it in. However, you both need to speak to Ramsay, get what's coming to you. The Edinburgh lot are the dedicated officers for the Plague of Crows, so we can't really argue it.'

A final glance between us and then he nods at the door and we're dismissed. Gostkowski leaves. I follow her out.

*

Five hours. Interview three members of the great British public charged with assault. Make further various investigations regarding battery and theft. Squeeze in a few hurried phone calls on my three suspects, but make no progress on narrowing them down. Probably what I need is some time to have a bit of measured thought, and I'd be able to eliminate one or two of them on the basis of realising that I was sucked into adding them to the list just through natural dislike on my part.

Don't get the time for measured thought.

Gostkowski walks past my desk at some point after eleven, glances at me and shakes her head slightly on her way by. That's a reasonable call, and I'm old fashioned enough to think that it's the lady's prerogative to make the decision.

Nevertheless, as the evening has suddenly changed from complete rubbish followed by delicious dessert, to just complete rubbish, I can't help but be disappointed. I'd enjoyed the release of the past two nights, and had been looking for it again.

Sergeant Jones catches me looking at her as she sits on the other side of the office. She smiles, which is unusual, and I smile awkwardly back and then turn back to the ever-growing mountain of paperwork. She probably thinks she caught me staring idly off into space, but really I was looking at her, wondering if it might be worthwhile suggesting that she and I become fuck buddies for the duration of the investigation.

Despite the illicit smiling that took place across the office, I'm never likely to suggest it. I don't have that kind of relationship with Sgt Jones.

*

Leave the office just after midnight. Go home, make myself some tea and toast, wash it down with vodka and tonic. Drink the first one quickly, make another. Fall asleep watching a Danish movie about the aftermath of child abuse. Have vague thoughts that I oughtn't to be so hard on all the fucking awful people that live in Britain, because there are fucking awful people in every country. Fall asleep as I'm having the thought that there are plenty of people who would think that I'm fucking awful, as fucking awful as all those members of the public I so detest.

Wake up suddenly, darkly, shockingly, sweat on my face, mouth open, a strangled cry in my throat, flailing hand knocking over the near-empty glass, which lands on the carpet and silently spills the dregs. Sit bolt upright, trying to bring myself back down from the high of fear.

The forest is already fading. I'm not naked. I'm not naked. Still in yesterday's clothes. I look down, see it rather than feel it.

Peed myself. Sit staring at the damp patch in my trousers for a while. I peed myself. What the fuck is that about?

I know. I know what it's about. Not the first time since Bosnia, but the first in a long time. Stand up, feel a drip down the inside of my leg. Look down at the seat. Already damp.

What did I dream?

I don't want to know what I dreamt. I know what I dreamt. Walk out into the hall, tired, sore, hot, miserable, encased in fear and gloom and darkness. Tired. Tired more than anything else. I could just go and lie down in bed. Me and my damp trousers. Hesitate. Seriously consider it for a moment, and then head for the bathroom. Look at my watch as I turn on the light.

Aw fuck. Couldn't be worse. Already after half-five. No time, no point in going back to bed. Isn't that just the worst feeling in the world? No time to do what you desperately want to do. No more time. No time for sleep.

Lean on the edge of the sink and look up at the mirror. Look fucking awful.

You know that thing that happens in movies where people look up into the bathroom mirror and then suddenly there's someone there behind them, waiting to bury a knife in their head?

I'd jump, and maybe I'd even pee myself again, but I wish that person was there right now. I wish he'd come. From nowhere. The man with the knife to finish me off.

The man with the knife.

Come on, you fucker. Come on.

30

Sitting in the office. A little before seven. Everyone looks tired. I feel more awake now than most of the rest of them look. Do I look awake though, or are they glancing at me as they walk past thinking, *fuck he's knackered*, or *what happened to him*? They don't know. They don't know I slept for less than four hours on a chair and woke up scared and miserable, trousers soaking like some incontinent old bastard.

Cried in the shower. Falling to pieces. Exhausted.

They don't know I cried in the shower.

The tears were dried off after the shower. The piss washed away, trousers stuffed in the washing machine. I drank coffee, I drank cold water, I cleaned my teeth. I'm awake. I'm not scared any more.

I'm still miserable.

I know what today brings in terms of the Plague of Crows investigation. I have five more people to talk to, and I need to reduce my list of three suspects to one. More than likely, to none. Finally got my few quiet minutes to think about it while I ate breakfast. And when I say ate breakfast, I didn't actually eat anything. I'll grab something later, probably on my way out. If I get the chance to go out. Cleared up all the outstanding crap last night, although mostly that means I found somewhere to park it, allowing me to work on the case that really matters, so the morning will depend on how much other stuff comes my way.

Hopefully, and this is of course a wild stab in the dark, people won't have been trying to kill crows during the hours of darkness, because that *would* be a wild stab in the dark. No crow killings, less chance of inadvertent murder. Of course, it might well be that the collective, intent on increasing the crime rate because they know the police are otherwise occupied, will have been even busier because it was too dark to kill crows.

Constable Forsyth passes by. Now there's a man who looks tired, and it's pretty obvious he's been working the night shift. He nods.

'Busy night?' I ask, as he's about to pass by without saying anything.

'In a word...' he says, 'fucking hell, aye. It was. Never stops.'

I'd question his maths, but to be honest he doesn't really look in the mood. Anyway, he doesn't stop.

Doesn't look good. Better grab a few minutes doing some research on my three fellows from yesterday. Or one fellow, as it happens. On further thought I decided to ditch the rapist. Partly this is because he spoke to his lawyer the minute I was out the door. He's just a money-grabbing shit. The Plague of Crows isn't in it for the money. He's here for the sport.

It also wouldn't be in keeping with the obvious desire for anonymity. It's one thing the police turning up out of the blue uninvited – like Adele and Alanis – but to then keep the contact going, make them mad at you again, get your face in the newspapers if at all possible. That's not the Plague of Crows.

I've also realised that I need to chop the footballer off the list. Sure, he was an odious little bastard, but he's also a footballer, dyed-in-the-wool, which is to say he's thick as fuck. This guy probably hasn't worked out yet how to tie his boot laces, which is the real reason his career stank up the lower divisions of Scottish football. I was just keeping him on the list because I was in a bad mood and he's an obnoxious arsehole. If I did about ten more minutes of investigation on the bloke I could probably find at least three reasons to arrest him, but none of them would be for having the wit to carry out the crimes of the Plague of Crows.

That's what we're talking about. The crimes may be

vile, horrendous, brutal, vicious, depraved, whatever you want to call them, but they're the work of a man who knows what he's doing, a man of creativity and acumen, a man who knows how to play his audience. A man of quality, who has decided for one reason or another to put those qualities towards perpetrating the most appalling murder. So, whoever he is, he ain't some dipshit footballer.

Which leaves the guy with the ugly kids in the big house to the north of the city. Married to a woman who used to be on *High Road*, that's what he said. There was no sign of the wife, and for all the photographs of the bloody spawn, there were none of the missus. Or of him. It was all about the kids.

Maybe that was why he went on the list in the first place. These people with endless photos of their damn kids all over the place. Fair enough, if that's what you want to do, once the damn kids have left home. Maybe you actually want to be reminded of them. But while they're living in the house with you? Really? What's the point? You finally get the little bastards off to bed after they've spent the day torturing you and ripping out your soul, then you look round and there's a fucking photograph of them smiling back at you. Laughing at you. Mocking you, letting you know that there's no escape. They will be there, sucking you dry, for all time.

Whereas, give yourself a few hours without the evil grinning faces of your kids garishly looking down upon you like some insane, murderous clown in a Stephen King novel, and you might be quite glad to see them when they get up the following morning.

Haven't seen my own kids since two days before Christmas. Some days I miss them. Some days I never give them any thought. Some days I feel guilty. Maybe that's what leads me to feel resentment against the brigade who fill their home with evidence that they've reproduced.

There was no sign of the wife, however. The wife who had been on *High Road*. And there was a smugness about the guy. Like he was laughing at the police for being so lost. Being so desperate that they're searching around for any old person to interview.

And maybe he's right to be smug, maybe he's right to hate the police, and maybe he's right to be laughing at us and our desperation. But the fact that he's laughing, the way he was laughing, it was just the way that I'd expect the Plague of Crows to be laughing when he's sitting watching our press conferences on the TV.

So, that's what I thought while I was drinking coffee. That I'd discard the rapist and the idiot footballer and concentrate on this guy. The guy who does something in stationery, the guy who was accused of murdering a schoolgirl, but who was never charged, and who makes enough to keep the large house he bought thanks to the police and who has a Lexus parked on the front driveway.

*

I read the files, but it's always best to get the subtext, get the information that was never written down. Twelve years later, and the officer in charge of the investigation has been retired about nine years. Ex-DCI Lynch isn't old. At least, he didn't retire because he'd hit pensionable age. He just chucked it because he'd had enough.

Find him at a trout farm up by Larkhall. Comes here twice a week. Four of the other days he splits between river, sea and loch fishing. Doesn't fish on a Saturday. Goes to watch the Celtic. Divorced. No kids. As miserable a bastard as you could wish to meet.

He's flicking his line over the water. I'm standing far enough away to avoid getting a hook in my hair. He clearly did not enjoy being interrupted. Acted like he was being forever questioned about old cases, although the sergeant I talked to at his station pretty much said that none of them had heard anything about him since he left. He wasn't easy to track down.

'But you didn't catch the real killer?'

So far he's answered most questions with one or two

words. Coming to be of the mind that I might just push him in. And he's yet to look me in the eye.

'We did,' he says.

'You did what?'

'Catch him.'

There's a fair amount of disconnect going on here, which would be helped if he'd put down the fucking rod, speak to me properly and stop answering questions in mini sound-bite size chunks.

'I thought the case remained unsolved? That that was part of the suspicion that continued to hang over Clayton?'

'We solved it,' he says. 'Just couldn't nail the bastard.'

'Who?'

He finally glances round at me. He's looking at me like I'm the idiot.

'What?' he says, continuing the theme where he thinks I'm the one being obtuse.

'Who couldn't you nail?'

He continues to stare at me with the clear implication that I'm being thick as shit. And he's right. Finally sinks in.

'Ah,' I say eventually. 'Clayton…'

'Thank Christ,' he mutters, and at last he can drag his contemptuous look away from me back to the dark water of the pond, then he flicks the line over his shoulder for all the world like he's Brad fucking Pitt in that fishing movie.

'You sure it was him?' I ask, risking opprobrium by even continuing the conversation.

'Aye,' he says. 'But he was good. Knew what he was doing. Covered up after himself. A real pro.'

I stare at the miserable old bastard. There we are, the kind of thing that we've been looking for. Knew what he was doing. Covered up after himself like a pro.

'You been following the Plague of Crows business?' I ask.

He snorts. I wait for him to say something. He doesn't.

'You been following the Plague of Crows business?' I say again.

He grunts, this time says, 'Aye. Fucking glad it's

nothing to do with me 'n' all.'

'You think Clayton is the kind of man who could be pulling this off?'

He'd been about to cast the line again, then lets it fall and lie limply in the water. He stares straight ahead of him, although his eyes are vague, looking at nothing.

'That's what this is all about, is it?'

'Yes.'

He's still thinking, still looking at an indistinct point in the middle of nothing.

'What led you to him?' he asks.

It would be fun to answer him with a grunt and few words, but one of us has to be a grown up.

'Fishing around. Pretty clueless, to be honest. Ended up talking to people who might resent the police and the media, as the Plague of Crows appears to do. Spoke to several people yesterday, he was one of them.'

'Why'd he stand out?'

'He was an irritating, smug fuck,' I say. He snorts again. 'Lived in a nice house, seemed to have done well for himself...'

'Fucking too right, he did.'

'... just something about him. Didn't like the cut of his jib. When I think about all the people I've talked to in the course of the investigation, he stands out. You sure he killed that schoolgirl?'

'Yep.'

'Why?'

'He told me.'

'When?'

'When we'd let him go and he'd successfully sued the police, the Sun and the Daily Express.'

'Bravado? Rubbing it in? Just making shit up to try to piss you off?'

'Maybe.'

'So what made you believe him?'

He turns and looks at me again.

'He knew. He knew things he couldn't possibly have

otherwise known. But he was good. Covered his tracks down to the last detail. Every time we thought we might have him, he had an out. Every track.... Bastard.'

We stare at each other for a few seconds and then he slowly turns away. Lifts the rod, flicks the line and the bait darts out over the water.

I look away. There are two other middle-aged blokes fishing on the other side of the pond. A chill day, low cloud, no hint of rain, not cold enough for snow. A flat, grey day. In the distance you can hear the traffic from the M74. A constant low sound, occasionally penetrated by a loud exhaust or an unnecessary charge up the outside lane.

'You there yet, Sergeant?' he asks.

'What?'

'You at the stage where you wonder what the fucking point is? You're there to catch criminals, to keep order, then you catch one and you're immediately hit with paperwork and human rights lawyers and all the rest of the crap. Fucking signs up on every wall of every station telling you how to conduct every single moment of your life in uniform. And you're always the bad guy. The scum... the bastards who rape and steal and assault and murder... they're the ones with the rights. The human fucking rights. Isn't that a joke? You there yet? You got to that point where you think, what in the name of fuck am I doing this shit for?'

No answer to that. I've been there a long, long time. I've just never had the guts to get out. What else am I going to do?

'He was the final straw. Clayton. Pushed me over the edge sure as I was standing on a cliff. Knew what he was doing as well. Picked his moment. Then he told me. Told me what he'd done to her, all that shit that hadn't been in the papers. Told me, as he was walking away with his three quarters of a million quid.'

'He told me it was a couple of hundred thousand.'

Another snort. 'From us, maybe, but he got more from the papers. He did all right out of it. Slaughtered a young girl, and earned seven hundred and fifty grand... Is that what it takes to be rich?'

'Did you wonder whether this might be him?' I ask. 'All this stuff with the crows, did you ever think it could be him?'

He's still flicking the line, although I can see that it's a more mechanical movement now than it was when I first arrived.

'Hadn't even crossed my mind,' he says. 'I'm not wrapped up in him, or my old work. Barely ever watch the news. I just do this... go and watch the Celtic at the weekend. Sometimes I can't even be bothered with that. I don't watch the news. I don't think about Clayton. He beat me, that's all. He beat me, and I've had to live with it. I don't think about him.'

'Now that you are,' I say, continuing to push him, although it's not like I'm unsympathetic to the oppressive weight of defeat that hangs over him, 'what do you think?'

He continues the movement of the line, but it's becoming less and less focussed. Suddenly realise that I'm completely fucking him up as I stand here. He'd been doing fine, and now I bring him this. And if this guy, this Clayton, turns out to be the Plague of Crows, then there are now a great list of victims who wouldn't have been killed if Lynch had been able to get his man in the first place. How shit is that going to make him feel?

I have a vision of Lynch at home, hanging from a light fitting, the cord around his neck, his face black and purple, tears dried on his cheek, a bottle of vodka on its side, the dregs having dribbled onto the carpet.

Or maybe that's me.

'Yes,' he says. 'Now that you make me think about it. Yes. He was intelligent, knew everything we'd try to uncover, and he had it all taken care of. He was on top from the start, and he stayed there. And...'

Finally he stops the continuous movement of the rod, the flick of the line.

'... and he was a sick fucker. The things he did to that

girl. Is he sick enough to carry out this weird stuff that your Crows bloke is accused of doing....?'

'There's no accused about it,' I mutter.

'Yes,' says Lynch. 'It could be him. Let me know when he walks away and laughs in your face.'

He coughs, stares down at the water.

'Nothing's biting the day,' he says, then he lays the rod down on the grass and looks around. There's a bench a few yards away, and he lifts his small bag and walks over to it. Glance at my watch. Lunchtime, more or less, and he's taking a break. I realise that we're finished. He's not about to ask me to join him. He's said all he has to say.

Think of something else just as I'm about to leave.

'Has anyone else been asking about him?'

He turns and looks at me. Just a glance. Curiosity mixed with contempt, before moving quickly onto complete disdain. Doesn't even bother answering.

I'll take that as a no.

I watch him for a few moments and then turn away as he takes a small flask from his bag.

31

Back in the office with Taylor and Gostkowski. Ramsay tried to grab me on my way in, Gostkowski had already been grabbed, but I put him off and managed to get Gostkowski out of her interview with some little wanker who assaulted a couple of pensioners, so that the three of us can have a chat about Clayton.

More work to be done, more research into his family and what he's been doing for the past eleven years of his life, but for the first time since last August we actually have someone to investigate.

I've just finished laying it all out. My senior officers have listened without interrupting.

'Either of you know DCI Lynch?' asks Gostkowski when I'm done.

Shake my head.

'I remember the case,' said Taylor, 'but it was nowhere near us. Didn't know the guy. I might have had an opinion on it at the time but...' and he waves a dismissive hand in the air. 'And no sign of the wife?'

'None.'

'And no photos...'

'No photos. But, she was on *High Road*, apparently, so that might make her slightly easier to track down. Although, it's liable to have been in the early days of the internet, maybe there won't be too much online. We'll need to go and find someone at STV.'

'If there's a wife, if she's still around...'

'He said she was out getting her hair done.'

'Well that proves bugger all. If there's a wife then she's pretty crucial to it. We know how well executed this whole thing has been,'

He hesitates to glance at Gostkowski, who has reached over and taken the iPad that was lying on the edge of Taylor's desk. Fairly confident that she probably isn't checking the weather, the football transfer window or a recipe for that night's dinner, he ignores her and continues talking.

'She's going to be aware of him having been away for a while. Presumably she's thinking he's on some business trip or other.'

'He said she was a victim of the press as well. Maybe she's involved.'

He stares at the desk as he thinks about it.

'Maybe. Maybe. Don't like it. Everything we think about the Plague of Crows is based around him being in control. The second you bring someone else into it, no matter how much you trust them, you start to lose the control. There's also the matter of someone else being able to, in some way, moderate your insanity. This guy... this guy is a fucking basketcase. You've been married. Take the stupidest, weirdest, ugliest thing you ever did before or after your marriage, and then imagine if you'd have done it if your wife had known about it.'

We look at each other while we think about weird, ugly, stupid things we've done. Gostkowski glances up with a curious smile on her face, then looks back at the tech.

'Fair point,' I say. Didn't actually think of anything. Didn't want to.

'The whole thing is difficult enough to imagine, but the idea that two people – one of them the mother of two young children – would get carried away with this... I'm not convinced.'

'You're very old fashioned, Sir,' says Gostkowski without looking up.

'And I shall stay that way,' says Taylor.

'You have her name?' asks Gostkowski, turning to me. 'The wife?'

'Caroline...' I say, then realise I don't know her maiden

name.

'There's a list on imdb of everyone, well, a shitload of people at least, who appeared in *High Road*.'

'Jesus. Who takes the time to write down that shit?' mutters Taylor.

A pause while we both look at her, then she nods.

'There's a Caroline Strachan, appeared in one episode at some point. Doesn't say when. There's no link to anything else.'

'I'll get the second name. Got the impression, from the way he said it, that she'd done a bit more than that. That she was some kind of regular. Maybe she used a different name for her acting career.'

Gostkowski's fingers are flying over the small keypad, then she starts nodding at it, understanding something that she's not letting us in on.

'There's the same plethora of information on the internet that there is about anything. We can look at it later.' She switches off the iPad, lays it back on the desk.

Taylor taps a quick beat out on the desk.

'Right, get going. I'll speak to Ramsay, make sure he leaves you out of the rest of it. You two get digging on Clayton and the missus. Discretion from both of you, no blundering phone calls. Obviously he knows we have some interest in him, after yesterday, but don't let him know for the moment that we're following it up.'

'You going to speak to Edinburgh?' she asks. 'Assuming Clayton wasn't winding the sergeant up, Edinburgh have already talked to him. It'd be wise to find out what they know.'

Taylor taps his fingers again. He's already been thinking about it. Ever since they were brought in they've been part of every one of his thoughts on the investigation.

'Yes,' he says. 'Wise. You're right. I'll run it by Montgomery, see what he thinks. Say enough so we don't look like we're over-reacting, but not enough to make him swoop in and take the thing off us and then do a shit job...'

He waits, and when we don't immediately stand up, he

nods in the direction of the door and turns side on to us to look at his monitor. I glance at Gostkowski as I get to my feet, but she's already on her way out.

'We going to split this up?' I say, as we walk across the office.

She stops, stares at the floor while she's thinking about it.

'Yes, makes sense,' she says. 'I'll do the wife. I used to watch that stupid show when I was younger, maybe something'll ring a bell. I'll track down the story that her husband says ruined her career, and then find out what she's doing now. You stay on Clayton. Where he works, what he does in his spare time, that kind of thing. What about the kids? What age were they?'

'Photos looked pretty young. Both under five, I'd have said.'

'And there was no sign of them?'

'None. So maybe they were at school or nursery school, the mum took them to the hairdresser's…'

She's nodding, already mentally getting on with the job.

'Fine,' she says. 'See you later.'

She turns, then stops and looks back, a little unsure, as if that last line had been a slight overstep of the fuck buddy rules. We stare at each other, she shakes her head to lose the moment and turns away.

See you later. Those three words. That's all it takes, and I'm already there, thinking about the night ahead. Take a moment, a delicious moment to sink into it, to think about the two previous nights of fuck buddy heaven, and to think about what it might be like this evening.

Sigh, switch back on to the general tumult of an open-plan police office, get the image of Michael Clayton in my head, the image of a naked DCI Gostkowski out of it.

*

People don't entirely realise the extent of it these days. The amount of information that the police – and no end of other bodies and organisations – have at their fingertips on virtually everybody.

Doesn't take long, and I can tell you where Clayton goes shopping and what his favourite type of breakfast cereal is, how often he plays golf, how much money he has in the bank, the last time he went to the theatre, what kind of movies he likes. If I wanted to do the Sherlock Holmes shit I could probably have extrapolated that he and his wife don't have sex any more and that his kids don't love him. But then I'd already found out that he and his wife split up three years earlier and he hasn't seen her, or those ugly kids of theirs, since then.

Those picture-perfect images of two young children adorning every wall and every mantelshelf in the house are at least three years old because he's had no contact with them.

Living in a big house, earning a decent amount of money working self-employed as some kind of sales consultant in the stationary business. He's a big thing in paper clips. I mean, even if I didn't have my suspicions about this bloke being some kind of deranged crow-controlling super-villain, I'd still hate him. A theatre-going, golf-playing consultant. In my world, punching people like that in the face would be an Olympic sport.

Of course, the more your read, the sadder it looks. Come across a lot of lawyers letters from three years ago, and quite a number since then. Split from the wife, she didn't want anything to do with him, didn't want the kids anywhere near him. She left in the middle of the night, he hasn't seen them since.

I suspect that Gostkowski will have trouble even finding where she is now. He wasn't married when he was previously arrested, but he managed to take the money he made out of that scandal and put it into a nice house, a wife and a decent job. Been earning quite a lot since, in the usual money-follows-money kind of way.

But whether or not he turns out to be the Plague of Crows, this is just a portrait of a sad little life. Of course, if

Lynch is correct, then a sad little life is far more than he deserves. But this is the trouble with police work. So much of it revolves around people whose lives have been fucked up, or who have chosen to fuck up their own life, that you end up wallowing and trawling through these endless sad stories. Your days become one long episode of Eastenders. And every now and again, such as when you're looking at a divorced bloke who never sees his kids and whose life is filled with all sorts of pointless shit in some desperate attempt to compensate, it's like looking in a mirror.

*

At the Costa across the road, me and Gostkowski, two cups of Americano. Just because we're having sex, doesn't mean we can't also hang out and talk and stuff. That's part of the contract. The things you don't do are have expectations, fight, and get neurotic.

Boiling bunnies is also right out.

'So, no sign of the wife?'

'She did a Lucan,' says Gostkowski. 'And a pretty spectacular Lucan at that. Middle of the night, fleeing the country with the kids. Nice job.'

'You think he looked for her? I mean, I know he got his lawyer to write a lot of letters to the courts and police, but…'

She shrugs. 'Presumably. But did he ever get on a plane? I doubt it.'

'Well, he doesn't have a passport.'

'Ah. Well, there's your answer, because I'm pretty sure that she left the country.'

Sip the coffee. As usual there's too much coffee in the cup, not enough space for milk. Even though I asked. There must be people who complain if their cup isn't filled to the last millimetre.

There are always people who complain. And then there are the people who complain about the people who complain. Like me.

'And *High Road*? Turn up in one episode, did she?'
'No episodes,' she says.
'What?'
She shrugs.
'Really, it was hard to find out about his wife, because there wasn't a lot to be found. Regular family life. There was a sister and a brother. Studied mathematics at Glasgow, couldn't get a job, eventually worked for a while in an office job for Woolworths, etc., etc. She'd been a bit political at uni, kind of anti-government. You know, she was a student, they're supposed to be anti-government. Maybe she still had some of that when she met Clayton. Sympathised with him for having been manipulated by the system.'
'Maybe she never knew.'
'Maybe. Although, he never changed his name and it was in the papers, a lot, at the time, so she'd have to have been walking around with her eyes shut. Which doesn't tie in with her having been reactionary. At least to some level.'

A waitress hoves into view, clearing one of the other tables, so we stop talking for a second. Drink coffee. Look out of the window. Late afternoon, low cloud, street lights already on. Chill in the air. Snow would be nice, I suppose. At least it would brighten up the drabness, but you can tell this will be a winter without snow.

'Everything all right for youse?'

We look round at the waitress. Late thirties. Slim. Attractive. I know, I know, but that's just how it is. Look at a woman, and my brain makes an instant judgement. Just as well I don't project.

I nod. Gostkowski says, 'Yes, thanks.' The waitress shimmers off to another table, laden with the detritus of mochaccinos and muffins.

'You're a piece of work,' says Gostkowski. Smiling.
'What?'
'You just undressed her.'
'No, I didn't.'

'Yes. You. Did.'

Funny. She actually just did that. Said three words as individual sentences. I'm not playing that game.

'I just said everything was fine.'

'Actually, you said nothing, and while you were saying nothing, you were deciding whether or not you'd sleep with her.'

'Maybe. But that's not the same as undressing her.'

She stares at me. I am, of course, drawn to look round at the waitress, but I make sure I don't.

'So, was she slim?'

I give her the look. 'Yes,' I say eventually.

'Hair colour?'

'Mousey blonde, kind of tousled, shoulder length.'

'Nice breasts?'

I'm not answering that one.

'All you're proving is that I have decent powers of observation,' I say. 'And what with my job title 'n' all...'

'Sergeant, I'm just teasing, not going all high maintenance on you. But honestly, have you, or have you not, just imagined what that woman looked like naked?'

I stare across the table. So, that thing I was saying about not projecting...

'Yes... all right, I did. And she looks damned good without clothes on. You know...'

'All right, Sergeant, I've got the picture. You're not down the pub with your mates.'

'You started it.'

'You were the one undressing her, while thinking you were being discreet.'

She's got me there. I hide behind the cup of coffee, then say, 'Anyway, I never talk to men about naked women. That's... I don't know...'

'Vulgar?'

'Yes.'

'Well, I'm honoured. We should probably get back to talking about the investigation now.'

'Yes.'

'So Mrs Clayton leaves her husband, taking the kids with her. I spoke to a couple of people who weren't very forthcoming. Also spoke to the brother, couldn't get hold of the sister. I'll keep trying. But I think we can take it that he wasn't necessarily abusive, just not a nice bloke to live with, and pretty demanding. She felt threatened ultimately, but was never actually harmed. Bottom line is, she's not part of this, and he told you quite a lot of lies. Which is odd.'

'Maybe if your whole life is a lie, if you're always lying, lying to your family, lying to the police, lying to yourself, you forget what the truth is. You forget what can be checked.'

'Yep,' she says, 'that makes sense... But does that tie in with the Plague of Crows? The meticulous killer, the man who makes sure he covers every track?'

'Maybe he's very focussed on his work. That's... his work, his murder, is one thing. Cold and clinical. He can control everything. But his home life, his private life, he hasn't been able to control. It's fucked up so he's constructed stories around it to make it work, to make it appear as orderly as his work life.'

She's nodding. 'Not bad, Sergeant, that makes sense. So classic a personality type that it's almost a cliché; seemingly ordered on the surface, but full of turmoil and shattered confidence underneath. Yet, here, applied to this, it really fits, and it doesn't seem clichéd at all. This guy is potentially so screwed up, it seems... it seems likely.'

'Nevertheless, we have to be careful. We're talking ourselves into this guy being him. Every piece of information we unearth seems to back it up... have to be careful, that's all.'

She nods again. 'Yep. So, let's keep digging. The alibi or not is unlikely to prove anything, given that the bulk of the work was done late at night, early morning. Living alone... it'll be easy enough for him to say he spent the night in bed, and there would be no one to back him up even if he is telling the truth.'

Drain the coffee, still quite a lot in the cup and some of it dribbles down my chin. Grab a napkin and wipe it away before lowering the cup from my face. Like a seasoned professional.

*

Late night, Taylor's office. He's standing at the window looking out at the car park, although there are more lights on in here than out there, so he's mostly staring at his own reflection. Gostkowski and I have just laid it all out for him. A day spent rooting around after Michael Clayton. He's listened to it all, asked a few questions. Even as we explained it, I wasn't sure that there was enough to be making sure we went back to see him.

'All right,' he says, 'you've identified a certifiable liar, fantasist maybe, an unpleasant husband and father. Possibly, if we listen to Lynch, a murderer. The fact that he managed to get away with all that shit before, if it was him, doesn't make him any more unpleasant, but it does make him smart. Smarter than most of the fuckwits we end up dealing with in this job.' Ain't that the truth. 'So he seems right – fits the bill – but we have nothing to connect him to the Plague of Crows. No doctor's training, no particular social media expertise…'

'No,' says Gostkowski. 'Social media is one thing, he could be spending five hours a night working on that and no one would ever know. But the ability to remove part of the skull without killing the victim…'

'I know,' says Taylor. 'Spoken to a few surgeons. They're all impressed with the quality of work when I show them pictures and describe it to them. Ballingol's certainly impressed with it. It implies training.'

'Maybe he trained himself,' says Gostkowski.

'I've given that a lot of thought,' says Taylor. 'Spoke to a few people about it. Not impossible, and it would explain why I got absolutely nowhere chasing after medical students and doctors last year.'

He turns to face us, leans back against the window ledge. God he looks shit.

'So, it doesn't rule out our guy, it just doesn't help us. We have nothing definite that helps us. It's all supposition. We're the ones joining the dots, they're not being connected for us.'

A joining the dots analogy. It comes to this.

'I don't know how much more there is to find without speaking to him, Sir,' says Gostkowski. 'Or, at least, speaking to people who might well let him know that we're nosing around.'

'Time to make a decision,' says Taylor, and it's not a question. It is time to make a decision.

'You spoke to Montgomery?' I ask.

He nods without looking at me.

'Not at all helpful. Said he'd look into it and get back to us in a day or two.'

Useless fucker. This is like being in government in America. Too many people running things, no one wanting to help anyone else.

'I think we'll go and see Clayton tomorrow,' says Taylor, 'but I'll sleep on it.' Checks his watch. 'You two go home, get some sleep. Don't be late tomorrow morning, start getting our shit together.'

'You should get some sleep too,' I say, getting to my feet.

'Aye, I won't be long,' he says, and he waves a dismissive hand in the direction of the door.

And we're gone.

*

Long day. This time I think she falls asleep for a while in my bed, but when the alarm goes at 5.30 she's not there.

32

Me and Taylor off to see Clayton. We're opening up the investigation, letting Clayton know he's under suspicion. Gostkowski has been dispatched to his golf club and other places where he makes himself known and pretends that he's always had money rather than getting it from being a sordid, murdering bastard who just happened to be smarter than everyone else. She seemed quite happy with the division of labour, but she's a team player, Gostkowski. Will do what she's told. Not bothered about who's making the arrest, just interested in doing a decent job.

Part of my trouble is that I don't think I'm interested in either.

Sex was great again, which is a positive. I think falling asleep at my place might have been a little outwith the terms and conditions, but we'll get over it. Business as usual today, which is always slightly surprising when one considers the things we were doing to each other last night.

'Nice place,' says Taylor, pulling the car up in the driveway. 'Paid for by the police and the newspapers.'

'Well, the Express and the Sun,' I say glibly.

Out the car, stand and take in the surroundings and the air. Cold morning. Damp. Miserable. Look back out onto the street and up and along the road. A lot of trees. Arboreal. Large Victorian homes, set back from the road, large front and back gardens.

'Fucker,' mutters Taylor, and he turns towards the house.

*

'How many times have you been married?'

He smiles. 'Just the once.'

He's wearing the same clothes as yesterday. What does one make of that in an investigation? But then, maybe the shirt beneath it and the underwear are different. The same trousers and jumper doesn't really tell us anything.

Burble burble.

'You told the sergeant your wife had been involved in *High Road*. Called her a fellow victim of the press. Your wife doesn't appear to have been an actress.'

Clayton stares across the short distance of the Axminster.

'At any time in her life,' adds Taylor.

Clayton smiles, shakes his head.

'Wife,' he says. 'My wife is gone, I'm afraid. Didn't work out. It's…' and he lets the sentence trail off. 'I've been seeing someone for a few months. Nothing… you know, it's nothing. She used to act. Nothing much, you know. But she did a few episodes of *High Road* back in the day. I suppose everyone did.'

Taylor stares at him witheringly. Always interesting to watch the reaction of the interviewee at this moment. The bitter middle-aged copper staring at him with complete contempt, not believing a word he's saying. Taylor and I went over everything Clayton said to me yesterday, so he knows that the man's lying. Or, if he's telling the truth, then he was previously lying with some amount of bravado.

Clayton, of course, looks like he's discussing that morning's fourball over a pot of lapsang souchong at the club.

'That flatly contradicts what you told the Sergeant yesterday afternoon,' says Taylor.

Clayton continues to stare amicably, as if Taylor has just complemented him on his four iron approach to the fifteenth; and, as if he's too humble to know what to do with praise, he sits in his amicable silence.

'You and your wife have the same lawyer,' says Taylor, 'as you were both victims of the press. That was how you met. That was what you told the sergeant.'

Interesting character study. You know, if you study characters. I prefer really just to bludgeon characters, or to squeeze them into some neat pigeonhole that exists in the prejudiced part of my brain.

Clayton is being cool. Attempting to show that he's not at all rattled by being caught with his honesty trousers at his ankles. Attempting to show that he's not rattled by having two coppers in his house, because he has nothing to hide. Having some fantasy about your wife or your girlfriend, mixing them up for whatever reason, isn't in itself illegal. Nevertheless, he just looks all the guiltier for his suave urbanity in the face of an interrogator armed with the facts.

'How does that tie in with your girlfriend, who you've only known a few months, and who was in *High Road*? Your girlfriend has the same lawyer, or your wife has the same lawyer?'

He smiles now, as if Taylor is the simpleton, not really understanding.

'I do apologise, Detective Chief Inspector,' he says, and already there's a tone about the apology that says, 'between you and me I just said any old shit to your monkey here, because he's not terribly important and I didn't think it mattered. Now that you're here, obviously you'll get the truth.'

Maybe I've got a chip on my shoulder.

'You don't need to,' says Taylor quickly, 'just tell me the facts.'

'Obviously,' says Clayton, as if any of this is obvious, 'I meant my girlfriend. She did some acting a long time ago, but the press really did for her very early on. It wasn't just that they ruined her career, not really. It just made her realise that she didn't want a career. She's been very successful since then, in all manner of different enterprises. But yes, we do have the same lawyer, and yes, well, I'm rather afraid I do tend to tell people these days that she's my wife. A bit early perhaps, but she doesn't mind.'

'We mind that you tell the truth when you're being interviewed in relation to a murder investigation.'

Clayton makes a grand gesture with his hands, as if forgiving himself and acknowledging that we can now all be friends. I'd love to take a couple of strides over there, step on the edge of the sofa and bury my knee in his face. Wouldn't look so smug then, would you, you bastard?

'Once again I apologise,' he says. 'You can be sure that everything you hear today is the truth. I really must learn to keep my...' and he hesitates while he tries to conjure up the correct word to describe the fact that he's a lying fuck, 'my foibles and fantasies to myself.'

'What's her name?' asks Taylor. 'And where can we find her?'

'My wife?'

'This girlfriend,' says Taylor, 'who appeared on *High Road*. What's her name, and where can we find her?'

'Oh,' he says, as if he hadn't been expecting that. What now? Another apology, and a confession that in fact there is no girlfriend? I hugely want this guy to be the Plague of Crows, but of course, the longer this goes on, the more he comes across as an annoying prick who likes wasting police time. Generally, in life, you don't have to go too far to find one of those.

'Samantha,' he says. Of course. Suddenly I think of Grace Kelly in *High Society*. And you know, that's what this bloke aspires to. He found himself with money that he didn't deserve, and he used it to become part of a society to which he was never really meant to belong. 'Samantha Taylor,' he adds.

If he's just making that up, he's giving her the name of the officer asking the questions. Nice. That's one step from giving her the name of whatever object he just happened to be looking at, like Samantha Window or Samantha Turner Print.

Suppose Taylor's a common enough name around these parts.

195

'And was that her name when she appeared in *High Road*?'

'Far as I know,' he says. 'Obviously all that's behind her now. She doesn't talk about it much.'

'Where do we find her?'

Hesitation, then, 'Oh, I can get you her number. It's in my phone. She's working in the city at the moment doing some consultancy work for a firm of accountants on St Vincent Street. Parker & Howles.'

'And your wife?' says Taylor. 'What's the story there?'

'Ah,' he says. 'Well, it's as well you got me now, as a few months ago even, I doubt I'd have been able to talk to you about it. Still hurt too much. We met while I was at my lowest ebb during that dreadful affair. She knew what the police were like, what the media were like. She knew the lies they told. She gave me extraordinary support. It was really rather touching. We married in the middle of it all although, in retrospect, perhaps we shouldn't have done.'

Taylor stares coldly. Says nothing. The standard technique, playing the game of being cool just as much as Clayton's been doing it. Meanwhile I take my phone out and Google Parker & Howles. Without looking at him I notice the surreptitious glance in my direction

'You probably want to speak to her,' he says. 'Of course, of course. I can get all her details. They're in the other room, if you just bear with me for a moment. And I can get you the direct line for Samantha too, save you looking up the company on the website, Sergeant. She's just there temporarily, sorting out some client database or other.'

He leaves the room. I glance quickly up at Taylor.

'We're just letting the suspect walk out the room,' I say.

Taylor smiles grimly. 'He'll be back. And if he runs… if he runs, then he might as well sign a confession.'

'And we'll be the ones who let him get away.'

'I'll make sure you get all the credit, Sergeant,' he says. 'You find Parker & Howles?'

'Nothing,' I say. 'Don't exist according to Google.'
And then we hear the car starting.
'Ha!' barks Taylor. 'Got the bastard.'
We're both up and running to the front door, but that last remark proves to be somewhat premature.

*

I hate car chases. Sure, there's a certain adrenalin rush if you're driving, but the lead car is always the one with the odds on its side. It knows roughly where it's going, or at least can choose the way, and chances are that the chasing car is the police car. When accidents happen during car chases, the police get the blame. It's as if the guy running away, the criminal, well he gets a free pass, because he's doing what all fun-loving criminals do on the TV. He's doing what people expect him to do. Run. The police, on the other hand, have a duty of care to make sure members of the public don't get hurt. So when shit happens during a car chase, you can bet your arse it's the police who end up looking bad.

I particularly hate car chases when I'm sitting in the passenger seat. Then it's just like being on a fucking rollercoaster and usually ends up with me vomiting over the driver or out the window or onto the floor. Doesn't take much. And I'm usually petrified and spend the entire time with my eyes shut.

This time, however, I don't even get as far as beginning to worry about the car chase, or even as far as fighting Taylor for the honour of driving so that at least I won't be scared and I won't vomit.

The front door is locked.

Taylor barks, 'Fuck', no time to look for the key, and we run through to the front room. The library, he probably calls it. The white Lexus is legging it down the driveway. Taylor grabs the nearest wooden chair and smacks it into the window. It's some fucking glass, doesn't even crack. The chair buckles, and one of the legs breaks off. This is a man with money to spend on his windows.

Quick look around the room. There's a large glass paperweight or ornament or some such. Jesus, there's all sorts of shit on cabinets and sideboards and all sorts of middle-class furniture accessories. The paperweight looks the best option.

'Stand back, Sir,' I say, and Taylor edges away from the window as he looks over his shoulder. Hurl the paperweight at the window with the kind of ugly chuck that would usually precede a leg break on the sub-continent. The paperweight sails straight through the window, leaving an almost perfect cartoon hole, cracks emanating from it in all directions.

Taylor is still holding the chair, and now he attacks the window. I pick up some other piece of heavy ornamental junk – a bronze golfing trophy – and go over beside him.

It doesn't take long before we've broken out, the whole escapade taking barely half a minute. Of course, Clayton is gone, and as added insurance he's closed the large metal gate at the driveway entrance that was open when we arrived. Taylor climbs out through the window, cursing as he snags his jacket on the edge of the glass, and I follow.

We stand in the cold morning, and already the sound of the car is lost and we're standing still in stupid impotence, having let the man slip through our fingers.

'Fuck it,' mutters Taylor. 'Seriously, fuck it. What was that?'

He looks angrily at me, as if it's my fault we let the guy get out of here right enough.

'Is that the signed confession?'

'It feels like it,' I say, 'but we hadn't gone anywhere near the Plague of Crows.'

'No, we hadn't.'

He kicks the ground again.

'Bollocks. Get on the radio, Sergeant. Get the word out for that car. Time to call in the guys from Edinburgh.'

33

Three hours later. Still in Clayton's driveway. We've gone into overdrive. Currently about forty guys all over his house. Ours and Edinburgh's. A blitzkrieg of forensic examination. Other officers going door to door up and down the street. Found his car in the centre of town parked near Glasgow Central. That doesn't really help, does it? He could have got a train to anywhere. It wouldn't even have been that far for him to run up to Queen Street, thinking he was throwing us off the scent by parking near Central. Or he could have got on a bus. Or he could be sitting in a Costa just round the corner.

For the moment he's gone to ground.

Managed to get hold of a couple of cups of coffee, and me and Taylor are standing by his car looking at the surrounding crime-fighting stramash. So far no one has found any evidence that implicates Clayton in anything other than being a social climbing fuck.

We're not speaking, just standing there, one hand in pocket, the other clutching caffeine and both of us thinking the same thing. What was he thinking? Why attract attention to yourself when the only thing that really makes anyone suspicious is that you're attracting attention to yourself?

'You feel like we've been set up?' I say after a long silence.

Taylor doesn't immediately answer. Turns and looks at the house, and in every window we can see evidence of the investigating team. And on the ground floor there is, of course, the evidence of us smashing a window to try to get after him.

'I have that feeling, Sergeant, yes,' says Taylor.

'What about Montgomery?'

'Not sure yet. The jury's still out, but we can hardly be optimistic about a verdict in our favour. They're going to have to find something in there.'

'Has he gone national?'

'No. Needs to find something first. Something we can hang onto as proof.'

'And there's no proof.'

'Exactly. He just acted suspiciously. Strangely, in fact. Don't know what's going on in his head.'

We turn at the crunch of footsteps on gravel as Montgomery approaches. Looking round at the house I can see a few of the guys walking out the front door, and suddenly there's no evidence in the windows of the SOCOs going about their business. Like the ghosts have all left.

'Got a phone call,' says Montgomery.

Taylor gives him the eyebrow. I look away. Montgomery doesn't speak to me. Not worthy of his time. If I want to know what he's saying, I just need to blend into the background and he'll ignore my presence. I'm like the royal servant who got to hear all the shit from Charles and Diana because they just acted like he wasn't in the room.

'Mr Clayton has been to see his lawyer. Indeed, he's at his lawyer's office right now. Claiming harassment. Prepared to speak to us, if that's what we want, but only with his lawyer present.'

Montgomery and Taylor stare at each other, Montgomery searching for any sign of weakness or excuse from Taylor.

'You think he set us up?' says Taylor, which was what he'd already been thinking.

'Starts to look that way,' says Montgomery.

Taylor rubs his chin. Stares at the ground. Make the decision to chip in, even though the other DCI would prefer I keep my mouth shut.

'He thought that out pretty quickly,' I say. 'He didn't

know I was coming yesterday, had no reason to believe I was coming. Why would I question him, rather than anyone else? Again, he didn't know we'd be coming back today. So he told us lies yesterday to set us up for today, even though he didn't know that either visit was going to happen. That just… just doesn't seem right.'

'Hardly impossible,' says Montgomery. 'He's manipulated the police before, he could easily have thought of it again. We spoke to him two months ago and eliminated him from the investigation, but it wasn't as though we told him that. He might well have been ready for someone coming back.'

'He knows that we don't like him,' I continue. 'He knows he got the better of us before, and that we're not going to like him. So this could easily just be some kind of impromptu plan. Or even a well practiced plan to throw us off the scent should we get on it.'

'But why are you on the scent?' says Montgomery. 'He was just a name on a list, and then you blunder in full of accusation and bravado. You don't like the way he acts, and so he gets worse. Starts firing off lies. Maybe it's been his strategy since day one, ever since he got his payout from the police. If they ever turn up again, lie to them, make things up, let them act foolishly and see where it gets him. Goodness knows he might have tried it with DI Marqueson, but at least he had his wits about him. At least he didn't do anything stupid.'

Neither Taylor nor I speak.

'You two gentlemen, however, played right into his hands. Perhaps his actions suggest that he's guilty of something, but we have absolutely nothing to attach him to the Plague of Crows other than you getting over-excited.'

He looks at us, one after the other. He's not Taylor's senior officer, but he's spoken to him like he is. The tone was judgemental, the judgement being passed down from above. Glance at Taylor. He's not looking at him. I dare say he possibly never even heard him. Won't have been listening. Wrapped up in the case, thinking through

Clayton's actions, trying to straighten them out in his head.

Since he's not getting anything else from us Montgomery walks off to his car. All around us the police are starting their withdrawal. Immediate and all out. Complete capitulation in the face of a lawyer with some metal. I lean back against the car and join Taylor in staring at the ground.

*

Later on we sit in his office, the BBC news on his computer, and watch the lawyer in action. The usual beautiful stuff from any lawyer, fully implicating the police and fully casting his client as the victim.

Everyone's a victim these days. Everyone.

Even the Plague of Crows.

34

Long day. Shitty day. One of those long, shitty days you just want to end. It would end more quickly if you just got the fuck out of Dodge and went and sat in the pub from about five, but you've been made to look stupid, so you sit in work even later than normal, and normal's already become pretty fucking late.

Leave halfway between midnight and one in the morning. Got called into Connor's office, along with Taylor and Gostkowski, at some point during the evening. Informed that Mr Clayton was suing the police for £1.3million. Under the circumstances, and given that for the most part the superintendent is a complete bell-end, one would have expected him to tear into us, rip the fuck out of us, and at least kick us off the case, if not suspend us.

He did not disappoint, although he kept the red suspension card in his pocket.

'It's time to hand the case in its entirety over to Montgomery,' he said. Looking tired again. He looks tired every day. Sorting out this station was going to be the making of his career. It was going to get him his gong of whatever colour it is these senior plods get. He was going to be turning up at Buckingham Palace, Mrs Superintendent and two mini-superintendent kids in tow. Instead he got here, and immediately the Plague of Crows struck him down. The Plague of Crows has been the bane of this station since not long after Connor arrived, and now it is already too late. His time here has been dictated by it, and even if it gets solved in the next few days, his term in charge of the station will always be remembered for it and defined by it. And now, pretty obviously, the call has come from higher up to yank his men completely. So even if it is solved – and that's not looking very likely – it's someone else's officers that'll be doing the solving.

'Inspector Gostkowski and Sgt Hutton, you are reassigned with immediate effect. You will spend the remainder of this evening passing everything you've compiled on the case over to DCI Taylor. When you're done with that, then you can speak to Sgt Ramsay and begin to get back into the routine of the station. Chief Inspector, you can spend tomorrow with DCI Montgomery handing over the case files. I know you've done a lot on this. Ditch anything you think extraneous, hand over everything else.'

He looked at him, and having dealt with me and Gostkowski, we might as well not have been there.

'And I mean everything, Dan. It's finished. It looks like this Clayton character was just waiting for someone to come along, a police officer to come along, and it just happened to be you. Could have been any one of us, although I must say I do hope that if it'd been me I'd have been a little more circumspect, as Montgomery's man appears to have been.'

Fuck. You.

'So you pass it all along, and then you're finished. I don't want to see any sign of you continuing the investigation. The pictures on the wall, that absurd spot-the-forest nonsense, get rid of it. To be honest, don't even pass it on to Montgomery, he'll probably laugh at you.'

None of us spoke. Me and Gostkowski weren't really there to talk in any case – we were the seen and not heard children of the little drama – and Taylor was saying nothing. Presumably, sitting there wondering how he would go about continuing the investigation without the superintendent knowing.

He looked one last time at all three of us and then dismissed us with a flick of the hand. Then he added, 'Get out,' as he obviously thought the silence needed filling by a random sentence of futility.

We left.

Heard him having a quiet word with Taylor later on. So, you know, not that quiet a word. 'I'm a reasonable man, Chief Inspector, I realise this is bad luck. Bad timing. Could have happened to any one of us... I'm a reasonable man, I really am, but you have to acknowledge that the shit's hitting the fan on this.'

Wanker.

Shitty, long day. Spoke to Stephanie outside at the cigarette point some time around eleven. I was tired and miserable, feeling haunted. Feeling stupid. I needed my fuck buddy. I needed her to come back to my place. I needed to forget about the shitty, long day. And weirdly, I just presumed she'd feel the same.

'Not tonight,' she said.

'How come?' I said quickly, immediately breaking the terms and conditions. You wait for an explanation, and if none is forthcoming, you leave it at that and accept that your buddy is doing something she doesn't want you to know about it. Such as sleeping. Low maintenance rules the day, and whatever it is, it's none of your business. Move along.

I didn't think I was being high maintenance, but then, no one ever thinks they're being high maintenance. Even the most high maintenance person on the planet thinks that all their actions are justified. If you know your actions are high maintenance and do them anyway, then it means you're probably not high maintenance, you're just doing it out of badness. You're mean, vindictive, spiteful or malevolent maybe. Which is possibly worse, although I'm not sure.

'Just... not tonight,' she said. Sounded tired, which was natural, but in those few words I detected unease at being questioned on it, so I attempted to make a tactical withdrawal. It's hard, though, once the initial burst of high maintenanceness is out there.

'Sorry, fair enough,' I said.

I didn't immediately stub out my fag and head back into

the office, as that would have looked like I was throwing my teddy into all kinds of corners, so we stood there, smoking in silence, an awkwardness around us that hadn't been there before. Eventually she finished her smoke, pressed the stub into the metal ash tray attached to the railing like a good little soldier, nodded vaguely in my direction and went back inside. Didn't see her again.

So now it's one-thirty in the morning and I'm tired and miserable but my head's still buzzing, and there's something there, something right in the middle yet way out of reach, something that I saw today that's saying *Me! Me! Look at me!* but I just can't pin down what it is and it's driving me nuts and filling me with an ugly, spirit-sapping uneasy feeling, and I'm thinking about forests and all the things I've done that I shouldn't have and I'd presumed I'd have company and I don't, so instead of wildly fucking DI Gostkowski, I'm trawling through the internet looking for some decent porn, and having been here many times before, it's not like I don't know where to look. I've got Bob playing loud, you know those mid-sixties numbers that sound raunchy and laid back and hedonistic, *Temporary Like Achilles*, that kind of thing, that sound like he was getting sucked off while he was singing. Tonight, however, in the words of the blessed Saint Mick, I can't get no satisfaction.

Blessed Saint Mick. I'm such a stupid fucker.

March

35

Sitting in a school in Rutherglen. The headmaster's office. Called out after a teacher attacked a pupil. A bare-handed job, smacking the kid about the head. The kid fought back. The teacher ended up really laying into him, kicking him repeatedly. All in front of an English class, half of them horrified, the other half training their phones on the action and probably uploading onto Facebook simultaneously.

Badly hung over. Me, not the teacher. Again. Third morning in a row. Late for work today, and I could tell DCI Dorritt was annoyed. Can see I'm getting lax. Haven't made any mistakes yet, just managing to keep ahead of the game, but he's poised with his arse-kicking for when it happens.

And I ought to learn. Going to bed at three in the morning completely hammered out of my face isn't stopping me from waking up a couple of hours later, the image of those women in the forest in my head, the sound of their screams in the air. The silence of the woods with no birds and no insects. The silence that is always shattered by their screams. Their screams that become my screams.

Why am I screaming? Why do I always wake up screaming? Nothing bad is happening to me.

I can believe that if I concentrate hard enough. Nothing bad is happening to me. They can scream. The women can scream. They're dead now. All of them. Are they dead? What the fuck do I know? I just hope they're dead, that's all, because sometimes I can tell myself that I don't have to feel so bad anymore if there's no one left who I hurt.

It doesn't really work like that.

He's not talking. The teacher's not talking. His career is over. The press will get hold of this one. The press love this kind of shit. Teacher assaulting a pupil.

Morrow and I have spoken to most of the pupils in the class, although one or two of them said they were too upset to talk. They sat there blubbing. I have utter contempt for them. The minute our backs were turned, you can bet they were filming each other blubbing. They were filming themselves being professionally upset, so they could put that online.

This is me being upset.

My part in the Downfall of Mr Gower.

I'm going to need counselling. The school haven't offered any counselling yet. It's, like, so annoying.

It's a disgrace. And shit.

Pretty clear from those pupils willing to offer up their version of events, that while they were mostly supportive of the pupil who got a kicking, the little bastard deserved it. Had it coming for months.

This is what happens when you instruct teachers that they have to enforce discipline by engaging their pupils in dialogue. Now, I know walloping kids isn't really the way forward and is definitely off the agenda in these enlightened times. But in its place you have to have respect, because if you don't, then it doesn't work. And, at the same time as getting rid of an effective method of disciplining children, we've also allowed a society to develop where no one has any respect. For anything.

I blame Bob Dylan.

It's been coming since the sixties, and it's just getting worse and worse. Adults have no respect, kids grow up thinking that they don't really need to respect authority because adults don't, and so they do what they want. In schools it's particularly hard for those teachers who spent some years back in the good old days when you could physically enforce discipline. You could make kids listen to you.

What can you do now?

Once again I'm complaining, but I don't have an answer. Society had to slowly ease discipline out of the way, while maintaining a sense of respect. Too late now. Much too late. And it certainly is for the likes of Mr Gower who just finally snapped and beat the shit out of a fifteen-year-old who had it coming.

The boy's mates all had him pegged as some kind of angel, who spent most of his spare time helping disabled children go to the seaside. Reading between the lines, however – those being the lines that say he'd been suspended six times from the school, and had been reported for abusive and unruly behaviour by every single one of his teachers – one gets the impression that if he was an angel of any sort, it was Lucifer.

I'm sitting in the head's office. The teacher is in another room, watched over by a couple of our guys. I see it as some kind of suicide watch. This bloke, this poor middle-aged, middle-class fucker, isn't going to see out the week. A career teacher, and now that career is down the toilet. He faces disgrace, unemployment and, more than likely, prison.

The kid's been taken to hospital, although he was beaten up by an old duffer who'd never swung a punch in his puff, so the chances that he was seriously hurt are pretty low. The kid's stepdad has gone with him. You might think the mum would go with him, but the mum stayed behind so that she could sit in this room with the headmaster, the union rep and the investigating police officer.

Holy fuck.

'I knew something like this was going to happen,' she's saying. 'Fucking knew it, by the way, I says to Michael, I says to him, fucking knew it.'

She's directing her wrath at the headmaster, rather than the presiding police officer. She had been talking to me at the beginning, but I think the fact that I look like a complete sack of sunken shit has put her off. Realises she's not getting anything from me and so is completely ignoring my presence. The headmaster, on the other hand, rather looks like he'd appreciate some support.

'Where's that bastard now?' she says.

Now I would say that the bastard was currently in hospital having his injuries treated, but I don't think she was referring to that specific bastard.

'Mr Gower is in police custody and will be processed accordingly, Mrs Grantham. All we can…'

'I pure want to see him,' she says. 'I'm like that, I'm like that to Michael, they better let me see that cunt. Hitting a defenceless kid. I'll fucking see him off, see how he likes that.'

The headmaster looks at me. I take a deep breath and turn to the aggrieved mother. I would honestly rather someone was poking me in the eye with a chopstick.

'You are not going to see the accused, Mrs…'

'Accused! How many fucking witnesses do youse need?'

'He'll be taken back to the station, he'll be processed, and a decision will be taken on whether or not he's to be charged.'

'Whether or not he's charged?' She looks wonderfully red-faced and incandescent with anger. You know that way Penelope Cruz gets in movies when she gets all feisty and angry and starts shouting, full of Mediterranean passion and flair? Absolutely nothing like that. 'Fuck…' she says, because she seems to be having trouble articulating. She rises out of her chair. 'Are you… are you fucking with my… fuck?'

'Sit down, Mrs Grantham. Calm down.'

Are you fucking with my fuck? Nice. I think I might start using that one myself.

'Calm down? Has your son just had the fuck kicked out him? Well, has he?'

No, I think. But then, my son isn't a disruptive, horrible little piece of fucking shit either. I don't answer the question. She gives me the best Glasgow evils for a second or two, then turns to the headmaster to utter the words that any self-respecting, entitled bastard will utter in this day and age.

'See when my lawyer's finished with youse, I'm going to be loaded, and youse lot are all going to be out of jobs. You're shite the lot of you.'

Yes, madam, parents suing the education system is the way forward. It's weird that the government just doesn't plain encourage it.

36

The Plague of Crows is having fun. Enjoys the work. Likes a challenge. It had felt as though the police got a little too close in January, maybe there'd been a few too many chances taken, so this time the Crow will retreat a little. Go back to basics. Nothing too fancy. No live webcam. A simple, straightforward crime, much as had been perpetrated the previous August.

A social worker. A journalist. A police officer. Drawing up the shortlist had been time consuming, but entertaining, as usual. So many to choose from. Well, perhaps that had been the case with the social worker and the journalist. Not with the police officer, however. The police officer had been asking for it. The police officer had looked in the camera and had said, come and get me. The police officer had called out to the Plague of Crows, and the Plague of Crows was coming to get him.

*

Back at the station, the teacher downstairs. The media have arrived. They love a good beating in school. They can say that it's barbaric and Victorian. They can revel in it. They can be happy. I hate them all. It's because of people like them that the likes of Clayton even exist, that he can play the sport of manipulation.

They all know that the pupil pretty much got what was coming to him – if perhaps a little heavy handedly – yet they have come to execute the teacher. He will be the symbol of authority, the pupil will be the working class hero. No good will come of it.

On finding out the level of media interest,

Superintendent Connor immediately put DCI Dorritt on the case, to show how seriously we were taking it. And, of course, to make sure that I didn't get on TV, given that I look like three kinds of shit.

Sitting at my desk, getting the paperwork in order, typing up some notes on the case to hand over to Dorritt. He and I don't really get along so well. It's because I'm normal, and he's a total douchebag. Something like that. Anyway, typing up the notes will allow me to limit how much I have to speak to him.

'How was the school?'

Look up. Taylor's walking by. Slowly. In no rush to get anywhere, which is pretty much how he's been since we were removed from the Plague of Crows. It was like the whole thing with Clayton just sunk the careers of me, Taylor and Gostkowski overnight.

I presumed Taylor would continue to work on the case, even though he was ordered off it. I wonder if Connor thought the same. But no, Taylor stepped away. Completely. Realised what it was doing to him and turned his back. Killed him, though. It might have been a release for some, but not Taylor.

Inspector Gostkowski seemed to take it in her stride. She was taken off the case and given other jobs to work on and she went off to do that. Haven't spoken to her about it, but wouldn't be surprised if she hasn't thought about the Plague of Crows since then. That's who she is. She applies herself with the utmost diligence to the task at hand.

Another casualty of the Clayton fiasco was that great fuck buddy relationship we had going on. Didn't want to know me after that, as if being with me reminded her of that time when her career got completely shafted.

Maybe she blamed me. It was me who interviewed him in the first place. It was me who decided that out of all the people I'd talked to, he was the one. It was me who had her going off checking on Clayton's wife and then at Clayton's golf club, and had me and Taylor turning up at his house, to his obvious delight.

I believe I might have asked her for sex four more times after that first time she rejected me. She refused every time, and then finally said, 'Sergeant, it's over,' just to make sure I got the message.

I wasn't supposed to be upset, we'd just been fuck buddies after all, that's the point. So that night I nailed a hooker. She charged twenty-five pounds. I gave her thirty.

Gostkowski and I have had one case together, which we handled professionally enough. The case itself did not work out satisfactorily, but at least we didn't end up in some bitch fight.

Been thinking a lot about the waitress in Costa. The one Gostkowski made me picture naked. I've pretty much had that image in my head ever since. She seems like a good bet.

Asked her back to my place once, with little aforethought. She was pretty fucking cool, I have to say. Didn't say yes, didn't give me an outright no. Might, she said. Maybe.

That was it. I've been thinking about her naked a lot more since then, but trying not to go in there every night, because now when I see her it feels like there's some expectation. Is she looking for me to ask? And that kind of uncertainty makes me feel like a teenager, and who the fuck wants to feel like that?

Something's going to happen though. It has to.

'It was shit,' I say. 'A mess. If we just let teachers whack the shit out of the little bastards when they first caused trouble, this kind of thing wouldn't happen. Of course, the teacher's going to be the bad guy.'

'He thrashed the fuck out of a fifteen-year-old, Sergeant,' says Taylor.

'Yes, he did,' I reply. 'But in the same way that some twenty-one-year-old gets into trouble for knobbing a fifteen-year-old, when the girl has already got fake breasts and looks older than he does... things are not always as straightforward as the facts would make you think.'

'Aye, great analogy, Sergeant. I dare you to take that

one on to *Loose Women*.'

He starts to turn away. Looks fed up, as he does all the time at the moment.

'What have you got on?' I ask.

Me and Taylor haven't worked directly together since January. Connor is keeping us apart, as if the combination of the two of us will bring down the entire station with our collective stupidity. He's just waiting for the court case, wherein Mr Clayton is attempting to suck £1.3m from the public purse, and then, if we lose, Taylor and I might well be finding ourselves out of a job.

Might celebrate then. Not sure.

'Attempted murder,' says Taylor, 'with an added bigotry ingredient. Can't get enough of them.'

'And the other thing?'

The other thing is code. Nice, eh? No one is going to have the faintest idea what we're talking about.

'The other thing, Sergeant,' he says, 'is finished. At least, I'm finished. I'm not going back there, and when the Plague of Crows strikes again, it isn't going to be my problem.'

Nod. Look miserably at the floor. The Plague of Crows took three more victims, fucking up me, Taylor and Gostkowski along his merry way. Maybe Gostkowski doesn't think of herself as a victim, but let's see how long she has to wait for her next shout at promotion.

He loiters. Taps his fingers on the end of my desk. Nothing much else to say. We used to hang out. We used to go to the pub. Don't anymore. It was an odd relationship, I suppose, not friends as such, what with him being the boss. But really, that's what we were. That's what we are. Friends. But now we're not working together anymore, we never go to the pub. Neither of us will take the time to say, 'Pub?' so that the other one can say, 'Aye, all right.'

We used to go there to talk about work, and would end up talking about everything else.

'You ever speak to Montgomery about it?' I ask.

'No, I haven't,' he says.

I nod. I can imagine it'd be pretty difficult.

'Whenever you see one of them walking about the station, do you get the feeling they're looking at us? You know, like we're shit.'

'Aye. That might be because we've got a chip on our shoulder, but whatever it is, aye, feel it every damn time.'

Montgomery and his crew still haven't moved on, although they must be close. There isn't a lot of point in them being here as opposed to back at their own ranch, but this case is his nemesis – and we all know about that – and it's as though he feels he needs to stay here until it's solved. I've no idea what kind of behind-the-scenes manoeuvres have taken place to try to facilitate it or whether there've been any discussions on whether he should be replaced. What I do know is that three weeks ago there was a sympathetic lifestyle piece on Montgomery in the Saturday edition of the Scotsman. It was entitled something along the lines of *The Tortured Copper*. Fuck me. And that was the paper that in January printed a front page photo of him under the headline *Always The Last To Crow*.

Taylor taps his fingers again. Stares randomly at the desk. I glance around the office. The usual hubbub of noise, of police officers and administrative staff going about their business. Notice Mrs Lownes across the office, on her way to deliver something to the Superintendent.

'I miss hearing about your sexual exploits,' says Taylor, as if reading my thoughts. 'It's the closest I got to having sex in the last two years.'

He turns at that and walks away. Shoulders hunched.

The phone rings. The display indicates that it's DCI Dorritt. I stare at it for a moment, but given that Dorritt is sitting in Taylor's old office, which is no more than fifteen yards away and has glass walls, and therefore he will be watching me as I watch the phone ring, I can't really pretend I'm out of the room.

37

After the third Plague of Crows event, the police and local authorities across Scotland implemented a scheme whereby everyone considered to be under threat was issued with a panic bracelet. Yes, a panic bracelet. To be worn at all times.

They intended doing this after the second batch of killings, but of course, couldn't just go out and order some panic alarms or tags or whatever. They had to go through due process. A consultation to decide the best way to track each member of staff, and then an open competition to find the provider of the service. Can't do anything that's publicly funded without going out to tender.

All that meant the system wasn't in place by the time the third batch of murders occurred. However, it's now in order. They decided they couldn't track several thousand people on an individual basis, that the only sure fire way to do it was to put an implant in their head or something. Not really practical.

They considered a panic alarm that you'd have on your key ring or round your neck or something, but they sensibly realised that eventually you're going to forget where it is or what you've done with it or you'll get out of the habit of wearing it or taking it everywhere.

So they hit on the bracelet idea. You put it on, you never take it off. It contains a tracking device and an inbuilt panic button. So that it won't be constantly set off accidentally, there are two buttons, which have to be pressed in a short sequence of three to set off the alarm. The only way to remove the bracelet is to pull it apart, and if the circle of the bracelet is broken then the alarm is triggered.

Is anyone happy about this? Fuck, of course they're not. No one likes it. Virtually every officer you meet says he'd prefer to take his chances. It feels like some kind of weird futuristic shit. Fucking Blade Runner kind of shit. No one wants that.

They reckon it's foolproof, however, which of course means it won't be. Wherever we are, it should be with us, and if we get into trouble, then we call for help. Should we get the opportunity.

They were so up themselves with the foolproofness of the whole idea, they happily announced what they'd done on TV. Wanted to show Scotland how seriously they were taking it, and how much they were determined to protect their staff. Or, if you wanted to take a different point of view, they wanted to show the Plague of Crows what they were doing, so that the next time he could come prepared.

If they'd just shut the fuck up about the fucking bracelets, it might be that the Plague of Crows never even noticed. They're pretty cool looking. They're not some clunky 1970's piece of plastic, looking like they came off the set of *Blake's 7*. They look like they were bought out of a surfing shop, something like that, which no doubt was one of the things that contributed to them costing the government over £550 each.

But ultimately, that's what this is all about. That's what the government are thinking. They want to be seen to be doing something. Politicians are incapable of taking measures and not telling everyone what they've done. What would be the point in that? What's the point in doing good then the public not knowing anything about it? Being seen to get involved is even more important than getting involved in the first place.

A lot of muttering that the damn bracelets will stay even once the Plague of Crows is caught; if he's ever caught. They will argue that it's for the well-being of their officers. I doubt it, but at the same time, wouldn't put it past the bastards.

There was some discussion with the National Union of

Journalists about whether all their members in Scotland would be equally tagged, and they came back with a collective fuck off. They probably all want to be the next journalist selected, because they will all have that basic human belief in infallibility and will believe that they'll be the one to escape, and then they'll be the one to break the story.

Ultimately, they had the choice, so said no. We weren't given the choice.

For the first few days the bracelet was a pain in the arse. Felt like I had a camera trained on me. Now, of course, I don't care. It's just there. I presume there isn't someone sitting in a massive room somewhere – in India, if anywhere – following my every move, thinking, *ah, he's sitting in again tonight, the sad lonely fucker* or, *ah, I see he's made once again for Glasgow's infamous red light district*.

Same as everybody else, I've stopped caring.

The one positive of not working full time on the Plague of Crows is that work finishes at a normal time. We're doing twelve-hour days, instead of seventeen or eighteen. The bad part of that is that it shows even more how miserable and empty my life is, because I've got fuck-all to do with the extra time I have in the evening. I want to do something other than sit at home eating a fish supper, drinking vodka and watching crap TV, but I don't know what it is. Anything I think of just makes me feel like some desperate middle-aged loser having some sort of mid-life crisis, and trying to think of something new and worthy to do now that the autumn years of my puff are fast approaching.

So, instead, I do nothing, and in dark moments tell myself I'm happy doing nothing, and that the reason I don't try to give myself anything more interesting to do is because I'm happy being a fat, slobby useless bastard who hates his job and does fuck-all with himself.

Last summer, long weeks of climbing hills and sleeping under the clouds and stars, and of hunting food and living in the wild, seems like more than a lifetime ago. I rarely think about it, and I never, ever, wake up dreaming about it.

The other wild living, the feral living, that I did in a forest nineteen years ago… that still comes to me at night. All the time. And during the day.

I know I need to face up to it, to look at it, think about it, talk about it, accept responsibility for it, but deep down I just hope to fuck that I die before I have to do any of those things.

*

Sitting in Costa. Bad day today. Bad evening ahead. I'm here to hit on the waitress, no other reason. It's time. Time must be running out. Whatever the fuck time is.

Sometimes I come here because I'm positively trying to drink coffee instead of vodka. Today I feel reckless and depressed and I don't care. I don't care what happens. Tonight is an evening for getting completely hammered, for falling asleep with a kebab in my lap, and waking up at four in the morning in a cold sweat, feeling like complete shit.

Feeling recklessly horny. So before I go home and get wasted and stupidly drunk, fuck it, I'm going to get laid and if I have to pay for it, then to hell with it, I'll pay for it, and I'm not going to think about the ways in which I might have to do the paying.

I asked Constable Grant. That was fate avoidance right there, that's what I'm talking about. Just out and out asked her. Nothing subtle. Do you want to come by my place tonight? She said no. Didn't even feel that she needed to give me an excuse.

Couldn't blame her. What was I thinking? And I look like death. Nothing attractive about me. Whether there normally is, who knows? Maybe. A certain look of having been places and done stuff. Now I just look tired and old and fat. Three stone heavier than I was last summer, an increase that's showing no sign of abating. That's what being middle-aged does to you, especially when you eat fish suppers, drink vodka and do sod-all exercise.

'Everything all right for you today?' she says.

I look up at the waitress, having been staring morosely at the floor. She's smiling. A nice smile. I like that she smiles and that she asks if everything's all right. It's not in her job description. She's not singling me out or anything, I hear her asking all around the shop. Happy in her work. A genuineness and generosity about her that the rest of society could do with picking up on.

No, really, it could. It's easy enough to see your own faults in others.

'Pretty miserable,' I say, breaking the conventions of polite conversation.

'Aw, too bad,' she says. 'What's up?'

Look up at her. She's holding an empty mug and a plate with muffin crumbs on it, the wax casing twisted neatly at the side. She has a small towel over her arm, as if she's the waiter in an expensive London hotel bar.

This is the moment to ask. This is the moment to come out with the latest clumsy approach. The latest desperate attempt to get laid; or the desperate attempt to grab the future. And it all just disappears. Whatever it is that it takes, it all vanishes with a snap of the fingers. Seeps out of me, runs out of me, courses out of me, races from me. The confidence, the chutzpah, the desperation, the energy, the desire, the lust. It all goes, leaving behind a wave of suffocating darkness, the kind of sorrow that bleeds you dry, makes you want to collapse to your knees. Vomit. Makes you want to vomit. And give up.

I answer with a small wave of my hand. Nothing to say. Nothing to do. Nothing.

'You want to come back to my place tonight?' she says.

Look up at her again. She's taking pity on me. That's my first thought. I'm sitting here feeling utterly pathetic, wallowing in self-fucking-pity, and she's been sucked in. I don't think about the other thing.

'You don't have to do that,' I say.

'What?' she says, and she's smiling, that lovely smile, although this time there's a bit of an edge to it. Not a nasty edge though. Not sure what the word is for the kind of edge it is. Naughty maybe. A naughty edge.

She lowers her voice.

'I don't have to take you back to my place and fuck the life out of you?'

Now that is not something I've heard her say to the other customers.

'All right.'

Life is sucked back into me.

'I get off in about half an hour. I'll get you another coffee while you wait, Sir. On the house.'

And off she goes, flashing that lovely smile again.

*

I like lying on my back in bed because it makes my fat stomach flatten out. Five minutes earlier I was behind her, ramming my cock inside her as far as I could, my hands on her hips and loving every second of it, every moan and every thrust and every gasp from her as my cock slammed into her. It was absolutely glorious, but I'd look down and my bloated fat middle-aged stomach was there in front of me, fatter than I'd ever noticed it before.

Now she's on top of me, ten years younger than me at least, and slim. Beautifully slim, with delicious small breasts. The breasts I've been thinking about since Gostkowski made me picture her naked. And there they are, moving around in front of me as she fucks me with fabulous, wonderful energy, an energy that I seem to have lost.

She started off slowly, just for half a minute or so, half a minute of complete deliciousness, but then she got carried away, as you do, couldn't stop herself, and for the past couple of minutes she's been frantic, closing in on her orgasm, moaning loudly, taking all of my cock, taking it as hard as she can, her hands all over me in her frenzied, erotic desperation.

I'm watching her face, watching her breasts, watching the movement of her nipples, trying not to come. Don't want to come yet. This is just what I needed and I want it to last so much longer. There are so many other positions I want to fuck her in, I want her tongue all over me, I love listening to her orgasm and I want to hear it again and again.

And then, with an 'Oh fuck, yes!' she reaches her climax, her shoulders straight, nipples pointing into the air, her hands raised to the side like she's just scored the winner in the World Cup Final.

Holy crap, I wish there was video. I really wish there was video.

Finally she stops moving, after grinding on to me for another short while, and she lifts herself off and kneels down beside me. She looks at me, that smile even broader.

'Fuck,' she says, then she leans over me and takes the entire length of my shaft into her mouth, and I gasp and squirm and am so glad I stopped myself coming.

I've just put my hand on her hair, when she straightens up and looks up the bed at me, devilishness in her eyes. She hesitates, I smile.

'What?' I say.

'I've got something,' she says, and she looks so wonderfully fucking naughty I could spank her.

'Go on.'

She giggles. She actually fucking giggles. I could shag that laugh of hers.

She reaches down under the bed, struggles to find what she's looking for, and so steps onto the floor. I lie there waiting for her, my cock hard and aching and desperate

She stands up. She's holding something in her hand. So completely out of context is it that I don't immediately recognise it. If I'd seen it in the office, I'd have known straight away, obviously. Fuck, I've even used them. Not only that, when they were first introduced, I had it used on me as a demonstration. So that we'd all know what we were doing when we used them on the drunken scum of the streets of Glasgow.

A taser.

She smiles. This smile is different.

She aims the taser at my cock and does not hesitate. In an instant I'm hit by the most incredible, debilitating, excruciating pain. I've never had anyone try to bite my penis off before, but Jesus fuck, it must feel like this. Imagine it. You have an erection, and then someone bites it as hard as they can. Feel it.

Except the pain doesn't stop at my cock, it travels. It shoots over me, every part of my body. The worst is the point where it strikes, but the rest of it is abominable. A monstrous agony.

When we zap our customers we do it for less than two seconds. A quick blast. She holds it, sustains it. I don't know for how long. The pain is awful, and when it's done, I'm lying there, completely washed out, genitals throbbing with the worst pain I've ever experienced, and I can't fucking move. Can't move.

That's the point.

Everything's hazy and sore, pain and numbness and torture are washing over me. I look at her. She's leaning over me again. This time she's got a large tool or instrument. Not sure what it is.

I'm not even thinking about the bracelet. The panic button. I'm not thinking about anything yet. But she is.

She takes my left hand and places it between the jaws of the pliers and then squeezes. Swiftly, brutally, powerfully. Vaguely I can see the muscles in her arms tense, and then all I know is the horrendous pain in my hand as she crushes it. Crushes the bones between the jaws of the pliers. I can hear them crack. All those bones in the hand.

I try to cry out, but nothing comes. That's what happens with a taser. You can't do anything.

My entire body is wracked by pain, the agony fizzing

out and spiralling around me from the two main points that have been attacked.

The pain in my left hand is so great that I don't even notice as she removes the bracelet from around my wrist.

38

Just after nine in the morning. DCI Taylor at his desk, the remnants of a cup of coffee cooling at his right hand. His morning will be spent speaking to various family members of a man who lies in hospital after being attacked with a knife. Given that it was someone from within his family who attacked him with the knife in the first place, it made sense to keep the investigation close to home.

Funny, he often thought, television crime drama. Crime novels. Movies. There was always a case to investigate, a killer or a rapist or a thief to unearth. Real life? It was usually the brother or one of the parents or the best friend, and you knew right away. You always knew.

'What the fuck is the Plague of Crows, then?' he mutters, staring past his coffee. 'Someone who's related to all the victims?'

'Talking to yourself, Sir?'

He looks up. DI Gostkowski is standing in the doorway. Taylor looks at her with no trace of embarrassment, although he does lift the cold coffee to his lips and drain the cup.

'I was just thinking,' he says, and then he smiles ruefully and adds, 'discussing with my other insane half, obviously, that it's usually someone from the victim's family. That's who we always end up looking for. It's not about catching someone, but about compiling the evidence against them.'

'And how does that work with the Plague of Crows?' she says.

'Exactly. I hate it...' He glances at her, wondering if it was all right to talk the way he usually did with Hutton, before continuing anyway, 'I hate it when the day–to-day stuff ends up being like an episode of Lewis.'

'And that's what the Plague of Crows was...'

'Aye,' he says. He rubs the bridge of his nose as if he's just removed a pair of glasses. 'I like your optimism,' he adds.

'How d'you mean?'

'Saying that's what he was.'

'I meant it more from the point of view that it's not our problem anymore.'

'Well, Inspector, that's optimistic in itself. I may never officially work another day on that case in my life, but it's going to bother me for the rest of it.'

'Officially? You're still working on it? I mean, surreptitiously?'

'No... Thought I needed to deal with Clayton before I could move on, but it was just driving me mad. How could I do that without talking to people? The ex-wife, the girlfriend. All that stuff he told us... for all the stuff you get on the web these days, all that information, you can't just put into Google, *was this man talking shit*? and it'll spit out the answer. God knows how many lies he told us. Was he just taking the piss, or was he covering up?'

She shakes her head. No answer.

'You never checked up on the girlfriend, found out if she really did work on *High Road*?' he asks.

He had never asked Gostkowski. Knew what the answer was going to be, not sure why he's asking now. Hadn't wanted to drag Gostkowski back in once she was well out of it.

'I just left it alone, Sir,' she says.

Just as she'd been told to do.

'Of course,' he says.

A slightly awkward silence. They don't often work together, have only been involved in the same investigation twice in the past two months.

'What is it today, Sir?' she asks.

He drags himself back from some aimless wandering and indicates the notebook on his desk, in which he's been making a few random notes about what needs to be done.

'This attempted murder,' he says. 'Need to get to the bottom of all the claims and counter-claims about domestic provocation.'

'Sounds lovely,' she said.

'Oh, yes,' says Taylor.

*

Trees. It's always trees. That's what I see first. That's why the Plague of Crows business has had such an effect. The trees. That's why it's had an effect, more than any other crime I've had to deal with since I got back from Bosnia and started this shit-awful career.

It's not the brain-being-eaten-by-crows thing. Fuck, the press love that shit, they love to wallow in the horror of it. I don't think it's horror. It's, I don't know, gauche maybe. It's gauche. Showy. It's Grand Guignol, that's all. It's almost too horrible, too ostentatious, to produce genuine horror.

Too horrible to be horror? What? *Crow got your brain?*

It's just the trees.

I arrived in Bosnia with the same prejudices as everyone else. The prejudices that the government wanted us to have. The Serbs were the bad guys. The Serbs were the bringers of war. The other guys, they were all victims. When the Bosnian Muslims were fighting the Croats they didn't want to talk about it. That was a horrible civil war, victims on all sides. Massive reluctance to join in with that. Nobody wanted to take sides, because there wasn't a bad guy. Just two good guys. We wanted to be on both sides. Neither of them was particularly nasty. That was our view. No one said it, of course. The British government weren't issuing those kinds of statement.

It was easier when the Serbs fought them, because they were the bad guys. Suddenly it was easier to take sides.

I went out there properly brainwashed, knowing who the bad guys were. The first fighting I came across was

Croat-Bosnian. It was fucking horrible. My first experience of war. First-hand war. It'll fuck you up as soon as you look at it. There was no honour here.

At some point I decided that the Serbs were the victims. I know. Victims of a particular kind. Victims of the world's prejudice. Victims of the west's desire to show the Muslim world it could come in on their side. Just fighting for their land.

That close to the action, that close to the war and the horror of it, you missed so much. I began to distrust the other journalists. Thought they were all playing along with the government and editorial line. Saying what they'd been told to say. What they were expected to say.

The truth? Was there a truth? It was war. There was no truth. They were all fucking bad guys, but the Serbs were bigger and better armed than the others, so they were the worst. They certainly didn't need my sympathy.

But they had it for a time, and that was how I ended up hanging in the forest with a small company of them. Bosnian Serbs. They were fucking rogue, man, but that whole damn conflict was rogue. No one had any control. There were scores of guys, teams of them, at large in the forest of Bosnia doing what the fuck they liked. It was feral. Mediaeval.

Thought I'd get some good photos, and oh fuck, but did I ever. But if I'd wanted to be doing a piece on how the Croats and the Bosniaks could be just as horrible as the Serbs, I probably wanted to be hanging out with the Croats or the Bosniaks. Or maybe living in a small Serb village populated by Serb women, children and old guys with no teeth, hoping that one of those rogue bands of Croats would come through and kick all kinds of fuck out of everyone.

Roaming with a band of thieves was never going to do anyone any good. In the end, instead of reporting on them, I became one of them.

I became one of them.

When they sat in the forest, drinking, talking about

women, masturbating, casually firing their guns at trees, whatever the fuck they were doing, I wasn't sitting on the sidelines taking a series of great shots. I was with them. I was drinking and shooting and talking about women.

That was how it started.

It was never going to end well.

I was drunk that night. I like to think that it could have turned out differently if I hadn't been, but fuck, I was drunk every night.

We came across a family of Bosniaks making their way through the woods. A family trying to survive. Who knows where they were escaping to, or why they'd chosen that night in a war that was already two years old.

There were three younger men. Several women, I don't even remember how many, from teenagers to a couple of grandmothers. Then there was the grandfather. I remember him. Jesus, I remember him.

None of them were armed.

The first thing that happened was the murder of the three younger men. My guys, my band of happy thieves, tried to rile them, tried to make them fight, but they were having none of it. They seemed to think that if they kept their heads down and avoided confrontation, they might be allowed to pass unhindered through the forest.

In the end, all that keeping their heads down meant, was that they each got a bullet in the top of their skull rather than the forehead. That was the moment when I started to sober up, but it took a while.

Genuinely hadn't seen it coming. Thought my guys were having a bit of fun. It was cruel, yes, but I was drunk, I was one of them, I was laughing with them. After the three shots, the three bloody exploding heads, after the screams from the wives and daughters, the alcohol started to weep slowly from my system. I didn't think of myself as one of them after that.

They didn't immediately notice. Too busy enjoying themselves.

They made the grandfather watch. I think that was what

they took the most pleasure in. The humiliation of the head of the family. The respectable leader, brought to his knees as his family was put to death and shame.

They raped the women. Gang rape. I sat and watched. What a useless, pathetic, complicit sack of shit. They were laughing, having fun. The animalistic nature of the horde.

I sat there intending to do something. But what was it I was going to do against four guys with guns?

I couldn't even lift my camera.

'Come on, Tommy.'

I can still hear them. The first exhortations to join in. One of them said it, then they all did, in the same high pitched mocking voice.

'Come on, Tommy!'

I could have run. Maybe they would have shot me in the back, but they were drunk, there were trees, they all had their trousers at their ankles. Odds were in my favour.

I can barely claim any honour, but I know I didn't run because I thought I should do something. I can't turn my back on these people, I thought. I'm the west. I'm representing the west here. All of it. The responsibility of the NATO alliance rests on my shoulders. I should do something.

I sat and watched, that's what I did. Getting less and less drunk with every second.

If that was it, if it had ended there, I'd still be living with it. I'd still be consumed by what a bloody awful, pusillanimous arsehole I'd been. A coward.

If I couldn't have saved those people, I ought at least to have died trying.

The mood turned. I don't know what it was that turned it. Perhaps they'd had enough. They'd had enough sex, enough fun debasing the Bosniaks. Or perhaps they'd finally realised that there was someone there who was neither a victim nor a perpetrator. There was a witness.

What happened next plays in my head on a continuous loop. Over and over and over. Like a television drama, stuck on the same ten-minute scene, playing in the corner of every room you're ever in. You can try to ignore it all you like, but it's loud and demanding. It insists that you watch it.

Look at me! it screams. Look at what you did.

They encouraged me to join in. They wanted me to join in. At some stage they realised they needed me to join in. That was when everything changed. I was no longer to be defined by my pusillanimity.

I never knew their names, these four guys I got drunk with for a few nights in the forest. They told me they were John, Paul, George and Ringo. Funny. John was the leader, that was all I knew him as.

John aimed his gun at me. Suggested that I might like to take a turn. He offered me one of the women. The prettiest, curled in a heap on the forest floor, clothes torn, blood on her thighs, dirt on her face. Tears running through the dirt. Not yet at the place where she could shut down and accept that she would be better off dead. Still wanted to live.

'Do it,' he said.

I couldn't speak. I didn't look at her. I shook my head.

'Tommy,' he said. 'Come on, come on. Look at her. Now do it.'

I didn't look at her.

He smiled. He pointed the gun at the pathetic abused woman on the forest floor.

'I can tell you don't care about yourself, Tommy,' he said. 'But you don't want her blood on your hands. Now do it.'

I didn't move. Sat there, head down, just as pathetic and paralysed as I'd been for the past half hour.

He kneeled down beside her and put the gun at her head.

'Tommy,' he said, and just like that his tone had changed. He'd been mocking beforehand, and suddenly, there it was. Business-like. Mundane, almost, but full of threat.

'Tommy, you need to have sex with the girl. Now.'

I looked at her at last. Looked her in the eye. She never spoke, but her look said everything. She was begging me. That's what her eyes were doing. Begging me. What did she care if another man raped her, if another man came inside her? She didn't want to die.

I got to my feet. One of the other three started a slow hand clap and then they were all laughing, clapping slowly in unison. John wasn't laughing. He kept the gun at her head.

Her eyes begged me. Her eyes said, come on. Rape me. Don't think that I care. I don't care. It's not rape, not really. I want you to do it. Come on. Come on! Please!

I stood there. The laughter and the clapping increased. I was wearing jeans, no belt. A button, a zip. What was I thinking? Right there, at that moment, what did I think was going to happen?

I was never going to be able to have sex with her, whether I'd decided that I was going to do it or not. I couldn't.

I'd been sitting there in fear and abject poverty of spirit, consumed by self-loathing, for all that time. And now they were laughing at me and mocking me and threatening this woman, and the responsibility of whether or not she lived was on my shoulders. It was up to me to enter her. To fuck her. On their command.

I couldn't get an erection. I was never going to be able to get an erection. Did I think that by dropping my trousers they'd feel some sympathy for me? By showing them that I was incapable, that they'd let her go?

The clapping stopped, the laughter increased ten fold. The look in her eyes became ever more desperate. In a final pathetic gesture, she even squeezed one of her dirty, bite marked, bloody breasts in an effort to get me excited.

I fell to my knees. It felt like my penis shrivelled into nothingness.

John put a bullet in her head.

'You could have saved her, Tommy,' he said. 'But you're not a real man.'

He put a gun in my hand. That seemed strange at the time. He took a gun from one of the others – think it was Ringo – and put it in my hand.

'Kill the old guy,' he said. 'If you don't, the other women will die. If you kill the old guy, I'll let them go. You think you can do that much for me, Tommy?'

I had a gun in my hand. That's the moment I think most about when I think about that night. The moment he gave me a gun, knowing I would do nothing with it other than what he was telling me to do.

I should have shot him. John. I should have shot John when I had the chance. Then I would have died. Or I should have turned the gun on myself.

Except, I believed him. The whole idea was to mock me further, to complete my humiliation. He fully intended to let those women live if I killed the grandfather, so that I would know that he would have let the first woman live if only I'd been able to penetrate her.

I looked at the grandfather. His dead eyes looked back. His dead eyes. I stood there, my trousers still at my knees, my pathetic, impotent penis resting woefully on my balls, and I shot him. Twice. In the chest.

John didn't kill the other women. A man of his word.

*

Right from that night, that first night, I woke up gasping, my voice straining, silently screaming into the dark. In the forest, in the dead of night. Woke up, sweating, the guilt of a million years crawling over my skin like cockroaches. I'd wet myself.

They were sleeping. One of them was supposed to be the guard, but he was keeled over as well. The Bosnian women were gone. They weren't a threat.

They were gone. The bodies of the dead were gone.

I stood up. The dead of night in a forest in the middle of a war. Picked up my bag, picked up my camera, and stinking of piss and cheap booze and shame I walked out of there. Didn't look back. Some part of me wondered whether I should pick up a gun and kill the four of them while they slept. Then I could have turned the gun on myself.

I didn't pick up the gun. I kept on walking. I wondered if they'd come after me, or whether they'd search through the forest for the women. Didn't even look over my shoulder. Didn't care. They could have come after me if they'd wanted. They could have caught me, tortured me. They could have come invisibly from behind, a sniper in a tree, and taken me out.

I walked on. Every now and again I came across evidence of the war. I realised I wanted to see the women. I wanted to see them, wanted to apologise, as if that would make everything all right. As if that would bring back the old man, as if that would mean I'd stood up for them, or at the very least, that I'd been able to save her. The woman who'd been desperate for me to penetrate her. I'd apologise, they'd forgive me and I would receive absolution. Instant. There and then. Or else I could give them a knife and offer myself to them for vengeance.

I wake up. There is no sound. I can open my eyes, but there is total darkness. Darkness so complete that it appears solid. As if I'm inside a solid block. Wonder if I've been buried alive. Maybe I'm not alive.

But then there's the pain.

39

Taylor looks at his watch. Just after two in the afternoon. His heart sinks, although he immediately questions himself. The day is already dragging and there's a long way to go. But what is it he's looking forward to that evening?

Gostkowski beside him, they walk back upstairs from the interrogation room. An ugly day questioning people, most of whom were lying; or, at the very least, skewering their stories as far as possible from the truth.

What is Gostkowski doing that night? He's never wondered before. He knows she's not married, but that's all he knows. He would probably have heard from Hutton, but they haven't seen much of each other. Even when they were working together, he didn't talk about her. Which was peculiar, for Hutton.

Taylor glances at her and understands. Of course. He smiles ruefully to himself. Fucking Hutton.

He envies him. A carefree life, happily drinking and shagging. Slight glitch every time the possibility of getting back together with his wife comes along, and a moderate amount of remorse about the fact that he rarely sees his children, but that aside, a guilt-free life devoted to indulging himself in his pleasures of women and alcohol, both of which he finds in endless supply.

'You talk to Sgt Hutton much since the Plague of Crows thing?' he asks.

Hasn't seen Hutton and Gostkowski talk at all, but knows that his sergeant is capable, on occasion, of a degree of discretion.

Gostkowski glances briefly at Taylor, then looks away as she surprises herself with a rare moment of candour.

'We got a bit too involved during the Crows investigation, Sir,' she says. 'It was unprofessional. I haven't really spoken to him since.'

'Hmm,' says Taylor.

That they'd had sex in the first place was entirely in keeping with Hutton's character, that the DI had ended it because it was unprofessional in keeping with hers.

They come to the front desk, Ramsay holding dominion over his territory, never seeming to be off duty.

'Sergeant,' says Taylor. 'We'll release Masters later, but I'm not in a rush. Leave him for another hour or two, make him think the worst.'

Ramsay nods.

'Hutton around?' asks Taylor.

'Haven't seen him today,' says Ramsay.

Taylor has talked as he walked, but now he takes a couple more paces and then stops.

'What's he been working on the last couple of days?'

'Principally the school beating.'

'He passed that onto Dorritt,' says Taylor.

'He was writing up a report on it for him. I presumed he was continuing to work for the DCI…'

'What else have you given him?' asks Taylor sharply, aware that Dorritt would no more have wanted Hutton working for him on the school beating than the other way round.

'He had several ongoing cases, and I know it was logged in yesterday evening that he was given first sight of an insurance fraud case involving a small building firm in Westburn,' said Ramsay firmly. Undaunted by his superior officer's sharpness of tone, having been many years in the job.

'You didn't think to check his whereabouts this morning when he didn't come in?' said Taylor.

'If he was late,' said Ramsay firmly, 'it would hardly be the first time. He has prior. If he was out on a case, then I can't be expected to keep minute-by-minute checks on all our detectives.'

'These are hardly normal times,' says Taylor.

'It's been two months,' replies Ramsay.

'Jesus,' says Taylor, 'it was two months between the last two. There isn't a set length of time after which it's all right.'

'And there isn't enough manpower in the station for us to keep any kind of regular check on the precise whereabouts of everyone who works here. There has to be a certain amount of personal responsibility. Sir.'

Taylor stares for a little while longer then turns away, takes out his mobile. Gostkowski stands slightly awkwardly. She thinks Taylor is overreacting. Thinks that the men are having some kind of ridiculous, testosterone-laden alpha male power struggle. Also believes that Hutton is liable to have been too hungover to come in, or is off on some absurd tangent of an investigation.

An unreliable officer, that's how she sees him. Does not feel very good about getting carried away in January and allowing herself to be added to Hutton's absurdly long list. The sex was good, once or twice. The third had been too much.

Taylor turns back. Softened a little. Holds his hand up to the sergeant.

'Not answering his mobile or home number. I know on some level I'm probably being melodramatic, but the Plague of Crows is coming back, and some police officer somewhere is going to end up under the knife. Would you mind calling the folk running the bracelet scheme and finding out where he is?'

'Not at all, Sir,' says Ramsay.

'Thank you,' replies Taylor, and then he leaves him, heading back to his office.

Gostkowski and Ramsay share a glance as she follows.

*

There are in Taylor's office three minutes later when the phone rings. Taylor lifts it abruptly, barks, 'Yes?'

'The Sergeant is at his house, Chief Inspector,' says Ramsay.

'You have confirmation of that?' says Taylor.

Slight pause.

'The bracelet is at his house, Sir. There's no alarm gone off to suggest it's been broken or tampered with, so we can assume that the Sergeant is there with it.'

Taylor hangs up without saying anything else. He looks across the desk at Gostkowski.

'The bracelet says he's at his flat.'

'So that's where he'll be,' she says.

Taylor looks at her while he lifts the phone. Dials Hutton's home number, lets it ring. No answer. Uses his mobile to dial Hutton's mobile. Waits for a few rings, then hangs up. Has looked at Gostkowski throughout.

'I'm sure it's nothing, Sir,' she says. 'He's not the most reliable.'

'It's two in the afternoon,' says Taylor, 'he usually isn't that shit.'

Another glance at his watch, a quick look around the station.

'I'm going round there. Only take a few minutes. You stay on the domestic. You know where we're going with it anyway. I'll call in, let you know when I find him.'

Some glib comment comes to Gostkowski's mind, about not killing Hutton when he finds him, but it's not her way to utter any of the occasional glib comments that enter her head.

Taylor leaves.

*

He stands at Hutton's door. No answer. Waits impatiently. Has a bad feeling. Was aware of having had a bad feeling even before he came out here, even before he began to enquire after Hutton's whereabouts. Pointlessly checks his watch. Looks along the short corridor. Tries the door handle. Locked. Another glance along the corridor, and then he puts his shoulder to the door.

Nothing. This is what he needs the Sergeant for. Does it again, and again. Kicks it with the sole of his shoe, hard next to the lock. Nearly falls over. Someone along the landing sticks their head out the door, looks suspiciously along the corridor.

'Fuck off,' mutters Taylor, words vaguely aimed in their direction. The door closes again.

He's not counting. Eventually the lock starts to give and the door opens, screws pinging away into dark corners.

He enters the flat. Smells of cigarettes. Taylor shakes his head. Genuinely thinks at this point that he will find Hutton dead. For all the worry, he's not thinking about the Plague of Crows. He's assuming something much more prosaic about Hutton. Alcohol poisoning, perhaps. A binge too many. Fallen asleep in his bath and drowned.

Would he have killed himself? There was a darkness in him. A depth of some description that he did not talk of. A past. The war in Bosnia. Never talked about it. Never talked about it to the point that it was significant him not talking about it.

'Sergeant?' he calls. Despite the ill-feeling, still wary of walking in on the sergeant, drunk and naked in bed with someone or naked in front of the TV.

Glances into the bathroom. Nothing. Slight feeling of relief, yet the wariness and anxiety grow. Into the bedroom. Clothes dumped everywhere, the bed unmade. A full ashtray. An empty bottle of vodka on the floor beside the bed. Taylor's heart sinks at the sight of it all. And then, there it is, and his heart sinks even more.

The bracelet. The bracelet which was supposed to be impossible to remove without setting off a string of alarms, sitting humbly and quietly on the bedside table.

He stares at it, then carefully takes out a handkerchief, lifts the bracelet and puts it in the pocket of his coat.

40

You might call it sensory deprivation. Can't hear, can't see. There's no smell. Hands and legs bound, can't touch anything. Trouble is, that leaves pain.

A lot of pain. The after-effects of the taser still linger, particularly in my groin, but the worst is my hand. She crushed my hand, while I lay, impotently, consumed by pain. And the pain in my hand has not lessened.

I don't know what the body does to try to combat pain. I presume it does something, releases some chemical or other. Whatever it is, it ain't up to the task of dealing with a crushed hand. The most God-awful screaming pain I could ever imagine.

She crushed my hand to get the bracelet off.

You know? You know what? I deserve it.

I wake up, blinded by darkness, and all I can think is that I've had this coming. I don't know who she is. At least, I'm not sure. I'm not sure, but there was something trying to click in the middle of my brain. I'd been thinking about it, something about her. She seemed familiar. I walked into this. Something about her face.

I saw her in my dream. The dream that's not really a dream, the dream that's a flashback. She was there. She was one of the women, sitting on the sidelines, watching their men being butchered,. She was there, getting raped, several men taking her in turn. She lay on the forest floor as her sister or cousin was shot in the head because this pathetic, complicit coward could not get an erection. And then she watched as the coward put two bullets in her grandfather's chest. She was there throughout.

I lie, bound and gagged in the dark, no idea where I am, no sounds, no smell, and that's all I can think. Really, she doesn't look like any of those women, but she could easily have been one of the younger ones. Maybe that's what this is. Revenge. She was a sixteen-year-old girl being violated, physically forced out of her youth.

My hand throbs. My penis aches. Feel a bloody, useless miserable wreck. But lying here, lying in this abject state of despair, I don't feel fear at the horror that's to come, I don't feel regret, I don't feel any kind of self-pity.

Relief.

Is that what I'd say? I feel relief. At last, it's come. Revenge has come. Revenge will be brutal and unpleasant and agonising, but at the end of it I'll be dead, and when I'm dead I'm going to be free. I won't have to live with that night in the forest in Bosnia anymore.

Any day now, I shall be released.

Bob comes into my head. Fuck, I almost laugh, except I can't laugh. My mouth is gagged and anyway, I'm not for laughing. Not like this, and not with those images in my head.

I've been wanting release for so long. Suicide always seemed a chicken's way. Running from it. Not facing up to my past. I knew it was coming eventually. The time when I would have to stand up and face the consequences of what I'd done.

Every time I saw the war crimes tribunal in the Hague, I wondered if they were going to mention me. Mention the Scottish journalist who stuck his nose in, got involved, went too far, couldn't get himself out, sat and watched and even then, when all he had to do was have sex in order to save a life, couldn't even do that.

There seems to be a blanket over me. Why is there a blanket? That seems like a consideration, when none has been previously given.

I'm lying here, tortured, aching. Everything hurts. My past has caught up with me. And I feel relief. And I can't help thinking that I shouldn't be feeling relief. Relief is something else to be feeling guilty about. I couldn't save that woman. I killed the old guy. I don't deserve relief. I

don't deserve to feel relief at this torture.
  I just deserve to suffer, and to go on suffering.

41

Taylor is in Connor's office. Montgomery sits to the side, nominally more an observer than a participant, but he is about to get involved.

Taylor is incredulous. Connor uncomfortable. Montgomery contemptuous.

'You're fucking kidding me?' barks Taylor.

Connor has been getting gradually weaker as the months have gone by, as the Plague of Crows has turned his great opportunity into the dead weight that will sink him. He will call it his bane, Connor's Bane, when he writes his memoirs. The memoir that no one will want to read or, indeed, publish.

'Chief Inspector,' he says, although as words of admonition they are bound to receive no respect.

'What's the point in these stupid bracelets,' says Taylor, dismissively holding up his wrist, 'if we don't follow up when there's an identifiable issue? He's missing. The sergeant is missing. Why are we here? Why did the department spend God knows how much money if we're just going to ignore it when it happens?'

Connor glances at Montgomery. Montgomery looks dismissive of Taylor, although he has little more respect for Connor as he can see he wants him to argue his case for him.

'It's not the fact that there's a rogue bracelet, or there's potential for something to have happened to a police officer,' says Montgomery. 'It's the officer in question that's the issue.'

'Aw, come on to…'

'Chief Inspector, by all account your sergeant has been going off the rails the last couple of months. Regularly late for work. Two weeks ago he missed an entire day after a night when he was seen pouring into a taxi, completely out of his face on vodka. He's sleeping around the station like he's on some demented bender of sexual destruction. And this despite being suspended last year for inappropriate sexual behaviour.'

'During none of which,' says Taylor, 'did he remove his bracelet or actually go missing.'

'It's not too great a logical progression to imagine him taking it a step further and wanting some peace and quiet. He's probably sleeping with someone else he shouldn't be, and doesn't want to be traced to their house.'

Taylor rages. Closes his eyes. Could take two steps over there and land a punch on the fucker. And not some pointless, painful blow to the jaw. A punch to the neck, just under the chin. Let's see the bastard get up from that.

Part of Taylor's annoyance, of course, comes from the fact that he knows Montgomery might be right. It is odd that Hutton has just vanished, and he really cannot explain how he would have removed the bracelet without damaging it. Nevertheless, it would be in keeping with how it's been going with him. They hadn't been talking about it, but clearly the Plague of Crows business, something about it, something intrinsic at the heart of the case, had got under Hutton's skin.

'Have you checked what *your* wife's doing today?' says Montgomery.

He looks coldly at Taylor, knowing full well that Taylor had been divorced in the past year, his wife leaving for a younger model.

Taylor looks at Connor, ignores Montgomery. It's the only way to deal with him, punching in the throat being off the agenda.

'Sir,' he says, reigning back the tone, 'can you explain to me how he got the bracelet off?'

Connor stares across the desk. He doesn't look at Montgomery, as he has fallen so far back into the pits of insecurity that he can't stand to be undermined any further.

'I don't know,' he says. 'Butter?'

Taylor stares disdainfully across the desk. Look at the bracelet, he thinks. Look at your stupid, fucking bracelet you pathetic, ignorant fuck. It's tight around your wrist. Butter, for crying out loud.

'Chief Inspector,' says Montgomery, 'let's be realistic here. It's not just the unreliable habits of your sergeant that are the question. I know if the Plague of Crows returns, chances are he will take out one police officer as part of his ritual, and it's always possible that that one police officer could be from this station. However, it seems highly coincidental, highly coincidental, that it should be one of the previous investigating officers. If he wanted to make a point then surely he would have taken one of my men, one of the men who are actually involved in the case at this time. This... doesn't make sense. It doesn't make sense for the Plague of Crows to take Sgt Hutton. That the sergeant has gone somewhere he knows he shouldn't, that quite possibly he's with someone that he knows he shouldn't be, is far more likely.'

He stares at Taylor. Taylor has looked at Connor throughout. Connor sits uncomfortably looking at Montgomery.

'There's no place for talk of coincidence in police work,' says Montgomery.

'Coincidence?' barks Taylor. 'Two months ago we had the Sergeant in front of the cameras, taunting the guy, trying to draw him out. This could be it. This could be the drawing out. And what are we doing to handle that?'

He looks between the two of them.

'Maybe two months ago,' said Connor. 'But he's tipped too far over the edge now for anyone to trust him.'

'Jesus,' mutters Taylor. He stands quickly. Hesitates. Sits back down. Addresses Connor, although realistically he knows that he's speaking to Montgomery.

'On the obviously farcical off-chance that Sgt Hutton has been taken by the Plague of Crows, would it be possible for you to ask G4S to run a check to make sure that all the social services staff currently covered by the security check are accounted for?'

Connor knows that this is not within his remit. He has power over a small section of south-west Glasgow, and not much power at that. He looks to Montgomery.

'Chief Inspector, do you know how many false alarms there have been in the past two months?' says Montgomery.

He pauses. Taylor again contemplates walking out, but knows that it will look churlish.

'Oh, G4S are happy to do it when we ask, but you know how much it costs? How much it costs the police every time we ask them to make a 100% check?'

'Isn't that part of the contract?' says Taylor. 'Didn't someone think to make that part of the contract? That they would check when we asked? What, in the name of God, is the point of this thing if we have to pay them every time we ask a question?'

'We can ask questions, Chief Inspector, but we are required to provide extra funding for 100% checks. That's the contract as it stands.'

'Jesus Christ...'

'I doubt either of us has experience of writing a government contract, so let's not get into that.'

'So the system is set up in such a away that it discourages us from using it?'

'If you want to be jaundiced about it...'

'A police officer is missing under peculiar circumstances...' says Taylor harshly.

'Not just any policeman,' says Montgomery. 'A wayward officer. An officer out of control. A maverick.'

Oh, for fuck's sake, thinks Taylor. He didn't just use the word maverick, did he? Jesus.

'Prove to me that Sgt Hutton is not just out sleeping with someone's wife or some prostitute or some wanton... trash of a PC, then I'll take your request higher up the chain and see...'

Connor lets the sentence drift off as Taylor gets up

quickly and walks from the room, slamming the door behind him.

*

Door shut, he's alone with Gostkowski. Hutton's security band is on his desk between them. It dominates the room.

'They think I'm over-reacting. I don't need to know the full details, Inspector, I'm just looking for an opinion. This doesn't make sense. Hutton's band lying here without him attached to it, doesn't make sense. Montgomery thinks he's taken it off so that he can go out... shagging. Or that he's on the piss somewhere. I don't think so. For all that he's a fucked-up sonofabitch, this isn't him. He would know what taking this off would mean, he would know that removing it, and it being found, would get people panicking. Although, Jesus, that only appears to be me...'

'I agree.'

He exhales, aware that he's getting slightly breathless in his annoyance and excitement, his feeling of dread.

'The sergeant and I had a brief fling, just a few nights,' she says. 'I'm one of them, one of the long list that he's had around here. I won't explain it. Can't. Just happened. He is reckless, there is something there, something buried in his head that he doesn't talk about. But this isn't part of it.'

'How d'you think he got the band off without activating the alarm?' says Taylor.

Has only been able to think of one way. Gostkowski studies her own band, studies for the hundredth time how little give there is around her wrist. Presses the bones of her hand together.

Taylor watches her. Knows what she's thinking.

'That's going to have hurt,' he says.

'Yes.'

'Shit. Where do we have to go with this?' he says. 'For all the work we put in, what did we have? Where were we two months ago?'

She shrugs.

'The only lead we had was Clayton, and it might not have been a lead at all,' she says.

Taylor nods, as it's what he'd already been thinking. Taps his forefinger rapidly on the desk.

'I need to go and speak to him again,' he says. 'When I think about it, I really don't know what to do, where else to go, yet my thoughts always seem to come back to him. He beat us, but he knew what he was doing. I don't trust him, and not just because he was so intelligently manipulative.'

'Do you think that's wise?'

He makes a small gesture.

'I'll go,' she says.

'You can't.'

'Why? Are you saying that I can't take care of myself while you can?'

He doesn't answer.

'I could make a complaint about that,' she says. 'Discrimination. We don't have other available officers to go, it's inadvisable for you to go given that you've already been named in a lawsuit by Mr Clayton. I have my panic band, if I suspect anything I'll activate it.'

Taylor looks at Hutton's panic band. She follows her eyes.

'The sergeant was probably caught unawares.'

Or drunk. Or asleep. Or naked. She leaves them all unsaid.

'I'll be fine, Sir. I'll let you know as soon as I've spoken to him.'

Taylor nods slowly. Doesn't like it, yet knows it makes some sort of sense. The chances of him getting anything out of Clayton are nil. And if he seemed to get something from him, how would he be able to trust it? Although, that also applied to DI Gostkowski.

Maybe there was just no point in going to see him.

'Aw, bugger it, Stephanie... Be careful.'

'Yes, Sir.'

'I'll go back to Hutton's flat. I foolishly rushed back here because I thought they might be interested. See if I can find anything. After we've done those two things, we need to get back on Clayton's case. I know he's at the heart of it. Where he works, what he does, who he talks to, what happened to his wife, everyone he's slept with, everything…'

'Right,' she says. 'I'll take a quick look at the file, then I'll get over there.'

Taylor settles back in his seat. Takes a deep breath. Looks at the security band, lying on his desk in the middle of the room. The fear grows. The Plague of Crows is still out there. He never caught him, and eventually it was guaranteed to get personal.

'Thanks, Stephanie,' he says, and Gostkowski leaves quickly.

42

The door opens. A door. How can I say *the* door when I didn't even know there was a door. Obviously there's a door. I'm not outside, I'm not in a cave. There must be a door.

Open my eyes, there's still barely any light. Little illumination from outside the room, although there is some sort of light, the light of night, seeping into the corridor outside.

I can see her outline coming towards me. The last woman I'll ever fuck. The woman who came for revenge. Will she tell me? Will she say what's she doing? Will she let me know about her long search for me, and how she spent so many years waiting for this moment? Will I find out why her face was stored in some remote part of my brain?

I don't care. Won't make any difference to my wretchedness. Won't make any difference if she extends this sorrow. She's planning something. Perhaps she's taking me back. Perhaps I'll be put in a crate and sent to Bosnia.

Perhaps, in fact, this is what I want. To be taken back there. To that exact spot, which is so burned in my head. To face her again, one of those women. Any one of them. A sister, a mother, a granddaughter. Any one of them, if any of them survived. Maybe they're all dead now. Why wouldn't they be dead? What did they have to live for after that?

Fuck. What did I have to live for, and I'm not dead. Not yet.

She's pushing a trolley with a large, low level rack. Something that you would use in a warehouse. She stops next to me, manoeuvres the rack beneath my prone body. I get the feeling I'm attached to something, but I really can't tell. Cannot move an inch, my body expertly bound and strapped.

She removes the blanket. Can hear a slight sound of exertion as she tips the trolley back and lifts me off the ground. Ha! That extra couple of stones in weight is fucking you up darlin'...

Get to the door, she has trouble manoeuvring me through sideways. Bangs my forehead off the door frame. Grunt. Groan. More pain. The pain in my hand has started up again, somehow worse, after I'd been able to get used to it on some sort of level, lying alone in the darkness.

She bangs my head again as she works the trolley out of the back door. Outside now. Feel the cold air on my head. Seem to be wearing clothes, which I hadn't thought about before. I was naked when she attacked me at first, wasn't I? Of course, naked. I was naked, erect.

She stops beside a dark shadow. Large dark shadow. Get a glimpse of a tyre. She's putting me in a van. Taking me somewhere. Hospital? Ha! Still got a fucking stupid sense of humour.

She tips me off the trolley onto the ground. But it's metal. The metal ground. Then a slight humming sound and I'm being raised on a platform at the back of the van. Short trip. Then she's shoving me along the floor of the van until I hit something. Something not particularly solid, and there's a muffled grunt.

A muffled grunt. My head is swirling with confusion. General confusion. All over the place confusion. I'm not alone. Why am I not alone? Who else has she got in here?

I'm being punished for what I did in Bosnia. I know I wasn't alone, but surely those other guys haven't been living in Scotland. That doesn't make sense. They would have stayed on to fight for a Greater Serbia, or whatever the Hell it was they were after. If they had fled, why would they come to Scotland?

My mind is set. Feverish with the pain and the cold and

the sweat. Hallucinating. Maybe I'm just hallucinating. Maybe there was no grunt.

Fuck! Just think, man. Think clearly, think straight.

But I don't want to. I want to get out. Get out of here. Not the van. I don't want to get out of the van. I mean life.

And I don't want to know, not really. Suddenly realise that I'm not that bothered who this other person is. Maybe there's more than one. Even so, I'm not interested. This isn't about them. Not now, not this time. This is about me. My part in my downfall. This is about me getting my comeuppance. I don't care about them, I don't care why they're here. I don't even care if I'm imagining it, and they're not even here in the first place.

Another moan. Low. Low groaning. I'm definitely not alone. How many more are there?

Footsteps around the outside of the van, the cab door opening and closing, the growl of the diesel engine, and then we start to move. A slight reverse, and then the van shudders forward and we're off.

I'm not thinking clearly, although I don't think it would make any difference if I was. In my mind we must be heading to the woods. I know that's where we're going, because that's where my last judgement will be.

My last judgement. Fuck's sake.

My head rests against the floor. I need out of here. Out of this life.

43

The darkness seems to be coming early. A grim day. Drab and cold. Gostkowski stands at Clayton's door, ringing the bell. Suddenly wondering what she was thinking. Did they really think that Clayton was guilty? If he wasn't, then there was no point in her being here; if he was, then she'd come on her own to interview a man who had already murdered nine people.

Not thinking straight. Is she suddenly nervous? Are those nerves?

Deep breath. She has to be more worried about tact and diplomacy than about Clayton lurking behind the door with a knife or some other surgical tool.

Clayton answers the door. He's wearing a t-shirt and a pair of jeans. Has an air about him that suggests he hasn't showered yet that day, that he's had a day of doing little around the house. Watching television and playing X-Box. Jeremy Kyle and Nazi zombies.

'Mr Clayton,' she says, and she holds out her badge. 'DI Gostkowski. Wonder if I could have a word.'

He stares at her for a moment and then snorts out a slight, rueful laugh. Shakes his head.

'Whatever,' he says. 'You fucking people…'

He stands back to let her in. And she has the impression straight away, an impression so strong that she knows it to be true. This guy has nothing to do with it. Nothing to do with the disappearance of Sgt Hutton. Whatever the Plague of Crows does when he spirits people away from their lives, he does not then go and play Call of Duty for several hours. He has the real thing.

He shows her into the sitting room, the room at the front of the house opposite the more business-looking lounge where he'd talked to Hutton and Taylor. The television is paused on a battle game. There is a pizza delivery box at the side of the large gaming chair which is positioned in front of the TV. There is a two-litre bottle of Diet Coke at the side of the chair, lying flat on the floor, top on, nearly empty. If you looked closely enough you'd see pieces of masticated pizza floating in the dark, flat liquid.

He sits in the large chair in the middle of the room, swivels it away from the TV and indicates the sofa for Gostkowski.

Everyone gets depression. Everyone has their day. This is Clayton's day. Not in the mood for playing games with the police, regardless of his guilt or otherwise on any previous crime.

'What?' he says.

In a way, she already has what she's come for. Really, she'd been thinking that if he is the Plague of Crows and if he's in the middle of putting together another crime, then he wouldn't even be home. She'd always known that she'd be making her mind up in the first few seconds.

'Your girlfriend not here?' she asks, perched on the end of the sofa.

He snorts quietly again, makes an ugly movement of his lips.

'She left.'

'Oh. That's too bad.'

A shrug. Another scowl. She wonders if he's been sitting here playing X-Box, eating pizza, since the girlfriend walked out. Has it so utterly ruined him?

'What was it you wanted?' he asks. 'You people can't stay away.'

She stares for a moment and then gets back to her feet.

'I think I've already got what I was coming for,' she says.

He looks at her. Quizzically for a moment and then he shakes his head. Whatever. Doesn't care.

'Sure,' he says.

She looks away. A glance around the room. Feels strange walking in and walking back out. What will she say to the Chief Inspector? That hunch of yours, about Clayton... it's shit. It's not him. Wherever we're going to find Sgt Hutton, it's not down at his place.

Clayton is all they have, and she is about to make the bold move of striking him off the list of one based on a feeling, and the fact that he's playing X-Box. It's going to be tough going back with nothing, but is there any point in asking?

What were you doing last night? What about earlier today? We really need to get hold of your wife so that we can ask her how much of a nutjob you are.

She stops. She stops thinking. The thought processes stop and are replaced by a slight confusion. Where has she seen that face? It comes back to her immediately, no searching around in the canyons of her brain for the information. One of the things that makes her a good officer. Instant access to everything she needs to know.

She crosses the room and lifts the photograph. Clayton standing with a woman on each arm. One of them is his wife. She recognises the other. The hair is completely different. The photograph is a few years old, but it's the smile. She knows the smile.

'This woman,' she says, turning to Clayton. He's watching her, annoyance beginning to stir him from his apathy.

'What?'

'This woman,' she repeats. 'Who is it?'

He snorts again.

'That's my wife,' he says. 'Or, at least, it was. Bitch. Don't ask me where she is now. Haven't seen her in fucking years.'

'Not your wife, the other one.'

He appears not to hear the question. He noisily rattles off several rounds of machine gun fire, his face expressionless. She waits for a few seconds, but soon realises that she'll be waiting forever.

'Not your wife,' she repeats.

He turns. He looks in the direction of the photograph, although she gets the feeling that he could be staring into darkness for all that he's seeing. He snorts again, another small and bitter laugh.

'You people are so shit,' he says.

Looks back at the screen, shaking his head. Enjoying knowing something that she doesn't.

'Tell me how shit we are,' she says.

She has to wait again. The sneer doesn't leave his face. He rattles off more gunfire. She glances at the television. He says 'fuck', as red is smeared across the screen.

'Tell me how shit we are,' she repeats.

He half glances in her direction, but his game is ended and now he's concentrating on what he's done and setting up another game.

'That's my sister-in-law. Jane. That's her name. Jane. Sounds so unassuming, doesn't it?' He laughs. 'Dick and Jane play in the woods, or Dick and Jane build a house. Then there was Dick and Jane fuck round the back of the studio while whacked out of their heads on crack.'

He laughs again.

'What?' she says. Becoming irritated. 'What?'

He doesn't reply. Clicking rapidly through pages. Concentrating on the TV.

'Would you look at me while I'm interviewing you?'

She has his attention.

He stops, stares at her. The sneer has died away and there's nothing on his face. Eyes are dead.

'Jesus…' he mutters. Shakes his head, turns back to the TV. Now, however, he stares at the set-up screen, but doesn't do anything.

'Tell me about Jane,' she says.

Slight movement of his fingers and he starts witlessly clicking and trawling, before the game sparks to life again.

'Met her through the lawyer. That's how I first met Caroline. Jane and I were going out. Jane was on *High Road*. There were stories about her on set, you know, fucking, drug taking, that kind of thing. The usual crap. Fucking press. They love that shit.'

'You went out with her?'

'For a while. I mean, like twice or something. It was nothing. She was a fucking space cadet. Introduced me to Caroline. Wasn't happy when we started seeing each other, by the way. Can't blame her…'

'She sued the press over her stories?'

'Lost.'

'Then what?'

He plays for a few seconds, then glances over. He shrugs.

'Not sure. She was fucked. No money. Didn't want to ask us 'cause she was fucked off at Lin. And me. She was a fucking fucked-up junkie crack whore. Don't know what happened to her.'

'What's her name?'

Another quick glance, this time annoyance mixed with disdain.

'Fucking Jane,' he says. 'What else are you looking for? Her designation? One of Two, some shit like that, some kind of Star Trek shit?'

'What was her second name? What name did she use on *High Road*?'

He snorts. Knew what she meant.

'Fucking police,' he mutters.

He's finished.

Gostkowski stands in the middle of the room, clutching the photograph of Clayton, and Clayton's wife and Clayton's sister-in-law, the waitress at the Costa across from the police station. The waitress who had spoken to her and Hutton. The waitress about whom she had teased him.

Then suddenly she's running out the room, reaching for her mobile.

*

Clayton stands at the window, watching her leave, DI Gostkowski driving hurriedly back down the long driveway.

Another fine job under his belt. Another solid performance being someone he isn't. Along the way he has perhaps forgotten who he actually is. Perhaps he doesn't want to know. It'd be pretty lonely being the only one in here. Most people are lonely, or desperate enough to do something about it. That's what he thinks. So he submerges himself in various people and does not think of the contradiction.

He wasn't pretending to have been dumped by a girlfriend that never existed. He was that person, sitting in pathetic, game-playing loneliness. He *was* someone who had been dumped by his girlfriend.

A few years ago it would have made him smile. To carry off something like that with such panache. Now it means little. He watches her go. He doesn't smile.

Maybe that's why he played the spurned, depressed lover so well. He was tapping into the part of him that had had enough.

He has things to do, but he's not in any rush. The police won't be back for a while, and it's not like he has to change anything around here before they come.

He slumps down into the chair in front of the TV and lifts the Xbox handset. Before he restarts the game, he lifts the bottle of Coke, unscrews the lid with one hand and tips the remainder of the warm, flat liquid, small pieces of chewed pizza and all, into his mouth.

44

It kicks in some time during the journey. The awakening. The realisation that I'm being an idiot. A fucking idiot, no less.

When you're guilty, when you've done something you're scared is going to be found out, then you look for it everywhere. Everything reminds you of it. You constantly think you've been caught. Each turn of events seems to be taking you back to that place.

That's why whenever I heard anything about the war crimes tribunal at the Hague, I was instantly there. I was waiting for my name. And there were many times when I'd be called into the office of the superintendent, and I'd be standing there thinking, fuck, this is it. This is where they tell me that an accusation's been made against me and I'm suspended pending an investigation. And a trial.

Even after I'd sorted out that stupid arse Leander, when I was called into Connor's office the next day, some part of me still thought, shit, this is it. It's not about Leander, it's about Bosnia. They know. Everyone knows.

So it was inevitable. When someone attacked me. When someone bit me on the penis. When someone punished me during sex. When someone came after me, when they had stalked me in a café and asked me out, when they had chosen their moment, it seemed obvious. They were getting revenge for what I'd done. They were having their perfectly understandable, their absolutely entitled, vengeance.

And I was wrong. Because that's not what's happening. If it was, then why wouldn't she just have finished me off there and then, in her bedroom? Maybe she doesn't want any evidence of murder, so she takes me elsewhere. What she wouldn't do, if this was about me, is put me in the back of a van with a group of other people.

Whatever this is, it's not about me. And it's perfectly obvious what it is about.

The Plague of Fucking Crows. I looked at the camera, and I said to it, *Come and get me. Come and get me, you fuck, if you're man enough.*

Well, she was more than man enough, and I was happy enough and stupid enough to walk into it. Eyes open. Penis erect.

And now I'm getting what I asked for. I thought it, as I looked at that camera, I thought come on then, bring it the fuck on. Come on! And here I am. Never stood a chance. Never saw it coming. Blinded by lust, blinded by being obsessed with sex.

The endless, ceaseless search for sex, to prove to myself, to prove to that great watching audience that has followed every grotesquely dull turn of the screw in my life, that I can still do it. That I can get an erection. That I can have sex. It'll never happen again. It'll never let me down again, I will never let anyone down again, as I try to expunge the memories of the time when I let someone down and they died as a result. As if all that sex was doing anyone any fucking good.

And I knew I'd seen her face. The waitress. But it wasn't in dreams. It was in a photograph on a shelf in Clayton's house. The day he did a runner and Taylor and I got to look through his stuff. Another day investigating the guy and his family, and we would have found out more about him, but we were kicked off the case there and then.

Still, when I saw her in the café my brain didn't make the connect. Well, it has now. Just a few hours and one desperate fuck too late.

The Plague of Crows. Fuck, I don't care. I don't care. Fucking crows eating my brains. I don't care. Serves me right, because what I've done is put my wish fulfilment onto my own kidnapping. I wanted it to be about Bosnia, because this was how I would get my absolution. This is what I get for it. I get pain and torture and brutal, bloody death. And no absolution.

*

Sat in a small triangle in a wood. It's dark. Late evening, early morning, middle of the night. I can't tell. There's a lamp to the side, casting just enough light for everyone to see what's going on.

She's cemented our feet and the legs of the chair, just as we saw in the three previous cases. Witnessing it first hand, she's as neat and ordered and organised as we'd assumed the Plague of Crows would be. If I get to come back in a *Randall & Hopkirk Deceased* kind of situation, I'll be a perfect foil for Taylor.

Stupid fucking thoughts. I'll be glad when the crows have rid me of them. We should all be glad.

We? Who the fuck is we?

Oh God, enough…

Look at the other two. Terrified, one of them in tears. The woman. The bloke isn't crying yet, but he will be. He looks in pain. Don't know them, but I'd guess the bloke is the social worker. Got the look about him. Annoyingly empathic. If he is the social worker, then he'll have had his hand crushed, same as me. The woman has the look of the journalist about her too, but she ain't looking switched on and sharp and hungry for a story now. She just looks shit-scared. Shit fucking scared. Ha! Fucking journalists. At least the Plague of Crows is doing something useful for society.

I don't look scared. I know I don't. Because I'm not. I am… alone. Full of sorrow. Flat and empty.

Flat and empty? Can you be flat and empty? If you're flat, then you have no volume, so how can that also be empty?

Funny the stupid thoughts that run through your head while they still can. Just before the end.

'I'm going to take your gags off for a few minutes,' she

says unexpectedly. She's standing slightly to the side. Realise that I'd drifted off somewhere and hadn't been paying attention to what she was doing. She has the taser in her hand.

'You can scream if you like, I don't care. No one will hear you anyway, and as soon as any sound passes your lips that is a clear attempt to attract attention, you will get this. You all know what it feels like, so let's avoid it.'

She's giving me a slightly resentful look. Don't know why. Don't care. Our mouths are gagged with thick silver tape and she grabs the end of it at the back of my head and unwinds it quickly, before ripping it off, the last pull tugging painfully at my hair.

I let out a low grunt and my head falls forward. Jesus. Nothing to say. It's just one pain after another. I realise that I'd known the position of our heads wasn't quite right as we'd been sitting there, not yet bound the same as those from past murders. Obviously some way to go in the process.

She quickly does the same to the other two. The bloke yelps, the woman sobs. The Plague of Crows, wearing thin rubber gloves, sticks the tape together while somehow not getting it stuck to the gloves, and places it in a black plastic bin liner.

She looks at the three of us in turn. This is the payoff for her. This is the moment when she gets to play God. She has complete dominion throughout, from the moment she zapped us with the taser, right to the crow-feasting end; but this is the moment when God will speak to her desperate, pitiful subjects.

'You all know what's coming,' she says.

'Please…' gasps the journalist.

I close my eyes and bow my head still further, as if closing my eyes is a way to block out the sound.

I don't want to hear. I don't want to hear the whining and the pleading and the desperation. It never works. It won't work in the woods with the Plague of Crows, just as it didn't work for so many people in the woods of Bosnia.

'Why?' says the guy, desperately. 'What have we done?'

'You assholes fucked me up from day one,' she says. Matter of fact. Cold. Not getting into it.

'What?' he says. 'We can talk about it. Make amends.'

In the silence that's only punctuated by the sobs from the journalist, I can imagine the Plague of Crows staring at him with utter contempt. My eyes are shut, my head is bowed. I'm not looking. I don't care.

She's not getting any tears from me. Nothing. I'm not scared. I'm not scared. I'm empty.

'Let the woman go,' says the bloke.

How can you appeal to the chivalry in a female killer, you idiot?

'You?'

I don't look up, although I know.

'You!' Voice sharper this time. Don't raise my head. Sinking. I just want to sink. Keep going down until it's all darkness. Dark and cold. And there's nothing left. I don't want there to be anything left.

I hear the crack and fizz of the taser as she lets it go just to my side. Grabbing my attention as it zings into a tree behind me. Lift my head slowly. It's coming. Death is coming. And pain. Maybe I don't even care if she hits me with that thing again. Yet I've lifted my head.

'You,' she says again. 'Look at me. Look at me!'

I'm already looking at her. But I know what she means. My eyes are dead. What's the point of terrorising someone if they're not interested? How can you instil fear into someone when they feel nothing?

'You invited me in,' she says. 'You looked in the camera. You asked for this. Now look at you. Not so fucking… tough now.'

I continue to look at her with dead eyes. So bereft of spirit that I'm not even interested in telling her that I couldn't care less about this. Go on. Kill me. Kill the three of us. Go on killing until you've got everyone in Scotland.

All those things that mattered. Partick Thistle getting into the SPL. Going to see Bob. Cigarettes and alcohol.

Perfect, redemptive sex. Italy beating Scotland 2-1 at Hampden in 2007. Archie Gemmill's goal against the Netherlands. Ullapool. Peggy. The kids. Alison and Jean. Stupid politicians. Stupid newspapers. Stupid questions. Arrests, charges, convictions. Getting wasted. Forgetting. Bosnia. Rape. Death. Guilt. Anger. Fear.

None of it. None of it matters.

Anyway, I always thought it. Right from the start. It's worse for people watching than the people to whom it's happening. It looks horrific. Sure, you know what's happening to you, but you can't really feel it. You can't feel your brain getting eaten. That's why she does it this way. That's why the victims are arranged like this. So they can watch the others, and know what's happening to them.

I suppose some people are going to be freaked by that. I just thought, fuck it. Fuck it.

I thought it, I really did. But not as much as I think it now. And she knows. That's why she's angry. I bet she's not usually angry. I bet when she does this she's committed and cold and calculating. Doesn't make mistakes. But this time she's angry. She's angry at me, and she's off her game.

Maybe she'll make mistakes. Probably will. Won't save me. Won't save these two sad fuckers sitting with me, but it'll allow Taylor to get that bit closer. Close enough to make a difference.

Do I want to make her angrier? Do I care enough about this to try to throw her off her game? Do I care if she gets caught? Fuck, I'll be dead. Like I give a shit about the rest of society.

'Sex was good until you ruined it,' I say.

Suddenly find myself glancing at the social worker. Did she get him into bed too? Bastard. Doesn't look like it.

I get the back of her hand across my face. Compared to the rest of the pain she's been doling out, this is pretty insubstantial. An angry gut reaction, rather than all the rest of the calculated brutality.

'Fucking police,' she says.

I've been holding her gaze for a few moments, but can't any longer. My head drops.

'Don't you pretend you don't fucking care,' she growls at me.

'Thought you were someone else,' I say.

My voice is dead. Has to be disconcerting. I hear a whimper, but it's from the bloke, not the journalist. The journalist has silent tears streaming down her face.

'What? What? What the fuck does that even mean?'

I don't look at her. No, I've thought about it. I'm not interested in getting her even more annoyed than she already is. It makes no difference. Yet, my indifference is what will get her more annoyed, whether it's what I'm after or not.

'Fuck!'

She screams. That's got to be upsetting to the crows. She turns her back. The other two are watching her as I look up. Two shit-scared people, as well they might be. She has lost control. Because of me. Because of someone who is hitting the exact opposite end of the scale. Someone who has switched off. Someone who is not as impressed as he's supposed to be.

She turns around. She's holding a vicious-looking surgical tool. This will be the GPC oscillating & rotary thing. Whatever. Quite familiar with it, having done our research on what equipment the Plague of Crows had been using, even if I can't think of its precise designation for the moment.

She obviously has some power source somewhere, although it must be running quietly. Can't hear anything. She's looking at me. Standing between the whimpering bloke and the journalist. She lifts the bone saw, so that's she's holding it like she might hold a gun, and presses her thumb down on the controls.

It buzzes into action with a low sound. An expensive sound. The sound of top of the range bone-cutting equipment. She snarls. Wonder, in an almost disinterested way, what she's about to do. My head isn't strapped down;

she'll never get the clean cut that would allow me to stay alive long enough for the crows to get involved.

'Fucking watch,' she says. 'See how you like it.'

Then she turns quickly and thrusts the bone saw into the eye socket of the journalist. Her mouth opens in a silent scream. No reason for there to be no sound coming out, except perhaps her vocal chords are frozen in horror. She wriggles her head desperately, but that just increases the damage as the Plague of Crows presses down tightly with the saw and it begins to cut down through her face.

She then draws it out and starts using it to stab at her, repeatedly, in the face, briefly drilling into her skin and bone. Chops off an ear. Drags it across the other cheek. A nick at the throat. Teasing her and taunting, a brutal display of torture.

The social worker guy is wailing. It's a horrible sight, the journalist crying out now in pathetic little squeals, blood flowing, as the Plague of Crows deprives her beloved birds of a kill. Slashing and thrusting with the saw, her own breaths coming quickly with the excitement and the anger.

'Fuck!' she shouts again, and soon, very soon, the journalist's bloody head falls forward into her chest. The Plague of Crows stands, engrossed in her slaughter, then holds the saw at the top of the woman's head. Presses down.

'Come on!' she says, exhorting it to cut through bone, as she scythes into the journalist's skull. Already dead, this one is just for show. Just for fun. Just for the Hell of it.

Suddenly she lets the power off and straightens up, gasping for air, her mouth dry, her heart racing. The bloke is wailing. Loud sobs. Jesus, what an awful sound.

'Would you shut the fuck up!' she barks at him, but he doesn't. I don't think he can. Probably hasn't seen that happen to anyone in real life before. I mean, you've got to see some amount of fucking awful shit when you're a social worker, but probably not that.

'God!' she shouts, as if exasperated with her children.

She lets the bone saw fall to the floor, then steps quickly to the side. Stands back between us with the masking tape, then ties it roughly and tightly around his mouth. Round and round she puts it, several times more than is necessary, until there's no sound coming out.

She hasn't strapped his head back yet though, and he continues to move it around frantically. Eyes wide. With all that sobbing his nose is probably full of snot and tears so he's going to have trouble breathing for a few moments. He'll likely get past it, but his future prospects aren't looking too great.

'Fucking happy?' she sneers at me.

The journalist's body drips blood onto the forest floor. I'm not looking at her. I look at the Plague of Crows.

'You killed her,' she says, which is some kind of fucking logic. But then, if you're insane enough to come up with her crows plan… 'You fucking killed her, and you're supposed to protect people. Didn't fucking protect her, did you? You're all the fucking same. How did you fucking like that, you prick?'

I hold her gaze this time. Eyes are still dead. I expect she was looking for some kind of movie reaction. I was supposed to be shouting, *no, no, leave the innocent civilian, take me instead!*

I missed my lines. If there'd been an actual choice, I would have been happy to take the saw. But there wasn't. She was just looking for some desperation from me, and she didn't get it.

'Seen worse,' I say.

It sounds Python-esque, but fuck it, I'm not lying. I have. I have seen worse. For all my guilt, I haven't done worse, but I've seen it. I've taken the photographs and I've sent them back to London newspaper picture editors, and they've said, *you are fucking kidding me, we're not printing that…*

'Seen worse,' I repeat, and my head drops.

45

She arrives first. Sits and waits. The house is dark.
She isn't usually so unsure of herself, but this is different. This is the Plague of Crows. Gostkowski is convinced. It's based on nothing more than a coincidence, because why couldn't Clayton's ex-sister-in-law be working as a waitress on the other side of Glasgow? But she knows, absolutely and without doubt.

She'd called it in; hadn't bothered going to anyone other than Taylor. The sister-in-law who worked at the café across the road. First thing he did was run over there to see if there was anyone who met the description. Then he was back and tracking her down. Jane Kettering poured out of distant police files in great torrents of disaffection. From an early age. He cursed that they had given up on the search when they had. Even just a couple of more hours of Gostkowski's investigation and she could have tracked her down.

There was an address, in the hills behind Gourock. Gostkowski was closer. He'd told her to wait for him. As he'd said it she doubted that she would, but now that she's here she hesitates. Turns off the engine and the lights, finds herself making sure the car doors are locked. Sudden fear. Where has that come from?

Five minutes pass. She wonders if she should go in. Starting to steel herself. Starting to prepare for it. Seven-and-a-half minutes and Taylor arrives. She hasn't moved.

She gets out her car as Taylor pulls up.

'Where are the others?' she asks, as Taylor walks quickly towards her.

'It wasn't enough,' he says.

That's all that is needed.

Gostkowski hadn't had much to tell him. A face in a photograph, Clayton's former sister-in-law in a café paying attention to her and Hutton. Now Hutton is missing.

Six months ago it might have been enough, but now there have been too many mistakes, too many conclusions jumped to that have not been proven. More than anything, Taylor has been working on this since the previous summer and has got nowhere in all that time. To believe that he's gone from nowhere to identifying where the killer lives in a matter of minutes seems preposterous. Neither does the connection to Clayton help. To anyone else it is going to seem like another plan from Clayton to fool the police. Only Gostkowski, who has been there, who worked it out for herself, knows that it isn't.

Perhaps there are doubts lingering, too deep yet to come to the surface.

They approach the door, ring the bell. A detached house, not too large, a small front garden. Taylor turns and looks across the road and around at the neighbour's homes while they wait. Quiet Scottish suburbia. The kind of place where the police would get called out to adjudicate over a hedge dispute or to answer a complaint about someone parking their car in front of someone else's house.

He steps away from the front door to take a broader view of the house, bathed in the orange glow of the street lamps. A few bare trees in the front garden lessen the effect of the lights.

'Open the door,' he says.

Gostkowski first of all tries the handle, then finding it locked looks around the garden. There are stones lining the border between the lawn and the path and she lifts one of them and quickly puts in the glass panel on the door closest to the lock. Reaches round, key in the lock, which is all just marginally less difficult than the door being open in the first place.

They enter quickly, Taylor moving in front, close the door and turn on the light. A regulation hall, stairs leading up ahead of them, door to the left and right, another door at the end of the hall beside the cupboard beneath the stairs.

Silence.

'What was it that was suspicious about her in the café?' asks Taylor.

Gostkowski pictures the woman chatting to them.

'Nothing,' she says.

Taylor nods.

'Good. It's good that you didn't miss anything previously.'

All the doors are closed. The floors are wood, a long rug from the Middle East lines the hallway leading to the kitchen. The walls are magnolia, hung with three or four original watercolours. Pastels. Sea and sand and old harbours.

'Nice place for a waitress,' he says.

Hutton had thought the same thing, but he had parked the thought. Sex first, plenty of time to ask questions later.

'Don't like this,' says Taylor. Not used to working with women. 'Stick together.'

Gostkowski doesn't know that he and Hutton would have split up.

When he starts moving he does it boldly and confidently. Having established his bearings he is not about to creep around.

First room, on the left; a study, generally used as a dumping ground for unneeded things. There's a baby grand piano, cluttered and unused.

Second room, on the right. Sitting room. Television. Photographs of the same two children, and of a similar vintage, that Clayton has in his house. Taylor scans the room, takes everything in, turns and walks out. Down the hall, stops to open the door under the stairs. The cupboard has been converted into a very small bathroom. He looks at the floor, wonders if this is where there would be a trap door to the basement. On first inspection it is tiled and solid. He will come back later if he finds nothing else.

Into the kitchen. Light on. Modern, redesigned and

fitted some time in the previous two or three years. Nothing obvious. This person lives alone with no reason to assume that the house is about to be infiltrated. There's no reason why she would have to keep secrets hidden.

Taylor walks out, back down the hall. Gostkowski hesitates a little longer in the kitchen, then follows. Up the stairs. A door straight in front of them, slightly open. Taylor walks right in. A spare room. A single bed. Everything very neat. He quickly notices the film of dust. There is a sadness and an emptiness about the room. Something about it, so great, that there almost seems a physical manifestation of the emptiness. A spare room that is never used because there are no visitors.

Perhaps there is something more fundamentally amiss with the room than that. Gostkowski shivers. They walk out. Quick look in the bathroom, nothing to see. They can rake through the cabinets later. Another door beyond that, another bedroom. The double bed has been made, there is order. There is no sign that this was where Hutton lay back, where Hutton was euphoric, where Hutton was so brutally immobilized.

Taylor turns, walks back past Gostowski along the corridor to the final door. She follows.

The third bedroom, but this one a bedroom transformed. All traces of the room's original use have been removed. Here is a large desk in the middle of the floor, the walls have been stripped and hung with maps and lists of names. Photographs are everywhere.

They both feel the jump of nerves. Taylor steps forward.

'Call it in,' he says.

Gostkowski doesn't move. Looks around the room. The wolf's lair. The operations centre, almost as if it had been laid out for them. Photographs of some of the previous victims on the wall. A large map of Scotland, pins inserted in various places around the central belt. Satellite images of woods. The desk is littered with paperwork, which Taylor is already looking through.

He notices the silence and turns.

'Inspector?'

'How do we know?' she says.

'What?'

'How do we know it's not a set-up?' she says. 'This is perfect. It's too perfect. I see the photograph in Clayton's house, and now we're here. He might as well have told me where to look, and now we pitch up and we find this. All the evidence we'd ever need, right there in front of us.'

Taylor stares at her, a piece of paper in his hand. Closes his eyes, tries to think it through.

'They could be working together,' she says, 'Clayton and this woman, the café woman, to get the police to make an even bigger idiot of themselves. For us to make idiots of ourselves. They want us to call it in, they want us to turn up here with thousands of SOCOs. This could just be...' and she lets the sentence drift off and waves a hand at the pictures on the walls.

Taylor opens his eyes, turns and looks over the evidence before them. Goes to the map of Scotland on the wall. There are seventeen pins in place, three red, fourteen yellow. Recognises the three red as being the spots where the Plague of Crows previously committed murder. The others are spread around the central belt.

What would they find when they got there, to these fourteen woods. Trees? Crows' nests? A jack-in-the-box, all part of Clayton's deception and joke? Hutton and two others, bound and gagged and scalped?

He runs a mental cross reference with woods that he's looked at over the previous few months. Some of these might only be useful for the summer. He quickly reduces the list of fourteen to six or seven. He turns back to Gostkowski.

46

She's been gone for a while. Not sure how long. Maybe half an hour. I've got under her skin, yet she didn't kill me. She's angry. Too angry to be coldly removing part of someone's skull, preparing the food for crows. She'll make mistakes. Something that she won't see coming, something she will miss because she's not in control.

She's been in command throughout every one of the murders so far. This time she's lost concentration. I know that's what she's doing when she shuffles around, out of sight. Occasionally there's the sound of footfalls on dead leaves, the noise of someone walking through the forest.

She is pulling herself together. Getting a grip. It's not about me, and she had made this murder about me.

The guy is still blubbing. Soft moaning, whimpering noises. Tears. He can't stop looking at the dead journalist. He is wrapped up in her, that bloody corpse. Occasionally I lift my head to look at the two of them.

I won't ask myself if I'm heartless. I know I'm heartless. Beyond caring, about me or anyone else.

The Plague of Crows flits in and out of my thoughts. It comes together, with wonderful clarity. I have none of the facts, and yet I know everything. Instinctively know that what is pieced together in my head is what brings me here, what brings the Plague of Crows out into the woods to avenge herself.

I see it in her face, just a flash, but it sparks the thought process. It's her eyes. The same as the look on photographs of Clayton's wife that we looked at.

If only we'd kept looking. If only we hadn't turned our backs on the case when Connor kicked us off it. Strangely I blame Taylor and myself, rather than Connor. He was just doing what he had to do. We shouldn't have taken his word. We should have kept at it. We would have come to the sister-in-law soon enough.

Clayton was just the way we found our path in. It was chance, but one of those chances that happen in life. Meant to be. I wasn't attracted to Clayton because he was the killer, but because the killer was connected to him. Quite probably he didn't know anything about it, yet it drew me in. There's no reason for it, other than some sixth sense saying that the path to the Plague of Crows lay through Clayton.

And so it did.

She comes back to the fray. Calm. Renewed. Concentration intact. She doesn't even look at me. The guy is whining slightly more loudly now. He must recognise the new coldness in her. She's back, she's determined, she's going to get on with the job.

She has the duct tape in her hand. Doesn't bother gagging me. Knows I'm not going to say anything. The social worker is already gagged, now she grabs his head and straps it firmly to the back of the seat. His eyes are wide with fear, tears flowing freely.

'You're next,' she says, without looking. Wants to be in control, but can't help herself.

Perhaps she's thinking some level of humanity will kick in and that I'll start pleading for the social worker's life. There would be no point, even if I felt like it. I'm not saying anything.

He looks at me. Beseeching, demanding. *You're the police officer! Do something! Do something, you fucker!* For all my genuine and heartfelt disinterest, I would be doing something if I could. But I can't. I'm as tied up as he is. Shouting won't get us anywhere.

Head strapped tightly, she moves away for a second and then returns with an electric razor. One of those big round fuckers with which you can shave your own head in seconds, if you're of a mind to not care what you look like afterwards. She's in her groove now, working quickly and efficiently. He has reasonably short hair as it is, receding slightly. I expect there's a bit of a bald patch, although I can't see from here.

Takes her less than a minute, then she rubs her hand over his shaved head to clear off the remnants of the cut. Turns away for a moment, replacing the shaver with the bone saw, and she's back a second later. She switches it on, the familiar low hum, holding it a couple of inches in front of his face. The eyes widen even more.

Terror. That's what terror looks like.

I've seen it before.

I look away. Head drops. Maybe she glances over to see if I'm paying attention, but I won't notice if she does.

The sound of the low hum is strangely all-consuming.

*

I wake up to her roughly grabbing my head and forcing it back against the chair, strapping it tightly. Quickly look over at the social worker guy. Scalped, skulled, still alive. His eyes are clipped open. His whole body seems to be trembling within the confines of his bondage.

I must have fallen asleep. Would have been perfect to just never have woken up. Gripped, immediately on waking, by a dreadful, oppressive feeling of desolation. Had been almost phlegmatic before. Sitting in hopeless impotence, the pain in my hand occasionally throbbing.

Now, the weight of it all is much heavier. The place I'd got myself into, the place where I didn't care and where pain could be ignored, has gone. Self-loathing has returned, much stronger than before.

A woman was just brutally murdered in front of me and I did nothing. I did not care. Now I hate that I was in no position to do anything. I blame myself. I'm a police officer, for fuck's sake. How could I have taken so long to find the Plague of Crows? How could I have gone to bed with the woman? How could I not know? Where was the gut instinct that I've been sitting here priding myself on?

Notice the first signs of grey light in the sky. Dawn's coming, then the crows will be unleashed. How will the crows be unleashed?

She's good. Sees it in my eyes straight away. The change. She stares for a moment, but she has nothing to say. Maybe thinks that I'll be the one to talk this time.

She moves away for a moment then returns with the razor. Bizarrely, it's quite a nice feeling as she runs it over my head. She's careful not to cut the scalp, as she doesn't want too much bleeding. It has to be as smooth an operation as possible. The crows will do the killing, not her.

When she's done, she runs her hand over the top of my head. Almost lingering. She was making love to me not so long ago. Jesus, not that I know how long ago that was. Lost all track of time.

So convinced was I that it had all been part of some sort of Bosnian revenge tragedy, that it's still hard to get it out of my head. I still associate that moment with revenge. The moment when she broke off the lovemaking to taser me. It was revenge. Except it wasn't.

'You spoke to the idiot,' she says.

Standing slightly back, the razor switched off and at her side.

I look at her. Anger going already. Had there even been anger?

'You spoke to Michael?' she says.

Michael. Clayton. Michael Clayton. Yes, of course I spoke to him. Michael Clayton. I spoke to Michael Clayton, didn't I?

'Yes.'

Can't nod, head strapped. But she hasn't gagged me again. Must want to chat while she slices my scalp off.

'What put you on to him in the first place?'

'Desperation.'

She smiles. Laughs lightly almost.

'Yet you didn't know I was the waitress working in Costa? Sloppy.'

I hold her gaze for a moment. Have I been lying to myself all this time?

'Maybe I knew,' I say. 'Some part of me knew.'

She laughs harshly.

'Yes, of course. You thought I was a multiple murderer so you lay naked on the bed with a hard-on as you prepared to make the arrest. It didn't work.'

'I'm not like other police officers,' I say, which, even under these circumstances, is a pretty fucking bad line.

She snorts and mutters, 'Fucking maverick cop. Asshole.'

Time I shut up. Silence is going to annoy her far more than glib comments. And if she thinks I'm asking her any questions, if she thinks I give a shit, then she's wrong. And I'm not stopping myself asking, so as not to give her the pleasure. I just genuinely don't want to know. I don't want to fucking know.

She takes another step back. On her way to get the saw. The bone saw. To remove the top of my skull, to let the birds in.

The sky is a little less dark, a lighter grey. For the first time I notice that it's cold. That'll be the air on my newly bald head.

'Michael's good,' she says. 'Doesn't make mistakes. I think he might have been a bit naughty. Probably time I moved on.'

That's nice. I don't want to think about Clayton and what she means, but it's lovely for her that she's got somewhere to move on to. There's no escaping the past, however. It goes with you, everywhere you go.

And here am I now, still unable to escape the past, right to the end, even though it appears I'm to die without it ever catching up with me. But it's always been there, burning away inside.

Still saying nothing, she starts to tire of it again.

'What the fuck is it with you?' she says. 'How can you be so... fucking superior? You're about to have your brains eaten out by a bunch of fucking... birds.... birds...

and you don't give a shit. What makes you better than this? What makes this beneath you? You fucker...'

She looks round at the social worker, forgotten in her growing violence of humour.

'Jesus, fuck the lot of you.'

She turns away.

He's still crying. The guy with the social worker moondog face is still crying, his eyes plastered wide open for the rest of his life. For fuck's sake, accept your fate will you, you fucking idiot? You were bound to die at some point anyway. At least this way you'll get on the news and a bunch of fuckers will go and lay flowers outside your front gate.

She's back, standing in front of me. Duct tape and bone saw in hand. She lays the saw down on the ground, then quickly wraps the tape around my mouth, tight, making me gag for a moment, a few seconds to adjust my breathing.

'I don't want to fucking listen to you,' she mutters, as she does it. Which is funny, really, because I wasn't saying anything. Then she pulls my eyes open and – one of those moments I hadn't really been looking forward to – pins the eyelids back with a staple gun. Rougher now than she was when she was shaving me, but she knows the blood spilled by the stapling is going to be minimal.

She bends, lifts the bone saw. Stares me dead in the eye and there's not a lot I can do now to avoid the look.

I feel relief. Now that it's here, I feel relief. No more waking up screaming, no more cold sweats. No more searching for the woman I can talk to, or the woman I can make love to, the woman who can erase the memories of what I've done. No more pointless crime solving, no more having to put up with the fucking public, the fucking public who have long since lost any sense of personal responsibility, the fucking public who demand everything from the police and give nothing in return. No more worrying, no more stress, no more having to get up in the morning, no more coming into work.

'You asked for it,' she says, as the buzz of the saw fills

the grey morning light. 'Now you're going to g—'

I guess the bullet must travel at roughly the same speed as the sound of the shot. A loud crack. A red hole opens up in her forehead. She stares blankly at me for a few moments, and then she falls backwards, a dead weight. The bone saw, still running, falls onto the social worker's leg and he silently screams.

My stomach wraps itself in a knot.

I wish I could close my eyes.

47

I can't speak. I don't want to speak. Maybe I've forgotten how. I'll probably speak again at some point. Montgomery was in for a long time, asking endless questions.

What a complete arsehole. Didn't seem to appreciate my silence. But I wasn't talking to him. I was barely even looking at him. My eyes might occasionally have been pointing in his direction, but I wasn't interested.

I'm in a hospital bed, but I'm not really sure why. The effects of the taser have worn off, I think. My head has been shaved, and my hand is in a cast, two things that don't normally make you bed ridden. Maybe I'm confined here because I'm not saying anything.

The Plague of Crows dropped like a stone and it was over. Just like that. Too late for the journalist, just in time for me and the social worker. Well, it ought to have been in time for the social worker. The police made the mistake of loosening his bonds before the paramedics got there, and he was freaking out. Started bleeding from his exposed cranium, dead by the time the ambulance turned up. If they'd just left him alone. If he'd just sat still.

They carefully cut away my bonds. I could have said, *just fucking rip them, I don't give a shit.* But I didn't. I didn't say anything. Still haven't. I expect that's why they think I might have gone a bit mental.

Montgomery really was an arsehole.

Have seen two doctors and several nurses. Lost track of time. Don't even know when they bandaged up my hand. It's not sore anymore, but maybe they've got me packed full of pain killers.

Maybe that's why I can't talk. Maybe that's why my brain is sludge.

But that's not it. I know. I thought I was going to get relief. I thought I'd be free, and that freedom was taken away.

I can't speak. I don't want to. My vocal chords, my brain, everything, is submerged beneath the weight of guilt and sorrow and self-loathing.

There's a television in the corner of the room. Small, placed too high on the wall. I haven't turned it on yet. A few nurses turned it on for me, as if they thought I was incapable. I put it off as soon as they left the room.

The door opens. Taylor walks in, looking slightly uncomfortable. Gostkowski is with him. I have no idea if this is the first time they've seen me. I don't even know what day it is, never mind who might have been in here.

They close the door. There are a couple of seats, but they won't be sitting down. I wonder which hospital this is.

'They think you've got PTSD,' says Taylor, after a few moments of silence.

Well, they're probably right. I've had it for nineteen years, it makes sense that someone would pick up on it eventually.

If I tell myself that's what I've had often enough...

'The Plague of Crows is dead,' he continues. Going straight for the facts, because he's not comfortable talking about me lying here like a dead weight. 'Stephanie picked up the fact that Clayton's sister-in-law had been working in the café across the road. We tracked her down, found where she kept all her stuff, did all her planning. She had a series of potential spots marked out for her next forest venue. I wasn't sure, but I realised that I'd been to all the places on the map that could be used during winter. She couldn't have known that I had already checked them out. We picked the six most likely and dispatched an armed unit to each. Not too heavy handed, didn't want the Crow getting away. Just ignored Montgomery on it, in case it was all a set-up. Given how much of an arsehole he'd become, he probably wouldn't have done anything anyway. So... you probably saw what happened. They were supposed to bring her in, but our guy... and I'm saying our guy, but it's not like I know who the fuck it was... made the call to take her out.'

I've been holding his gaze throughout. When he stops talking I glance at Gostkowski, then look away. Lower my eyes. Do I not want them to see me like this? Banged up and pathetic, silent and withdrawn, ready for the end? Bald?

I don't think it matters. Just got nothing to say.

'The other two are dead,' says Taylor. 'You were lucky.'

If that's what you call it.

Gostkowski's not saying much. Taylor continues talking, filling the uncomfortable silence with facts that I can't bring myself to tell him don't interest me.

'She had a shit life. Abused as a kid. We're still trying to find her sister, but it looks like the dad abused her as the eldest and not the younger sister. She became an actress, got a part on *High Road*, fucked it up. Took some newspapers and the police to court. Long time ago. We hadn't got that far back. Montgomery had, it turns out. They made some half-arsed attempt to speak to her, but no better than when they talked to Clayton. Never made the connection. She met Clayton through their lawyer, dated him a couple of times, made the mistake of introducing him to her sister. The sister seems likely to be pretty fucked up 'n' all. Just the fact that she went for Clayton in the first place.'

He hesitates, as if he might be leaving a gap for me to fill. That's probably it. A gap in the conversation that I can step into, thereby letting them know that I'm all right.

There's a fucking laugh.

'Maybe if she'd stayed with Clayton it might have kept her straight. But then, given what he'd done, it seems unlikely. He dumped her, she went off the deep end. Yet she managed to do it in a very cold, patient and time-consuming way. We've got the boys going over her computers, but it looks like she was planning this for years. It's all there.'

He pauses again. Maybe it's for me to speak, maybe he's finished. I don't have any questions. I ought to have questions. We spent months on this investigation. It had us pulling our hair out. But now that it's over, I don't want to know anything about it. The Plague of Crows is dead. Time to move on to the next thing. The next crime. Wonder what the next crime will be?

No, actually, I really fucking don't.

'Your hand was crushed to all kinds of fuck. That must've hurt. She broke fourteen bones.'

That would explain the screaming pain. I broke one bone in my hand once before and that was painful enough.

Taylor shuffles. No closer to his comfort zone. Doesn't know what to say to someone who looks fine, but isn't saying anything back. Of course he's not getting angry like that wanker Montgomery, but he's equally uncomfortable.

He walks to the window and looks outside. I don't know what he'll be looking at, or even what floor we're on. He turns back. Another glance at me, not really sure what to say, and then he nods at Gostkowski and walks slowly from the room.

My heart bleeds. He's my best friend. Maybe he's the one I should be talking to. Feel like I'm letting him down in my silence, but I can't say anything. How can I tell him what the terror in the woods reawakened in me?

The weight of depression rests slightly more heavily on me. Gostkowski does not immediately follow the DCI, yet she's not staying. I catch her eye. We stare at each other. I know she's not going to say anything. If she's trying to communicate through a look, then that ain't happening either. She bends over me and kisses me softly on the cheek.

Another look after she's straightened up, and then she walks slowly from the room, closing the door behind her. For a while I stare at the door, then I close my eyes.

I close my eyes.

*

'Hey.'

I'm back in the woods. For some reason I don't seem so upset, not as worked up as usual. I'm watching them, watching those other guys do their thing. But the women are different. I don't know who they are. I've forgotten. Perhaps that's why I'm not upset. It isn't my women that are getting raped, the women I've been so worried about and so remorseful over all these years. These are some other women who I don't have any feelings for. This is like watching the news. If they showed rape on the news.

'Hey.'

Open my eyes, dragged very slowly from sleep. The dream is gone in an instant, so that I have no memory of it.

'Hey.' Again. The voice is soft.

I manage to focus on the man beside the bed. It's Clayton. Michael Clayton. I hadn't been expecting him. I wonder what time it is. Dark outside. I wonder how he got past the policeman outside the door. How do I even know if there is a policeman guarding the door?

Why would there be a policeman outside the door? They got the Plague of Crows, didn't they?

'You intrigue me, Detective,' he says. Not that I've got anything to say to that. Not that he's waiting for me to say anything to that either. 'I was watching you. The way you manipulated poor old Jane. And, of course, I say manipulated, because I thought that's what you were doing. But you weren't, were you? You weren't playing a game.'

He's sitting down. He leans forward and places his forefinger in the middle of my forehead. Leaves it there for a second then leans back.

'You didn't need your brains eaten out, did you? There's already something missing. What is that? What did you mean when you said you thought Jane was someone else? What did you mean?'

He has the eyes of a crow. Clayton, with the eyes of a crow. Dead. Wanting. Expecting. Entitled.

'I wondered if I might kill you tonight, but there doesn't seem any point, does there? It's hardly sport. Like I always thought I'd kill the old man. Detective Chief Inspector Lynch. That's what I thought, but then... it seems so much more fun leaving him to live on, humiliated and broken.'

He pauses. Leans his chin on the palm of his hand, even though there doesn't appear to be anywhere for him to rest his elbow.

'You... You're already broken. What broke you? Not me. Not this. Not the infamous Plague of Crows. Not spending all those weeks searching for her. Hmm...'

He seems to get bored talking and looks around the room. There's nothing doing. Nothing to see. A bland hospital room. Could be anywhere. I wonder which hospital it is.

'You took your time turning up,' he says distractedly. 'I'd been expecting you right from the start. You took your time. I wondered if Lynch would put you on to me. Hmm... I expect he's got his head buried so far up his backside in self-pity he hadn't even noticed the news. Too bad... Do you care? I don't believe you care.'

I hold his gaze. *No, I don't.* He tosses an unconcerned hand in the air.

'I didn't come to kill you. I did come, after a fashion... to chat. Some might call it confess, I suppose.' He laughs. 'Ha! Confess... you know what I mean. Thought I might tell you the story, in expectation of it going in one ear, etc., etc. You'd never pass it on, and if you did, who'd believe you? You're a basketcase.'

He shakes his head, waves that hand again.

'What does it matter? You're not going to be impressed anyway. Lynch was impressed. Impressed enough that it got under his skin and it ruined him. But you... you're not interested in the minutiae, are you? You're not interested in anything.'

He casually looks away, makes another small gesture. Suddenly he seems terribly affected, in a way that I'd never noticed before. He's sitting here talking to me. It's a real conversation about things that actually happened, yet he's acting, and acting in quite an old-fashioned way. He's channelling Laurence Olivier or a touch of the exaggerated camp of Jeremy Brett's Sherlock.

He's been acting all along. We knew that. Couldn't believe anything he said.

'You used her?' I say. Found my voice. But really, I haven't found my voice.

Another casual throw of the hand, accompanied by a smirk.

'Things needed done, but I'd rather not get blood on my hands. She was very talented with... you know, she had talent. A steady hand. Yes. She had a steady hand.'

'So what happened?'

He laughs. A conceited, no-no-really-I-don't-want-to-talk-about-how-great-I-am laugh. Usually I'd be reaching out and putting my hands round the throat of someone with this amount of self-satisfaction. That's the laugh that Ronaldo makes when someone compliments him on his latest hatrick for Real. *Well, of course you recognise my genius, but don't for a second think I don't have better things to do other than talk to you...*

'I got bored. Who wouldn't have? I left the odd hint lying around. Not that you picked it up. Detective Gostkowski. Smart girl. She spotted it. Thought she might. Not that I wasn't prepared to hand out a much heavier hint if it was required...'

'How did you know...'

My voice tails off. I'm getting sucked in.

No, in fact, no I'm not. I really don't care. My questions are automatic, words falling out my mouth. I'm not interested, just asking because that's what he expects me to do, sitting there with the smugness of Whistler.

How did he know that the police would kill her, and if they didn't, what plans did he have in place? Those are the questions. But you know, they can remain unanswered.

'Oh, Jane, she was so... psychotic,' he continues, smiling, ignorant of or unconcerned by my ambivalence.

'Strange that we ended up back together. Mutual hatred of Caroline.' Another cavalier wave of the hand. Where's the woman with the pliers when you need her? 'Ha! Never healthy. Never likely to end well, was it? Hmm… I did all the computer work, of course, but I've set it up to make it look like she did it all. Rather splendid, computers. Wonder what I'll do with them next… Hmm…'

I'm keen for him to stop talking, but he doesn't appear to share my enthusiasm for silence.

I want to get off. I'm lying here, no interest in police work, no interest in the criminal case that has led me to a hospital bed, yet the only visitors I've had have been ones who've wanted to talk crime.

Where's my family? I suddenly think of the kids. What age are they now? How can I forget that? It's only three months since I last saw them. They're my kids, for God's sake.

My head is in sludge. I think about my kids. I picture them. I wish they were here now, and not Clayton. I wish they were here talking about school and music and movies, and acting shy on the subject of boyfriends and girlfriends and arguing over whether or not the science teacher they share is an idiot.

But my kids aren't here, and there's a reason for it. Because why should they be?

Maybe I fall asleep. I'm not sure. When I open my eyes Clayton is gone

Two Cups of Coffee

Me and Dr Sutcliffe.

I've lost weight. Not through living on the side of a mountain and eating rabbits. I'm just not eating. Don't feel like it. A little alcohol now and again when I've needed refreshment. Vodka tonic, with a squeeze of lime if I'm looking for one of my five a day.

Spending quite a lot of time in the public park at the top of Cambuslang. Sitting in amongst the trees, watching spring creep in on the land. Warm mornings in early May.

That's where she found me this morning. Sutcliffe. Sitting on a park bench, down by the pond. At the bottom of the hill where once thirty thousand gathered at the time of the Cambuslang Wark. It says so on the plaque behind me. Freshly mown grass all around, trees beyond that.

I wasn't thinking about the trees. Just enjoying the warmth, the smell of the grass. Dylan's *Black Crow Blues* still in my head. Could hear the lawnmower in the distance. There was a woman with a pram. A couple of boys on the skive from school. Another woman out for a walk with her elderly mum.

I didn't even see Sutcliffe approaching, then suddenly she was sitting beside me. Wearing a light, blue-and-white summer dress, a delicate floral pattern. A cardigan draped over her shoulders. She looked…

It doesn't matter how she looked.

'Sergeant,' she said. She'd found me here before. She was carrying two cups of coffee, and she handed me one. As I took the cup from her our fingers touched.

'Thank you.'

She smiled then looked away. Followed my gaze across the pond.

'The grass smells lovely,' she said.

I nodded. Sipped the coffee. It was still hot. The air was warm, so it wasn't as if I needed the hot drink, but it was reviving all the same.

'You all right?' she asked.

'Just the same,' I said, smiling. The answer she's come to expect.

'When are you going to talk to me?' she asked.

We've moved on from obfuscation and long silences, having long since acknowledged that there's something I need to tell her that I have no intention of ever saying.

I smiled again, didn't reply.

'You can't talk to me today anyway,' she said.

'Why not?' I asked without looking.

'I've got the day off.'

'Why are you here?'

She didn't answer. I looked round at her. There was a smile upon her lips.

*

At any given time, just over one in every ten police officers are off sick.

Taylor comes to see me every now and again. Slowly conversation is returning, although to be honest we have yet to really get beyond awkward.

A few weeks ago he told me that the police had settled out of court with Clayton and his high price legal team. £250k. Just like that. £250k because Taylor and I turned up and interviewed him, he ran away and we fell for it. Taylor has been reprimanded; he didn't mention what was going to happen to me. Maybe they'll wait and see if I ever go back. Maybe they'll forget.

At the time I didn't mention that Clayton had come to see me. Did the next time though. Felt a bit more like talking. Words were coming back.

I remembered it as best I could. Perhaps that wasn't very well. It was all a haze. And the more I thought about it, the more I wondered if he'd actually come.

Really? Was he really there, sitting by my hospital bed, admitting that he was the power behind the Plague of Crows' demented throne? Or was I just imagining it because somewhere in the depths of my head I needed that justification? I wanted to believe that my instincts had been right.

Taylor asked a few questions. Impossible to judge what he thought. Whether he believed me. They found all the computer files, all the techie skulduggery, all of that stuff, on her hard drive. Yet if Clayton had been doing it all along, and he was smart enough to cover his tracks the way the Plague of Crows had been doing, then couldn't he also have been smart enough to make it look like someone else was doing it?

So Taylor asked some questions, then he left. We haven't talked about it since. Maybe I'll get back to it when I'm one of the ninety percent, rather than one of the ten.

*

And now the doctor and I are lying in bed. It's probably unprofessional of Dr Sutcliffe to sleep with one of her patients. She could get cast out of the psych doctor cooperative.

I could tell she was getting interested after I left hospital. She realised there was something in my need to sleep with every woman I ever met. Perhaps she's justified it to herself. The only way to get to the bottom of it was to sleep with me too.

What the fuck do I know? Maybe she just needed to have sex. Although, if that was it, she probably ought to have found someone who isn't her patient. And who isn't a complete fuck-up.

She's lying beside me. The post-sex glow. (What women see as the post-sex glow, and what men see as the few minutes after sex before you fall asleep or go back to work or go and watch sport.) Her head is resting on my arm. Her fingers are making soft patterns on my stomach. Occasionally she kisses my chest.

A warm early afternoon breeze comes in through the open window. Summer is almost here. The leaves are coming. The woods are changing.

By Douglas Lindsay

The Long Midnight of Barney Thomson (Barney 1)
The Cutting Edge of Barney Thomson (Barney 2)
A Prayer For Barney Thomson (Barney 3)
The King Was In His Counting House (Barney 4)
The Last Fish Supper (Barney 5)
The Haunting of Barney Thomson (Barney 6)
The Final Cut (Barney 7)

Lost in Juarez

The Unburied Dead (DS Hutton #1)
A Plague Of Crows (DS Hutton #2)
The Blood That Stains Your Hands (DS Hutton #3)
See That My Grave Is Kept Clean (DS Hutton #4)

We Are The Hanged Man (DCI Jericho Book 1)
We Are Death (DCI Jericho Book 2)

A Room With No Natural Light

Song of The Dead (Westphall 1)
The Boy In The Well (Westphall 2)

Cold Cuts (Pereira & Bain 1)
The Judas Flower (Pereira & Bain 2)

Being For The Benefit Of Mr Kite!

Printed in Great Britain
by Amazon